WINGED

SHELBY RAYN

iUniverse LLC
Bloomington

Winged

iUniverse books may be ordered through booksellers or by contacting:

iUniverse LLC
1663 Liberty Drive
Bloomington, IN 47403
www.iuniverse.com
1-800-Authors (1-800-288-4677)

ISBN: 978-1-4759-9821-4 (sc)
ISBN: 978-1-4759-9822-1 (hc)
ISBN: 978-1-4759-9823-8 (ebk)

Library of Congress Control Number: 2013912944

Printed in the United States of America.

iUniverse rev. date: 09/04/2013

PROLOGUE

I t was a dark beginning. We were stuck in a dimly lit room, each of us locked in our individual cages.

The men in the white lab coats opened the cage across the aisle from mine. That was my younger brother's cage. The scientists took hold of my brother's limp body and hoisted it onto the gurney. They covered him with a thin sheet, but one of his arms hung off the side.

I reached through the bars of my cage to touch his delicate hand. I knew I would never see him again. As the scientists wheeled him away, the tips of my fingers only brushed his cold, lifeless skin.

Tears streamed down my face as they took him from the room. He had always been my little fighter. He was only seven years old and I was only a ten-year-old girl. We had lost our older sister only weeks before and, now, I had lost him.

As I cried, I felt a gentle hand stroke my back and right wing. I immediately turned. It was a girl, one I had never noticed before, in the cage beside mine.

She was older than I was and had a face similar to a cat's. Cat ears poked through her brown hair, and she had a long cat tail. What caught my attention most was her amazing cat-like eyes.

She also had wings that were a creamy silver. Her feathers were soft and fluffy. They were pretty different from my wings.

My wings were dark brown along the top rim and got lighter as the long feathers streamed down. My largest bottom feathers were tipped in black and gray.

The girl smiled. A few sharp cat teeth shone as she said, "It's okay. Everything will be all right."

I couldn't speak English, but I had a general understanding of it.

As my crying and shivering abated, she went on, "My name is Sara. What's yours?"

A name? I'd never considered giving myself one. I thought for a minute.

I tried my best to form words. After a couple of tries it came out as, "Iz-z, is Jay."

Hey, it wasn't the best but it was good enough. I'd said Jay because both my sister and brother had had beautiful blue jay wings and I wanted to remember them forever.

"Hello, Jay," she replied. "Don't worry. I'll be here to help you."

I had absolutely no idea what she meant, so I just smiled. I saw sympathy flood her bright green eyes.

"How old are you?" Sara asked. I tilted my head in confusion. "I'm eleven years old."

I held up my hands with fingers outstretched to indicate *ten*.

She was about to speak when the door opened and a white-coat stepped in. I slid to the back of my crate as he passed. He stopped in front of a cage, undid the latch, and opened the door to reveal fish-boy thing. His eyes were as wide as moons and filled with fear. The white-coat had to drag him out of the cage into the next room.

On the way out I heard the white-coat mutter in frustration, *Man, Subject 23 is a stubborn, slippery little thing.*

I stared after him. His lips hadn't moved yet I'd heard him speak really loudly. He'd practically yelled.

Sara noticed my confusion. "What's wrong? Did you hear something?"

I nodded and pointed at the white-coat as he turned the corner to the hall.

"You heard him speak or something?"

I nodded again.

"But he didn't say anything."

My eyes widened.

Then I heard her say, *Maybe she can hear people's thoughts. I've heard of some experiments that could.* Her lips didn't move either.

Maybe I can read thoughts. Something brushed my wing, breaking into my thoughts. Sara had extended her wing until her feather tips touched my own.

She and I smiled at each other. I didn't have to read her thoughts because we were thinking the same thing. We'd stay together till the end.

CHAPTER 1

We were trapped in the DNA Alteration Experimentation Laboratory, otherwise known as DAEL. It's a whack-job science lab whose location is unknown. There, innocent creatures are tortured for the "sake of science and the wellbeing of mankind." The scientists preferred to experiment on human children because we aren't fully developed and because it's easier to collect data.

The main experiments are human hybrids—humans whose DNA has been spliced and blended with that of another creature. I, for example, am a human-bird hybrid and Sara is a three-way blend of human, bird, and cat.

As a result of the experiments the two of us had wings growing out of our backs, right between our shoulder blades, and a thin trail of tiny down feathers growing along our spines.

The scientists would perform torturous experiments on us and then throw us back into our cages. Talk about inhumane.

Sara and I survived together for three years. We were each other's moral support. Many other experiments had long gone mad while we remained sane because we had each other.

Every day, we would wish each other luck as we were taken away for another test, and after it was over, we would silently talk about it through my telepathic abilities.

I wasn't the only one who had gained a new ability. Sara could make her fingernails turn into three-inch claws. I suppose it was one of the perks of being part cat.

All day we would silently talk and help each other through the pain. Not just physical pain, but emotional pain too. Day after day we would sit in our cages and watch the hybrids around us die.

Once, I thought angrily to Sara, *I can't take this anymore! We're just sitting here while innocent lives are taken by the day.*

She thought back sadly, *I know. This is driving me insane, but what in the world can we do?*

I straightened and said out loud, "We escape, that's what."

She stared at me like I had just said I was going to shoot myself. Other hybrid experiments turned to stare with wide eyes.

I thought to Sara, *I know that we can't save all of them. Just think about how many hybrids could be here. We could save a lot, though.*

There is no way it would work, Sara answered. *Remember, there are tons of cameras everywhere.*

We will *escape, or die trying. I don't care how long it takes. I just hope it's soon.* Just then a scientist entered the room and stopped in front of my cage.

"Subject 26, you are needed in Lab 9." He opened the cage door and led me out.

I'll be back soon, I thought quickly to my friend. She just smiled and nodded. I was led into the brightly lit hallway and past dozens of rooms. The scientist stopped in front of a door. It was labeled but I couldn't read it.

It was a large testing room with a huge, transparent Plexiglas box standing in its center. The scientist opened the door to the box, shoved me in, and locked the door.

He stepped back and two warhounds—half human, half wolves that were bred to kill—took his place, standing guard at the door, their amber eyes wide in hunger and their tongues swiping across their hairy gray muzzles.

Over a loudspeaker I heard, "Begin test in three, two, one."

The walls of the box began to close in on me, literally. I instantly panicked.

My heart pounded hard and my breathing was fast and uneven. I balled my hands into fists so tightly, my nails dug into my flesh and my right hand began to bleed. The pain forced me to uncurl my fist. As I held my hand out, not only did drops of blood fall to the floor, but so did a small metal key.

The walls were touching my wings when I thought, *I was never given a key*. I picked up the bloody key and fit it into the lock of the door. The walls were squeezing my shoulders and threatening to crush my wings.

I turned the key. With a click the door opened and I ran out. A warhound grabbed my arm, its ragged claws digging into my skin. Blood ran down my arm as I let out a pain-filled scream.

A white-coat stepped forward and yelled, "Stop! Don't damage it!"

I thought angrily, *I am not an it! I'm a person*.

Another white-coat ran up as the warhound put me down. "It's incredible!" he said. "It was able to scramble the atoms in the air to create its own way out."

"I know, it's amazing," the first scientist replied.

My eyes widened. Unfortunately they didn't say anything else before they took me back to Home Sweet Cage.

Automatically Sara asked out loud, "What happened?" I reached through the bars and slapped my hand over her mouth.

Shh! Be quiet, will you? I thought to her. *I think I gained a new ability.*

Her eyes widened like an owl's. *What? How?*

They tried to crush me in a giant box.

So, what's your new ability?

I'm not exactly sure. Apparently, I can make stuff out of these things called atoms that are in the air, I answered.

Wow! Do you think you can show me?

Um, I'll try, I thought back.

I held out my hand and concentrated on making a key to the cages. After a few seconds I began to see what looked like particles of dust clustering together in the form of a key. It looked almost solid, but then it shattered and the particles disappeared altogether.

The other hybrids had been watching. Their expressions turned from amazement to disappointment. They probably had thought I could have gotten them out if it had worked.

The boy in the cage across from me stared at me with light gray eyes. He was fifteen, two years older than me. He looked completely normal, but he could change the color of his hair and eyes, and he could completely change into a big black raven.

4

I accidentally picked up on his thoughts: *I thought she could get us out for sure but I guess that isn't happening.*

That's not true! I will get us out.

Oops. I shouldn't have done that. Understanding flooded into his widened eyes.

So that's why you and the Cat stare at each other all day, he thought.

Yeah, and she's not a cat. Her name is Sara. And yours is?

A name? I don't have one. Do you?

Of course I do! It's Jay.

He began to list different names in his head. At one point he had considered the name Max, but thought better of it.

I guess my name could be ... No. How 'bout—

How 'bout I just call you Sam?

He looked surprised at my suggestion but shrugged. *Why not?*

Footsteps sounded at the door and a white-coat stepped in. He turned the lights off and left. The door closed and we were enveloped in darkness. Because I had hawklike vision, for me it wasn't total darkness.

Sam sent one final thought. *Good night, Jay.*

After a few minutes of quiet, Sara surprised me by asking, *So who is the creepy raven boy?*

I turned to look. Her eyes seemed to glow in the blackness.

He's just a boy named Sam.

She smiled, closed her eyes, and went to sleep.

I didn't sleep. Instead I practiced making things out of that atom stuff in the air. By the time I blacked out from exhaustion, I was able to make a drop of water and an ant. *Cool, I can make living things too.* My training had begun.

CHAPTER 2

After a week of practice, I went from making a drop of water to a cup of water and from an ant to a mouse. Within weeks, I had made a bunch of stuff, like a gallon of water, a hawk-both of which dissipated once I released my concentration-, and a lot more.

I still couldn't make the key I needed though. Each time I tried it would just shatter and disappear again.

One day, when it was almost time for the food to come in, Sara and I were talking -I mean thinking- and I asked, *Are you sure you're okay? You look awful.*

Yes, I'm fine. They just worked me hard in the mazes earlier, she answered.

There's something you're not telling me. What is it?

Okay, Sara said, *you've got me. I have the weirdest feeling that something terrible and yet exciting is going to happen.*

What do you mean?

All I know is that it has to do with you. That's it.

Well that sure is helpful, I thought sarcastically to myself.

We looked toward the door as two scientists walked in, a woman following a tall man and carrying a metal tray. They both stopped in front of my cage. The man opened my door and grabbed my arm before I could squirm away. He took a hypodermic needle from the tray.

He sank the cold needle into my arm, injecting its mysterious contents, and then pulled the needle out in one painful movement. He slammed the cage door closed and he and the woman left. A warhound stood by the door. It leaned against the wall and watched me hungrily.

I sat motionless in my cage, wondering what would happen next. I felt Sara's and Sam's thoughts trying to reach me, but I blocked them out.

Suddenly my eyes grew heavy, and I lay down. Then... blackout. Nothing but a faint clang and some mumbling that I couldn't make out. Then absolutely nothing.

———————

As I gained consciousness, my senses slowly came back. First was my hearing, but all I heard was my heart pounding. I gained feeling in most of my body and realized my head was throbbing and my eyes stung like heck. I opened my eyes but I saw nothing.

I pushed up onto my hands and knees. Feeling around with my hands, I encountered nothing but the familiar metal floor of my cage. As I reached farther I felt the bars too.

I heard whispering as thoughts entered my mind. It was Sam and Sara.

Jay? Sam came through first.

Jay? Are you okay? Sara's thoughts came next.

I don't know if I'm okay or not, I thought to them. *I can't see! I can't see!*

I can't see either. The lights are off, Sam joked.

Sara and I can usually see when the lights are off, I answered. Now, my panic was rising.

There's something covering your eyes, Sara thought. *Bandages maybe?*

I felt my face. Yes, a cloth was wrapped around my head, covering my eyes. I was about to take the bandage off when I heard the main door open and then a small click.

Who is it? What's going on? I asked Sara.

It's just a white-coat turning on the lights, she explained. *There's a woman white-coat with him and she's walking this way.* I heard footsteps grow louder and then stop. *She's in front of your cage.*

I heard another click as my cage door was unlocked and then the sound of the door opening. My whole body tightened.

"Calm down," a woman said softly. "Let me just take this off." She grasped the bandage wrapped around my head. "Close your eyes." I did, and she pulled the bandages from my face.

She forced one eye open and she shone a small, bright light into it. The brightness stung, and I gritted my teeth. She did the same to the other eye.

She didn't replace the bandages but closed the cage door and left the room with the other scientist. I opened my eyes and blinked them into focus.

I turned to look. Sara was to my right, across the aisle was Sam, and to my left was an empty cage. Everything looked the same. Nothing had changed. My eyes began to sting and water again.

What did they do to your eyes? Sara asked.

Your eyes look fine to me. Sam said. *What did they do?*

I replied, *I don't know. I just don't know.*

CHAPTER 3

Scientists had come and taken Sam to one of the labs. That was, what I thought of as, hours ago.

Call me hopelessly paranoid, but I was preparing myself for the worst. Questions ran through my mind. What had happened to him? Was he hurt? Was he hurt and dying? Was he dead? Yep, paranoid.

Suddenly the door opened and Sam and a scientist walked in. He was still walking. That was a good sign. The scientist led him to his cage. Sam backed into it and the scientist closed the door.

Once the scientist left I asked out loud, "What happened?"

Sam yawned in reply. "Too tired. Tell you later." He turned away and for the first time ever, I noticed huge solid black wings on his back.

Once he fell asleep I thought to my cat-like friend, *Have you ever noticed Sam's wings?*

Yeah, what about them? She gave me a confused look.

Nothing. It's just that I've never noticed them before now.

Sara just shrugged and turned away. I decided to practice making keys again.

I held out my hand and focused as hard as I could. Particles clustered in the shape of a key. Just when it looked solid, the particles scattered and disappeared.

I tried again, but this time I was interrupted. A scientist stepped in. He carried a needle but he walked past my cage, stopping at one on the right about three cages down. I couldn't tell who or what was in it.

After he left I tried again to make a key, again, and again, and again. Absolutely nothing. The last time I tried, a white-coat came in and turned the lights off. I was exhausted. Hey, making stuff out of thin air is hard work. It had been a really long day and my eyes still burned. I lay down and was out like a light (no pun intended).

———◆———

When I woke up Sara was still asleep but Sam was wide awake. I sat up and stretched.

What are you doing up? I asked him telepathically.

He smiled and thought back, *Early to bed is early to rise, I guess.*

The lights were already on, my eyes didn't sting anymore, and Sam was obviously less tired than the day before. It was a good start.

A minute later Sara woke up with a wide yawn and stretch. "'Morning, guys."

'Morning Sara, I replied. *Sam, Sara, you hungry?*

Duh, Sara answered.

Of course, Sam thought.

I had had a strange dream that night that I could make food with my ability. Why id didn't think of it sooner is still a mystery.

I concentrated, and slowly but surely, three warm loaves of bread materialized. The other hybrids stared in hunger. Sam, Sara, and I nodded to each other. I made six more loaves and tossed three to Sam, who broke them into smaller pieces and passed them around. Sara and I did the same. Thankfully, all of us got the same amount to eat.

For the first time in ages I saw satisfaction on the faces of the hybrids. I felt all warm inside. That feeling quickly left when a scientist walked in, opened my cage door, and dragged me out into the hallway.

While I fought him, I overheard his thoughts: *I still don't get why she wants us to do this. It will only make them learn to plot against us.*

I was confused. How could a simple test make me do that?

He took several confusing turns, leading me down hallways I'd never seen before, until we came to a set of large double doors.

He pushed me through the doors. To my surprise, I wasn't in a testing lab but a huge forest. I took in a deep breath, and the air didn't smell of antiseptic. It smelled fresh and alive. It was blissful and green with the foliage and trees.

The view took my breath away. There were trees, small plants, and actual soil. Suddenly, a loud growl broke the silence. From what I heard, the animal that growled was big, very big, and very close.

Hearing a rustle in the nearby bushes, I crouched into a defensive position. The rustling stopped and a small gray squirrel hopped out. Its twitchy movements bothered me. It squeaked and scurried up the nearest tree.

"What the—"

A warhound burst out of the trees. It was *huge.* Its eyes glistened with rage and hunger as it stared at me. It licked its hairy doglike muzzle but otherwise didn't move. It just kept staring. I turned and ran as fast as I could. Adrenaline poured into my veins, giving me extra speed. My bare feet pounded against the earth as I pushed through bushes and trees.

The thundering sounds of the warhound's pursuit faded. I slowed down and looked over my shoulder but still kept running. Nothing.

With a roar the warhound burst out of the brush. I ran faster, still looking back. Abruptly the warhound stopped running. He drew his lips back into a twisted smile and waved.

Suddenly the ground disappeared from beneath my feet. I had fallen over the edge of a rocky cliff. The wind pulled and tugged my wings open. I jerked as my body stopped falling. It hurt, but it would have hurt a lot worse if it had been one second later.

I was gliding over the rocks at the base of the cliff. I tried my best to flap my wings and slowly I began to rise. Within seconds I was high above the cliff, the warhound, and the trees.

I'm flying! I'm actually flying! I thought with a huge smile on my face. I'd done it. I'd found the purpose of my wings. I was doing what they were meant to do and it felt right. It felt natural.

Then two bad things happened. First, a bug flew into my face.

Then, as I rose closer to the ceiling, big sprinklers turned on. Water poured down on me, soaking me and making my feathers really heavy. I began to lose altitude fast. Soon, my wings had become too heavy to move and I dropped like a rock.

I fell into the trees. The branches cut and bruised my skin. A thick branch hit me squarely in the stomach, knocking all the air from my lungs. I hit the ground with a sickening thud. I looked down and saw that I was bleeding badly. My breaths were short and uneven. The grass was stained scarlet.

A sudden cold filled me, inside and out. My vision doubled. The last thing I saw was the warhound towering over me with, what looked like, a smile on his face.

Chilling darkness dropped over me, and I was stranded in that cold, soul-sucking darkness. Nothing brought me out of it.

CHAPTER 4

I t had been weeks since Jay died …
Ha! I got you, didn't I? No, I'm not dead. But it felt like I really *had* died.

When I came to, I was lying on the hard metal floor of my cage. I sighed. Death only came as a blessing here.

I heard a soft crying. My head was spinning so I couldn't tell where it came from. I tried to sit up, but my head and body throbbed. I let out a pain-filled moan.

"Jay? Jay."

Sara's voice echoed and bounced in my head, making me feel worse. I cradled my head in my hands and curled into a little ball. It hurt to do anything.

Sara reached through the bars and touched my arm. I flinched. Everything made me hurt.

"Jay? Are you all right?"

Sam's deep voice hurt even worse. I clenched my teeth and managed to squeak, "No." Everything hurt, throbbed, or ached. Even my wings were numb with searing pain. I squeezed my eyes shut.

After what seemed like hours, which it probably was, the pain began to ease. My head and left side still throbbed, but

14

I tried sitting up. I became light-headed and thought I might black out again.

Lifting my hospital shirt a little bit, I looked at my side where it hurt worst. A bandage covered it. I moved the covering a bit and saw three parallel claw marks ripped into my flesh. I quickly recovered them and slid to the back of my cage as a scientist stepped into the room.

He removed Sara from her cage and she gave me a *don't worry* look. Sam looked at me after she left, and my head throbbed as his thoughts drifted into my consciousness.

So what made those scars? he asked. *What happened?*

Stop! Slow down. My head feels like it's going to explode. I slowly told him about the forest and the huge warhound and everything else.

I've been through that test but mine didn't go as bad, he thought.

What? I asked.

You know. Yesterday, he explained.

Oh! So that's why you were so tired. So did you really fly?

Yep! he thought proudly. *Did you?*

Uh, yes. I'm still here, aren't I?

Suddenly a blood-chilling scream of anguish split the air. I jumped and almost hit my head on the roof of my cage.

What's wrong? Sam asked.

Didn't you hear it? I replied, looking around in a panic.

Hear what? What are you talking about?

That really loud scream.

What scream?

I was so confused. How could I hear it and no one else? I'd heard it with my ears, not my head. That wasn't the weirdest

15

part. The weirdest part was that I felt like I'd heard it before, but I swore that I hadn't.

After about five minutes of silence, a scientist brought Sara back and locked her in her cage. She was uncoordinated and dizzy. I saw that she had many cuts and bruises across her body as she lay down.

So what's the story, Sara? I asked her.

Her eyes were bleary as looked up at me. *Inside ... whole forest. Huge warhound. Fell off cliff and ... I flew ...*

Don't worry. I placed my hand on her shoulder. *Sam and I have been through the same test.*

Huh? She had a glazed and confused look in her eyes.

Nothing, just go to sleep.

In less than a minute she was out cold.

So what's with this scream you heard? Sam asked.

I—I don't know. But I feel as if I've heard it before, I answered.

How?

Honestly? I don't know. Then I remembered the crying I had also heard. *I heard crying when I woke up. It was the same voice.*

Once again, I didn't hear a scream or crying, He lifted his hands to show that he'd given up.

Listen, I'm tired and I don't want to talk about it.

Almost as if I had called him, a scientist came in and turned the lights off.

Good night, Sam.

'Night, Jay.

CHAPTER 5

The next morning, I woke up early. The lights were still out and everyone was asleep. I decided to practice making things out of nothing.

I made very little progress before the lights came on. I tried making keys again and it didn't work the first ten times I tried. Some of the hybrids that were awake watched me at first but then became uninterested. Even Sam turned away to his own thoughts.

I was becoming irritated. I tried one more time and it shattered too. I felt like I was going to explode with rage.

Why can't I make a stupid key? I thought so angrily that my head hurt. I stared at my hand.

The particles formed really fast into the shape of a key. I expected it to shatter at any moment, but this time, it became totally solid and fell into my hand.

Stunned, I stopped breathing. Then I heard a little laugh. It was the same voice I had heard crying and screaming. I didn't care. I had the key.

I slipped my hand through the bars to release the lock, but a thought stopped me. I couldn't just unlock myself. I didn't know any exits. I didn't have a plan. If I tried to leave now,

I would just get caught and be brought back here. Instead, I tried to make a second key. It formed as easily as everything else.

Sara yawned and sat up.

Her eyes widened when she saw the keys, and she said out loud, "Oh my gosh! You've made the key."

Everyone turned to see. I heard excited whispers and voices ring from all directions.

"We can escape!"

"Pop that lock and let's get out of here."

I said over everyone, "Wait! We need a plan first. Otherwise it won't work." I thought a moment. "Okay, I'll need everyone to memorize possible exit routes."

Nods and murmurs of approval quickly followed that statement.

I continued, "We'll get out soon. We need to plan first and then we'll escape together. Got it?" That time I was given mischievous smiles and more mumbling.

For the next hour, the room was quiet as all the hybrids thought about the upcoming escape. We were going to escape. We were all going to be *free*.

CHAPTER 6

T he next morning, I was taken from my cage. The scientist I walked with had no idea I could hear his thoughts....

I still don't know who's getting the exercise here, the avians or the warhounds?

Being called "the avian" was better than being called "it."

I wondered what kind of exercise he was talking about. I was also thinking, *Crap! Warhounds in the equation cannot be good.* He opened a heavy steel door, and I blinked against the light. It was the outside. Not like the indoor forest but *really outside.*

Two more scientists stepped forward and clamped a heavy metal cuff around my ankle. The first one tied a rope around my torso, pinning my arms and wings to my body. He tied it so tight I couldn't move arms or wings, and he knotted the rope in the back so I couldn't reach it. Two of the scientists retreated inside. The remaining scientist stood behind me, brandishing a knife. He pushed me forward nearly making me fall face-down in the dust.

A ten-foot-high chain-link fence encircled us. Beyond the fence, was about twenty warhounds. A single gate stood between me and the deadly Warhounds.

Oh, crap! I couldn't fly and there was no way I could run away. *I am so dead.*

The scientist slit the rope and ran back inside. I loosened my wings as a loud buzz sounded. The gate burst open wide, releasing a tide of warhounds. I spread my wings and ran in the other direction.

I gave one mighty heave and my feet were off the ground. I turned and glided over the reach of the warhounds as I sped up. I gave another downward push and was almost equal to top of the fence.

I heard another buzz, this one from my ankle bracelet, and a jolt of electricity coursed through my body. I dropped about foot, but that wasn't going to stop me. Not this time. I gave another push and was almost the fence.

I'm home free! I thought, but then the completely unexpected happened. My vision shut down completely. I was blind.

Panicking, I lost my balance and rocketed to the ground. Within seconds the warhounds were on me, their claws tearing at my skin. I heard the snapping of jaws as they fought to see who would have the pleasure of killing me.

"Stop! Get away from it!" a man shouted.

"No!" one barked back. "This is our kill!"

A painfully high-pitched sound split the air, and I heard and felt the creatures back off.

A couple of scientists carried me back inside. They bandaged my cuts and then led me back to my cage. I was still blind. And you probably thought that the thing they did to my eyes wasn't important.

Sara's confused thoughts drifted to me. *What happened to your eyes? They look different.*

Are the lights on? Is there anything over my eyes? I asked I didn't know how they could have put something over my eyes while I was flying or how the lights would affect the outside where I had been when my vision cut out.

No, there's nothing on your eyes and the lights are on. Why? Sara asked.

Because I can't see anything. Nothing. Not color, not you, not anything!

So you're blind?

I guess so, I thought sadly. There was no way we could escape if I was blind.

What's going on with your eyes now? she asked.

I concentrated on my vision. Slowly, I began to see blurred colors, and then shapes, and then perfectly.

Your eyes look normal now, Sara told me calmly.

I can see now, I thought in reply.

She looked like she was going to say something but decided not to. Sara seemed happy, Sam wasn't in his cage, and I heard that little laugh again. It was mysterious but it made me happy.

------◆------

Later that night Sam, Sara, and I woke the other hybrids. I used my ability to make a dim ball of light.

"Okay, everyone. I have a plan," I whispered. "I've memorized an escape route that will get us out. It leads to the outside. I've been through the doors so I know it's perfect."

Gasps and whispers sounded throughout the room.

"What's it like out there?" one hybrid asked in an excited whisper.

"It's big and wide and there's dirt and grass and sun and sky, just like we've heard." There was a moment's silence. I added, "Tomorrow night, I'll make keys. Once we're all out, I'll lead you though the hallways to the door. We'll decide what to do after that. Everyone got that?"

Murmurs of agreement and acceptance told me that our freedom was near. But I also suspected it wasn't going to go as smoothly as I planned.

CHAPTER 7

One hybrid died the next day. It was the fish-boy two cages down from Sam. Few hybrids left their crates but the ones that did, came back okay. Maybe we would catch a lucky break. Yeah, and maybe Warhounds would learn to fly.

I waited until two hours after the lights were off and then decided it was time to get this thing started. This was going to be so easy. Sometimes when I'm excited, I can get a little overconfident.

I heard that little voice in my head again. It sounded the same as always, more like an innocent woman than a mysterious and evil person. I didn't hear a scream or cry or laugh this time, but words. *Something will go wrong.*

A hint of worry pricked my thoughts, but I set it aside. I concentrated on making three keys to unlock the cages. I had overheard the thoughts of two scientist a few days earlier, complaining about how long it was taking to get the cameras in this room fixed.

It's a shame they won't see us, I thought. *Not!*

It took me only a minute to make three keys. Sam and Sara both watched me through the dark. Did I forget to say that

Sam had gained hawklike vision? Finally! I tossed one key to Sam and handed another to Sara.

I felt around for the lock through the bars of my cage. Once I found the keyhole I fit the key in and gave it a turn. With a click the door was unlocked and I pushed it open. Sara and Sam had gotten their own doors open already.

I slowly stepped out of my cage and onto the cold linoleum floor. I walked free without a scientist for the first time. All three of us unlocked the cages of the other hybrids. I memorized each face.

One hybrid caught my attention. It was a girl whose big white wings had a single black feather on each wing. She was about my age but a little shorter.

"I'm Jay," I said as she stepped out. "What's your name?"

She didn't answer. I suspected she could not speak. I picked up from her thoughts that her name was Abbie. Her hair was long like mine, but hers had streaks of all colors—red, brown, blonde, and a little black. My hair was just dark blonde.

A few other hybrids intrigued me. One was a tall, thin, blond-haired kid named Alex. Another was a big gray wolf. Surprisingly, he spoke English but had no name. Over the years I had seen hybrids with deformed limbs, strangely colored skin, scales, fur, and feathers, and even some with bones and organs growing on the outsides of their bodies. (Eww! I know!) I saw a couple more hybrids who had wings like me, Sara, Sam, and Abbie. One little girl with wings was the most surprising.

She had long brown hair and big green eyes. Her wings were a beautiful russet-brown. She looked about eight years old.

I did a quick head count. Yes, Sara had taught me to count. Well, to fifty anyway. There were thirty-six of us total. It was a lot more than I had expected.

"I'll lead the way. I know the way out," I announced over the excited whispers. I walked over to the door and turned the handle just like the scientists did. It clicked and I pushed it open. The hallway was lit by only a few lights.

I reviewed the path in my mind. First a right, then another right, then a left and down a long hallway, a final right, and out the double doors at the end of the short hallway. I peeked into the hall, left and right. No one, great! I stepped out and motioned to the others to follow. We all went down the right side of the hall.

When we reached the first turn, I stopped and looked around the corner. Good, also nothing. I glanced over my shoulder. Everyone was behind me and no warhounds. I quietly continued down the hall. We successfully made it to the next right and down that hall. We were almost to the left turn when I heard a small beeping sound.

I looked to the source of the sound and saw a camera and a motion detector. My eyes opened wide in realization.

"Move it! Move it!" I yelled. "Run!"

We ran down the next hallway. Sadly it was the longest and the last right was almost at the end. Growls and thundering sounds echoing behind us warned that warhounds were on our tails. No offence to the hybrids with tails.

Looking back, I saw the warhounds were in the same hallway.

"Sam," I yelled, "take that right out the door! Make sure they're safe."

I motioned him to go on as I dropped to the back of the group, yelling at the slower hybrids to run faster.

I almost ran over the gray wolf as he skidded to a halt. He growled at the ten gaining warhounds.

"What the heck do you think you're doing?" I screamed at him.

"Helping you to escape," he barked. "I couldn't live outside this place even if I wanted to. This is all I've known."

His voice was gruff but I saw fear in his amber eyes. I stopped to watch in horror as he ran at the warhounds, tackled one to the ground, and bit into its arm. Six or seven warhounds piled on him. He scrambled and whined.

He stopped struggling and scarlet blood seeped from his lifeless body. I closed my eyes and started running again.

I reached the last corner and looked back. Three warhounds were right behind me. Hybrids were streaming out the double doors, and I shoved some to hurry them on. Finally I was out as well. It was dark and stars glittered in the sky, but what lit our path was a beautiful full moon.

Seconds after I leaped out the door, the warhounds thundered through it. The adrenaline flooding my body gave me speed. I was tempted to spread my wings and leave everything behind, but I decided the better of it.

As I raced toward the cluster of hybrids and away from the warhounds' snapping jaws, the little winged girl fell. I slowed down and scooped her up.

She squirmed in my arms. I tried to hold her tight, but she struggled free and jumped out of my grasp, spreading her tawny wings. She flew to the crowd and hit the ground running. I, on the other hand, had forgotten to speed up (if that's possible while running for your life).

A hairy warhound's paw shot out and grabbed my leg. I fell as it dragged me back, its yellowed canines dangerously close to my throat.

This is it, I thought. *I'm really going to die this time.*

Wrong again! Faster than a leopard, Sara leaped onto the warhound with her claws extended farther than I had ever seen them.

She clawed at its face till it let go of me. I scrambled to my feet to see the second warhound try to tear Sara off his partner. She managed to claw the first one's eyes before being pulled off.

I scrambled away, torn between catching up to the crowd and taking on a warhound myself to save Sara. The warhound lifted her over its head and threw her. She landed in front of me and I helped her to her feet.

Copy me, I told her. I spread my wings and did a running take-off. She quickly followed and together we caught up with the group. The hybrids had stopped, and within one second of landing, I realized why. The ten-foot fence blocked our path.

Why didn't I remember the fence?

The hybrids glanced around with worry. I turned to see the two warhounds just sitting there. Were they *laughing*?

Wait, I thought. *Weren't there three Warhounds chasing us?*

"I'll get us through."

The calm voice shocked everyone. It was Alex. How could a skinny eleven-year-old boy get us though *that*?

"Give me room," he commanded. Everyone backed up, attention torn between Alex and the two Warhounds.

Alex's blond hair grew longer and wrapped around his neck and chest. His canine teeth grew larger and sharper. Golden fur began to cover his body.

At first I expected a warhound, but he morphed into a magnificent lion. He was bigger than any warhound I had ever seen. He turned to the fence.

Rearing up on his back legs, he slammed his forepaws into the fence. At first it only shook. He tried a second time and a big section came crashing down. He turned and let out a fierce growl.

The third warhound had come back and he had brought about thirty of his friends. The small army of warhounds charged after us. I stood there doing my hybrid-deer-in-the-headlights pose as the hungry tide came closer.

Alex leaped over the crowd and landed in front of me. He let out a mighty, thundering roar. I swore I saw a small shock wave rise from that roar. Some warhounds slowed down and a couple even retreated, but most kept running. All hybrids turned and ran for dear life.

I ran too, and Alex caught up. "I'm going to scout ahead for a place to hide," I said. He nodded. I ran faster and took off. I spotted Sam and Sara in the lead. I had no clue how Sara had gotten up there so fast.

Sara, Sam, and a few other winged kids took off and followed me, Abbie and the little girl among them. With powerful strokes, we rose higher and higher. It was amazing. I felt light and powerful, like nothing could touch me. I felt free.

In less than a minute I could see a huge gorge in the distance. We picked up speed. We were almost on top of it.

Suddenly Abbie shouted, "Everyone, follow me."

Before anyone could reply, she tucked in her wings and rocketed toward the ground. I quickly followed her. She was so close to the ground I thought I'd see her go splat. Instead, she landed gracefully next to a hole in the ground. I landed beside her and looked up to see Sara hovering in the air.

I'll keep you up to date, she thought down to me. *Right now the lion-kid is trying to protect the others and is pretty much killing the warhounds closest to him and the other hybrids.* I signaled to her and turned back to Abbie.

She was climbing into hole. "Come on," she said irritably.

Sam shrugged and easily fit down the hole. I slid down next. The hole dropped about six feet to a wide, long tunnel. The tunnel led to a huge cave. Other smaller tunnels branched out of the big cave.

Abbie stood in the middle of the cave. "I found this in a dream. It's a safe place for us hybrids. The hole is too small for warhounds, and it's hidden by a bunch of bushes. These tunnels over here lead to smaller caves …" She stopped herself. "I'll give a tour later. Right now we need to lead the others here without the warhounds following."

"Right." I stepped up. "I'll bring a few of you with me and the rest need to stay here. We'll lead the others here and keep the warhounds away." I paused. Some of the hybrids looked determined and excited while others seemed reluctant and scared.

"Sam, Abbie?" I said. Abbie seemed surprised that I knew her name. "I need you to come."

I studied the other hybrids. There were thirteen of us in the cave, including me. I chose six of them. The one little girl looked upset that I didn't ask her to come with me. We all climbed back up and took off.

"Good," Sara said when we caught up with her. "Lion-boy can't take much more."

We reviewed the plan, and once we reached the still running hybrids, Sara and Sam took all of the other winged hybrids to keep the warhounds at bay while Abbie and I helped the other hybrids escape. Alex looked absolutely terrible. He was still a lion and was bleeding at the shoulder, with one of his eyes swollen shut.

"We've found a safe spot to hide but we have to hurry!" Abbie announced.

"Alex," I said, "can you carry the smallest and slowest?" He nodded, and I hoisted seven small hybrids onto his back.

"You fly," Abbie said to me. "I can run faster and you have better eyesight. You can show us where it is."

As she took position in the front and I got ready to take-off, I looked back at the battle.

Sara, Sam, and the other hybrids were fighting the warhounds in probably the bloodiest battle they would ever see. Sara's arm was bleeding and so was Sam's shoulder. Some of the others were hurt too. Blood and warhounds' dead bodies littered and stained the ground. Those fighting back fought with anger and rage. I turned, focused on my task, and did a running takeoff.

Within moments I was high in the air with the wind tugging at my wings. I looked down and focused. Sara had paused to watch me.

Keep them busy until I come back, I thought down to her. She nodded and went back to ripping the flesh off a warhound's face. Abbie was running in front of the group of hybrids as I flew over them. After a minute I saw the small hole and began my decent.

I landed smoothly on the rough ground. Abbie ran up, and she and I dropped kids into the tunnel. I took the little ones off Alex, and he morphed back into himself.

"Why did you bring us here?" he asked as Abbie disappeared into the hole.

"This is the safe place," I said, "so get your butt in there while I go get the others. Abbie will explain everything." I took off before he could ask any more questions and turned in the direction of the DAEL building.

As soon as the battle was in sight, I flew down, yelling, "Retreat! Get into the air! Let's go, now!"

Sara and Sam took off together, carrying other hybrids.

Sam carried a small fishlike boy, who cried, "Wait, my brother!"

He pointed to a small green kid on the ground being attacked by a huge warhound. I dived, turned so that I was leading with my feet, and double kicked the warhound in the face. Its head snapped to the side and it lost its balance.

I wasn't sure what to think. That was the first time I'd ever attacked anything. I instinctively scooped up the kid and aimed for the skies. Dawn was breaking and the sun was rising. The warhounds followed us as we raced to the tunnels.

"Oh, crap! They just don't give up, do they?" I shouted into the wind. I poured on the speed and in about a minute, we were above the hole. We landed and skidded to a halt.

The ground under our bare feet vibrated. The warhounds were almost on top of us. I shoved the last of the Hybrids into the hole. Looking around, I saw a big flat rock that almost completely blended into the dirt and sand. I dragged it close to the hole, lowered myself into the tunnel entrance, and covered the hole with the rock.

It was dark but I heard the terrified whispers of the hybrids. I quickly materialized a ball of light. I still had no clue what exactly I was doing when I created light, but it was helpful.

"Come on, let's go," Abbie whispered as if the warhounds could hear us. She led us down the tunnel to the big cave. I followed the crowd, taking up the rear. I heard the sound of something hitting the cold hard ground.

I turned and was immediately terrified. His clothes shredded and soaked with blood, Sam was pulling himself up to lean against the cave wall. The group had already gone to the Big Cave.

"Sam, you okay?" That was a really stupid question on my part. He looked more pale than usual and was extremely shaky. His silver eyes were dull and unfocused.

"I'm okay." What an obvious lie! Suddenly he collapsed onto the floor again.

"Sam!" I knelt down beside him, letting the light disappear. I could still see his crumpled shape through the darkness. He was conscious, but just barely.

I pulled him up, draping his arm over my shoulder and my left arm around his waist. He limped along with me about halfway down the tunnel. I had to drag him the rest of the way.

In the cave, everyone stared when we appeared. Sara ran over so quickly that a few of her feathers fell out.

I heard the little voice say, *"Find her... help him."* My thoughts on this: no freaking clue.

"L-let's see how bad he is," Sara said shakily. She slowly pulled off his shirt. No, it's not just a hospital robe. It's a shirt and, yes, we were given pants (thank goodness).

Deep, bloody claw marks ran from the top of his right shoulder to the bottom of his ribcage. Blood still flowed from the wound.

He was completely unconscious now. As I stared at him, thoughts began to flow chaotically into my head. I ignored most of them but one so terrifying, I couldn't silence it.

He's going to die. There's no way he'll be able to survive that.

This brought me to tears. Even as I watched, his breathing grow shallow, his heart rate slowing. It wouldn't be long. His end was nearing.

Suddenly the little girl with russet wings knelt down beside him. An odd pureness and sadness shone in her green eyes.

She rested her small hand on his wound. She sat motionless and then began to cry quietly. After a moment it looked as though the bleeding had stopped. I took a closer look. It *had* stopped. I looked at the girl's face with shock, and she seemed to brighten up as the wound began to seal.

When I looked back down, the claw marks had scabbed over. They were going to leave one nasty scar, though. She shakily removed her blood-covered hands.

Abbie tapped my shoulder. "Now, can I give a tour after you do a head count?"

I stood up and counted the hybrids. Only twenty-five, including me and the still unconscious Sam. Not including the wolf, ten had been either captured or killed.

"Twenty-five. We lost eleven," I reported.

Abbie turned and waved for us to follow.

CHAPTER 8

Abbie showed us a maze of smaller caves and tunnels. Some of them had openings that lead out to the gorge. The higher ones could be used by the flying hybrids and the lower ones by the nonflying ones.

When we returned to the big cave, Abbie led us around the still unconscious Sam and the little healer girl to a long tunnel that sloped downward.

A faint light shone at the end. The tunnel opened into a big, I mean *huge* cave. It was way bigger than the big cave. Several natural spring pools and one big pond in the center of the stone floor.

The water was clean. The many springs were shallow and warm and some of the water flowed to the outside through a small opening in the cave wall, allowing light to come in. The many springs were shallow and warm. The pond was wide, deep, had a few fish, and it was a bit colder than the springs.

"As I said before, I think a civilization could be made here," Abbie said. If you don't like lectures, you can skip the rest of this paragraph. "These caves and tunnels would provide food and fresh water. The forest below, in the gorge can also provide us with some food. The caves can also protect us from cold and bad weather."

The blue fish-boy and his greenish-colored brother ran to the nearest spring and climbed into the water. I only then noticed that a plant grew the green boy's back and small ferns grew from his wrists.

From what I sensed, the two boys *had* to stay together to keep each other alive. The fish-boy secreted water to keep the plant-boy from becoming dehydrated and the plant-boy provided shade to prevent the fish-boy from shriveling up in the sun and heat. Not surprisingly, the plant-boy was much taller than the fish-boy.

They both seemed to enjoy the warm water. I walked over, rolled up my pant legs, and stepped into the spring while I sat on its edge. It was amazing! It wasn't scalding hot but it wasn't freezing cold either. A few others joined us. Everyone seemed to like the springs, except for Sara, what with the whole part cat thing.

Suddenly the little healer girl ran into the cave, "He's awake!"

I jumped out of the water faster than Sara ever could and ran up the tunnel. I slipped once or twice on the sloped stone path. Sara was on my heels with the little girl at her side.

I burst into the first cave. Sam was still on the floor, trying to sit up. Sara and I helped him. He was still shaky and dizzy. He looked up at us with bleary eyes and blinked a couple of times to focus on us.

"Hey, w-what happened?" he asked groggily. He glanced at his long scabs and frowned in confusion.

"You were bleeding badly and you passed out," I explained. "You almost bled to death, but this girl here saved you." I motioned to the little winged girl. I knew he might be embarrassed that he'd had his life saved by a seven year-old girl but, he'd get over it.

"Thank you," he said to her. She smiled with a proud sense of accomplishment. "But does my little savior have a name?"

Yep, still a charmer. He was fine.

Her smile faltered. "I don't have a name," she said softly. We all looked at her as an expression of concentration crossed her face. "I still don't know," she said after a moment, "but I'll think of one eventually."

Sam tried to stand up but winced in pain.

"Are you okay?" I knew I looked and sounded like a worried mother, but I *was* worried.

"Ow! Very sore," he said.

I glanced at Sara, "I think we can help you with that."

We helped him stand and then walked down the tunnel to the huge cave. We found a spring that no one else was in. Sam tentatively stepped into the water. Once he was settled, he gave a pleased smile.

"Sara," he asked, "could you please find me a shirt I can use? I'm sure someone will give theirs up."

"Sure," she answered. She walked away and the little girl disappeared to a near-by spring.

"We kind of match now, don't we?" Sam smiled.

I had no clue what he meant. He motioned for me to sit down next to him. I sank into the knee-high water, on his right. He lifted the left side of my shirt to reveal the scars running along my side and then he pointed to his own. I simply smiled.

The healing girl walked up with Abbie. "I know what I want my name to be." She paused and continued, "It's May. What are your names?"

I turned to her. "My name is Jay and this is my friend Sam. And that girl over there" -I pointed at Sara who was still walking around- "is Sara."

I was about to introduce Abbie, but May said, "This is my friend, Abbie."

"We've already met," I explained. I looked out the hole where the water ran out into the gorge. The sun was still high in the sky. May and Abbie joined us in the warm water.

Sara returned. She threw a dry, clean shirt at Sam and then joined us, dipping only her feet in the water. I had a good feeling. We'd be friends, yes. Almost like family, yes. Have our differences, also yes.

I felt someone staring at me. Looking around, I saw that it was Abbie. Had she the same feelings I had? Maybe, maybe not.

We got into strange conversations about what our different abilities were. Abbie could turn invisible except for the single black feathers on her white wings. She also got hints from the universe about important things that would happen. That explained how she knew about the caves.

Other than her ability to heal people by touch, May could also breathe underwater. She proved it by going into the big pond and staying under for about ten minutes. When she came up, she had a fish that was almost as big as she was.

I smiled and laughed, "Looks like we've got dinner."

CHAPTER 9

After we ate, everyone went to sleep in the smaller caves. Most stayed in the caves farthest back in the earth, since they made us feel safer, more secure. The five of us: Sam, Sara, Abbie, May, and me stayed together in one of the back caves.

As I fell asleep, all I heard was the steady breathing of my friends around me. The stone ground was actually more comfortable than the hard metal floor of my cage. This night's sleep, however, was worse than any night at the DAEL.

———◆———

I was in a lab. Before me was the entrance to a maze. A metal cuff encircled one of my ankles and scientists were taping electrodes and sensors to my head and chest.

Suddenly, a scientist pushed me into the maze. I ran. I knew that if I stopped or slowed down, I would get zapped by the ankle bracelet.

One white-coat yelled, "The warhound is in!"

Oh, crap! I ran faster. No matter what I did, which way I went, I couldn't find the exit. The warhound wasn't far behind me.

I stopped to look behind me. A jolt of electricity coursed through my body, temporarily scrambling my thoughts. I ran again. I took a turn and came to a dead end. I whirled around, but the warhound blocked my exit. Growling menacingly, it stepped forward, one threatening step after another. When it was within a few feet of me, it bared its teeth and launched itself at me...

———◦◆◦———

I bolted upright. Slowly, my eyes focused. I was back in the small cave I had fallen asleep in. Everyone was still asleep, and my wings itched to be opened. I stood up and pushed the nightmare aside.

I silently slipped from the smaller cave to the big one. Standing in the center, I looked around. I could see the long tunnel that led to the surface, the sloping tunnel that led to the water, and a bunch of smaller tunnels that led to the smaller caves.

I walked down a tunnel that Abbie had led us through. It led to a chain of small caves that eventually opened into the gorge. I reached the last cave and looked outside.

Dawn was just breaking over the horizon. I climbed onto the rim of the cave opening and got ready to snap out my wings. I leaped from the ledge. Before I had fallen more than two feet, I unfurled my wings and gave a mighty push. I pushed down again to gain speed. The wind whistled through my feathers. It kind of tickled. An idea flashed into my head.

I flew higher and higher. Once I was hundreds of feet above the gorge, I rotated my body so I was head down and then pulled my wings to my sides. I began to rocket downward at immeasurably blinding speeds. When I was within a hundred feet of the ground, I snapped my wings back out and pulled up. Now *that's* an adrenaline rush.

Out of the corner of my eye, I saw something move in one of the cave openings. It was Sam, Sara, May and Abbie staring at me with wide eyes. I banked in their direction.

I hovered over the ledge and then pulled my wings in, dropping gently to the cave floor. Sara ran up and gave me a huge hug, taking me by surprise.

"I thought you were trying to kill yourself!" she said.

"Nope," I replied, pulling away. "I was just trying to wake myself up." I grinned, still feeling the rush of flight.

May tugged on my shirt, "I'm getting hungry."

I took her hand in mine and we all walked down to the big cave. Ten other hybrids were already there. May left me to join them, and I leaned against the cave wall. Hearing the sounds of wet feet tapping along the tunnel, I looked toward the entrance. A fishy-looking kid walked in with a big silvery fish in arms.

I crossed my arms over my chest. *We can't just eat fish,* I thought. *It's just not healthy, and we could get sick from it.* Huh, I guess you can learn something from hanging with doctors and scientists. A couple of the hybrids started gutting and cutting the fish. I won't go into the details. It's too disgusting.

One girl turned away from the fish gutting and looked at me, and gaped. The others looked as well when she gasped.

I looked around. Nothing wrong. I looked down where the others were staring and at my side was a lush green bush. It had small blue flowers and bright red berries. It was growing really fast and it was almost as tall as me when it stopped.

A large top branch snapped, cracked, and came crashing down. I moved out of the way just in time.

I had no clue how that had happened, but as I examined the branch, I saw it had only five small berries on it. This was unlike the other branches which were clustered with berries.

May ran forward, picked a big one off a low branch, and popped it in to her mouth. I held my breath. I didn't know if what I had created was poisonous or not. I half expected her to keel over and fall dead. Instead, she smiled, pulled another one off, and handed it to me.

I chomped off half. Juices squirted out around my lips. It tasted amazing. It was sweet and a little sour at the same time. I pretty much inhaled the other half. A few others joined us and ate some too. They seemed to like them as well.

I think that fixes that *problem*, I thought. I looked away from the bush to see Sam's silvery eyes staring at me intently from the other side of the cave. Why was he always staring at me? Perhaps, I would never know.

CHAPTER 10

"Jay. Jay."

The hushed voice was full of anxiety. My eyes shot open. I hadn't dreamed that night, but was still startled by someone shaking me awake. My eyes quickly adjusted to the darkness to see Abbie leaning over me. I sat up.

"What's going on?" I yawned and rubbed my eyes. I could just make out the restless anxiety written across her face.

"I've got to tell you something," she whispered. "It's really important."

"What is it, Abbie?" I asked softly. I leaned in closer so that I could hear her clearly.

"We need to leave. You, me, Sara, Sam, and May. We can't stay here." I was about to say something but she continued, "You know how I get clues from the universe about things that are going to happen? Well, I just got one. And it says that we have to leave."

"Without the others?" I whispered. She nodded.

"They have their own paths to take, but it's not ours. So we *have to go*." She paused. "Someone will lead them but it's not you."

I was confused. I didn't know if it was because of the total weirdness of what she was saying or because I was so freaking tired.

"Don't you see?" she went on. "The falling branch was a sign. It's telling us that we need to break away from the other hybrids."

Oh, was that the hint she was talking about?

I gave a wide yawn and laid on my side, "So, when do we need to leave?" My eyes were already half closed.

I only heard one word before I blacked out: "Tomorrow."

———◆———

I woke early and then woke the others and took them down to the springs. Sara didn't really wake up until I pushed her into one of the warm springs. She crawled out shivering, hissing, and spitting. She stared at me through narrowed eyes. I -being a nice person- apologized.

While the rest of us settled into the water, Sara sat on a nearby rock. Abbie and I exchanged knowing glances. Everyone else seemed to pick up on that and leaned in closer to listen. They were all silent as Abbie explained the sign she'd received.

Sam said after Abbie had finished, "So we're just supposed to leave because a stupid branch fell?"

I sighed. Even after a ten-minute explanation he still didn't get it.

"Someone else will lead and take care of them, so we can leave," I explained.

"So, who is this *magnificent leader* you speak of?" He crossed arms and squared his shoulders. I had wondered the same thing. I was curious as to how to find the leader.

I turned to Abbie, "Uh, Abbie, how *do* we find the leader?"

She shrugged. "I don't know. They're just going to show up, I guess. That part wasn't very clear to me."

Great, I thought.

CHAPTER 11

We didn't have to wait long. At lunch, the leader just stepped up. Most of us were in the big cave eating fish, berries, and deer. How did they get a deer? I don't know and never will know.

"I have something to say," someone said.

Everyone turned. It was Alex, the lion-boy, standing on a rock in a corner. "I think we should go back." Everyone gasped. "No, no, I mean go back for the others. There were other kids like us still there and I think we should get them out." His nervousness began to show in his voice. "I can feel energies, energies that come from living things. I felt a lot of them whenever I walked down those halls."

He started looking more leader-like and confident. "I know the first rescue will be tough, but then we will have more that can fight back. And with more rescues, we'll have more and more fighters. Then we can take control of that awful place!"

Many of the hybrids cheered this new plan.

We have a winner! I thought.

After everyone calmed down, I walked up to Alex and said, "I'm going to be leaving soon and a few others are coming with me."

"You can't leave!" he said. "You've led us this far! Who will lead us from here?"

"You. *You* will lead them and care for them," I replied calmly.

"N-no, there must some mistake. I can't lead them." He shook his head.

"You just gave the speech of a leader that I couldn't do in a hundred years and now you just say *no!*" I realized that my voice was rising and took a deep breath. "You're the only one who *can* lead them. I have to lead my own group and travel where the wind takes us. I know you feel you can't do it on your own and I know it's hard. Being a leader means making connections, having confidence, and... Well, you know. You have to do this just like I have to leave."

He looked as if I'd just handed him the earth and said, "Here you go, make sure nothing bad happens to this." He sat down on the rock. He had to take it in. I turned and walked over to my little group and explained to them what had just happened.

———◆———

I shook Sam's shoulder. He woke up quickly. He helped wake up the others as we'd planned. We were leaving right before sunrise.

We walked silently through the tunnels. I was happy for my hawk-like eyesight. If Sam and Sara had not been equally adept at seeing in the dark, we would've be tripping over hybrids and running into walls.

Upon entering the big cave, we jumped at a hushed voice. "So, you *are* leaving?" I turned. I could clearly make out Alex's form. I nodded, and he continued, "I've thought a lot about what you said and I decided. I've decided that I will lead them and make them stronger."

I smiled, leaned forward, and gave him a fast hug, surprising him.

I felt Sam tense at my side as I quickly pulled away but I paid no attention to it. I led my little group to a small tunnel near the back of the cave. We followed it until we came to a cave with an opening.

One by one, we leaped out of the opening, leaving me for last. I could feel Alex peering around the corner as I rose into the lightening sky.

The crisp, cool air filled my lungs and tugged at my wings. This was bliss. I pulled to the front and led. We were high above the gorge and heading in an easterly direction.

I didn't know where we were headed, but at the moment, I didn't care. That's the thing about flying. It's hard to explain but there's a reason why some people dream about it.

———◆———

We flew in that direction for about an hour or two. Eventually, in the distance I could see the faint outline of a clump of small buildings. I wanted to veer another direction, but something kept me on course for them.

As we sped toward the buildings, May asked, "What is that?"

"It's called a town."

Our heads swiveled toward Sam as he spoke for the first time on the flight.

"A what?" I asked.

"A town. Normal people live there. These places have food to eat, places to sleep, and places to buy stuff," he explained.

Okay, he lost me at *normal people*. He must have seen our confusion because he motioned us down to a grove of trees on the outskirts of this *town*. As Sam explained, we relaxed a bit.

He told us what money was, that people earned it by working, and what a store and a restaurant were. I thought it was beyond weird that slips of green paper had value and were exchanged for food and clothes and other stuff. I wondered how Sam could know all these things. Being locked in a dog crate all your life doesn't exactly include an education plan. There's a reason why *normal people* have schools.

We made a plan to get some supplies from one of those stores. Since we had no money, you can probably figure out what we meant by *getting* it.

———————◆————————

We had to wait for hours before putting our plan into action, but it paid off. The last worker left at sunset and locked the door of the store we had picked. Near the door, a pile of old paint cans leaned against the brick building. The man picked up an old, rusted can, dropped the keys inside, and set the can back down by the paints. *What a stupid hiding spot*, I thought. I don't think it even counted as a hiding spot.

After he drove off in a big, noisy metal thing Sam had told us was called a car, we sneaked over and took the key out of the can. *Ha-ha, moron.*

Sam unlocked the door, and we tiptoed inside. This place had lots of stuff. It had food, clothes, and even knives.

We all fitted ourselves into some loose jeans, T-shirts, and shoes. We had to cut long slits into the backs of our new shirts and jackets to fit our wings through. Sam kept the black-handled pocket knife. Meanwhile, Sara dragged her claws down a wooden wall, sharpening them.

"Heads up," Sam said as he tossed me a backpack. "Stock up on food."

I started shoving all the cookies, crackers, and bread I could into the bag while Sam got meats like hot dogs, ham, and sausage.

We all were ready to go except one thing. Where was May? I walked up and down all the aisles to find her, ending at a counter at the front of the store. Not there either. I turned to walk away and ran into a coat rack. It tilted, leaned, fell, and smashed right through the front window. Piercing alarms split the air.

I ran to the back of the store where the others waited. They were clustered together and wide-eyed, even May. We grabbed everything and headed for the back door. Then it got worse.

My vision went completely out again. *Great timing.* I tripped over something and fell. Now I was blind *and* helpless on the floor.

Someone picked me up and began carrying me somewhere. I felt cold air against my face, so I guessed we were back outside. I expected to hear the snapping of branches as everyone ran into the trees. Instead, I continue to feel the wind on my skin and the strong arms holding me.

Suddenly the person carrying me bumped into something, and I landed on the hard ground. I coughed and spat out the sand and dirt that had filled my mouth.

"Jay, are you all right?"

That was Sara's voice, full of panic and concern. I felt small hands roam over my arms, legs, and wings. "Is she hurt?" Sara asked.

"Is she okay?" That was Abbie.

"She's not hurt," May answered, "but something is definitely wrong. I can't figure out what it is."

"Hey, Sam, look at her eyes," Sara said. "They have that same look to them. Jay, can you see anything?"

"No," I mumbled.

Someone helped me sit up, propping me up against what felt like a tree. I could feel everyone staring and holding their breaths.

Slowly, my vision came back. First blurs and colors, and then shapes and forms, and then solid features and perfect once again.

May was still running her hands over my head and chest, trying to find an explanation. Abbie, Sara, and Sam were all staring at me with worried expressions. Sara released a big sigh when she realized that I was actually looking at her.

Sam leaned forward and gave me a hug. "I'm happy you're okay."

I was a little freaked by the hug, but what freaked me most was that I realized his arms were the same strong ones that had carried me out of the store. And I kind of liked it...

CHAPTER 12

We flew a few miles away to make camp for the night. We ate the food we'd taken. We'd been smart enough to not bring canned foods. They would have been way too heavy.

As was sat around the campfire, Sara, May, and Abbie all fell asleep quickly, leaving just me and Sam awake. I was still hungry and was cooking another hot dog. I held it over the fire, turning it on its stick as the tips of the flames licked at the meat.

Sam stood up and came to sit by me. "So, what happened today?"

I shrugged. "I don't know. How did you know all that stuff about the town?" It had been bugging me for a while now.

He sighed, "I haven't told anyone, but I actually went to school before I was taken from my parents." He paused for a breath. He knew I would want to hear the whole story. He continued, "I lived like a normal kid for the first seven years of my life, but I knew I was different from the other kids. I went to school up until the second grade. I learned to read and write. Then, on my way home one day, I was stopped by a strange car pulling up right in front of me. The back door opened and I was pulled inside. Then it all went black. Next thing I knew, I'm in a cage at that lab of horrors and I can hardly remember anything. After that, my wings grew out and my powers developed. Some of my memories came back eventually. And later, I met you. You know the rest. I was a little shocked that you had figured out my real name back there when we were deciding on a name for me."

An idea popped into my mind. "Do you think that you could teach me some stuff? Like how to read and write."

He smiled. He picked up a stick and began to draw in the dirt, strange shapes I'd seen before but had never known the meaning of. He made three shapes, and then another three underneath them.

"These are letters," he said, "and together they make out words." He pointed to the first set. "This one spells Jay. *J-A-Y.*" He pointed to the second set. "This one says Sam. *S-A-M.*"

He puts the stick in my hand. "You try. First the *J.*"

I drew a squiggly *J.*

"Now the *A.*"

I made a similar-looking *A* next to it.

"And now the *Y.*" I made that as well. "Good, now you know how to spell your name."

My heart fluttered at his praise. "Thank you. Good night, Sam," I said as I lay down.

"You're welcome. 'Night, Jay." He took off his jacket and laid it over me. I closed my eyes and drifted into sleep.

———◆———

Suddenly, my eyes popped open. No, I hadn't woken up from a nightmare. I'd just woken up. I didn't know why.

I looked around. *Uh-oh, fire's almost out.* I threw a couple of sticks onto the fire from the pile we had made earlier. I fanned it to get it going again. Soon enough, it was nice and warm.

Hearing a faint scratching sound nearby, I stood up. Sara was tossing and turning in her sleep. She was having another one of her nightmares. I knew what to do.

I sat next to her and rubbed her back between her wings, just the way she liked it. She calmed down.

I had almost fallen asleep again when Sara started thrashing around once more. This time more violently. She started growling and hissing in her sleep. She turned onto her stomach and clawed the ground with her lethal claws.

I had to wake her up. I shook her shoulders and shouted her name. I almost didn't notice the others rousing from their sleep.

Suddenly, Sara pushed herself off the ground and rammed into my chest, knocking the wind out of me. Her eyes were wide but unfocused as she launched herself at me, raking her claws across my right cheek and sending me crashing to the ground.

She skidded to a halt and turned back, her cat tail lashing. She was about to attack again, but Abbie tackled her.

Next thing I know, Abbie is on Sara's back with her knees in her wings, holding one of Sara's arms behind her back. Sam held down Sara's legs and tail. Sara lashed out with her free hand.

May was at Sara's side with a water bottle, splashing its contents on her head. Sara was still sleeping as she continued to thrash around. Slowly, she quieted and everyone backed off. Her steady breathing showed that she was sleeping normally again. I had expected her to wake up because of the water on her face.

One question ran through all of our minds: *What the heck was* that *about?*

CHAPTER 13

We kept our distance from Sara for the rest of the night in case she went on a rampage again. May fixed up my cheek, and let me tell you, it felt both good and weird at the same time. Weirdly-good, I guess. All that was left of the injury was a small scab.

After everyone woke up the next morning, we didn't talk about what had happened the night before. We just ate breakfast and got ready to move on. I started to pack the last of the food and water in the backpacks. We'd eaten almost half of it. It wouldn't be long before we had to stop again to get more.

"So, what happened to your face?"

I looked up. Sara was staring down at me with her curious cat eyes. She motioned to my cheek, and I sighed. I couldn't lie to her. Well, I could but it would be a really heavy weight on my shoulders.

I slowly explained what had happened last night, and she sat in stunned silence.

"I-I don't remember any of that happening," she whispered. She kept her gaze on the ground as she sat on a small tree stump.

I turned and continued to pack my bag. When I looked up again, Abbie was shifting her gaze between Sara and me. Her eyes were pools of fear and sadness.

Suddenly, Sam clapped his hands together, the sound ringing through the trees like a gunshot. "Let's get this show on the road, shall we?"

At least someone was *acting* like they were in a good mood. Soon after, we took to the skies.

———————

The wind whipped through my hair and tugged at my feathers. It was amazing. The only downfall about flying is that you have to yell to talk to each other, and you can't keep your mouth open for too long or you start choking on bugs.

We'd been flying for, I think, two hours. My wings radiated heat as I pushed up and down.

"So, where exactly are we heading?" Sam shouted above the wind. "And why?"

I had not really thought about that. I had just picked a direction and flew. We went with the flow, you know.

"I don't know," I answered. "Why do you ask?"

"Well, I was just won—" A loud coughing fit interrupted him.

"Are you all right?" I asked.

"Yep. Just … Ugh, just swallowed a bug."

We tried, we all *really* tried, but we couldn't help it. Everyone just burst out laughing.

Sara had tears in her eyes and May struggled to catch her breath. Even Sam laughed. I think I might have seen a speck of bug guts in his teeth. I had started to stop laughing, but started again when I saw that.

After we all calmed down, we flew on in silence. It had been a few minutes so I did a quick 360 to check on everyone. Sam had gotten the bug out of his teeth and was concentrating alternately on the horizon ahead of us and the trees below. Sara and May were deep in conversation a few feet back. Abbie was silent with a tired, zoned-out look in her eyes. She didn't look too good.

I slowed down till I was even with her. "What's up? You've been really quiet." She flinched. I guess she hadn't noticed me coming.

"Yeah, I'm fine."

Her tone told me otherwise. "Are you sure?"

She turned to look at me. Suddenly, her eyes rolled back in her head and she went completely limp. After that, she dropped like a rock.

"Abbie!" I shouted.

The others turned to look, staring at me and then at Abbie's plummeting body.

"Sam, take the lead. I'll go get her. Meet us at that lake a few miles up."

We had spotted the lake a little while ago. It was really big.

I pulled in my wings before anyone answer and I rocketed after Abbie. We were a good one hundred feet apart, and if I didn't hurry, she'd be one of those inkblots like the scientists had shown me a few years ago. Like this one ...

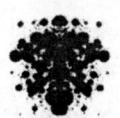

Not very pretty.

Now we were about seventy-five feet apart, and about a thousand above the trees. I pulled my wings flat along my back to make myself more aerodynamic.

Fifty feet apart. Now forty, thirty, twenty, ten … Five feet and closing. I grabbed her and held on tight. Opening my wings out, I let them fill with wind like sails. *Ouch!* We were only a couple hundred feet away from smashing into the dense forest beneath us.

I flapped hard to slow us down, but between the extra weight and how fast we were going, it would at least be a crash landing. At the most, it would be death. I pushed harder and tried to angle straight up, but it didn't help.

Abbie's eyes fluttered open and she spread her wings, slowing us down a little. We'd hit the trees in about five seconds.

Three, two, one … *SNAP!* We hit the first tree and I lost my hold on her. A thick branch smacked me in the chest, knocking the wind out of me. More branches whacked me, while smaller limbs and leaves smacked and scratched me. I almost thought I would never reach the ground.

I hit hard dirt—maybe it was a rock—and heard a crack in my chest. I think I had cracked a rib on my left side. Man, it hurt! I lay there for a minute gasping for air, no matter how painful each breath was.

I slowly stood up and looked around for Abbie. It didn't take long for us to run into each other. Well, let's just say that I walked around a tree as she was doing the same thing and we smacked heads.

We stood up and dusted off our new jeans. Abbie had a cut on her forehead, other minor cuts and bruises, and the occasional splinter. I could tell she was assessing my damage as well. Our damage looked about even, except I had a, most likely, cracked rib and she had a minor head injury.

My side began to sting and burn, and I gripped it where I thought my rib had broken. I noticed she was standing gingerly on her right foot, keeping the other one off the ground.

"I think I broke a rib," I said through clenched teeth. "What about you?"

"Foot hurts. Other than that I'm fine."

We began to walk, leaning on each other for support. I was struggling to breathe and Abbie could hardly walk. When we came to a big clearing, she stopped.

"What's up?" I asked her like nothing was wrong.

"I have something to tell you." She looked down at the ground, playing with a little brown leaf by her shoe. "It's about why I blacked out up there." She paused. "I had a premonition, a vision. It was about Sara." My eyes widened and I listened intently. She looked up. "Something really bad is going to happen to her. I don't know what it is or how it will happen. All I know is that it will happen very soon."

Tears welled up and pricked at the back of my eyes, but I refused to blink and let them loose. I said as calmly as I could, "Let's catch up with the others."

Abbie nodded. I'm sure she realized I was upset, so she didn't push the subject. She attempted to do a running takeoff but collapsed on the first step. I helped her to stand up. An idea came into her head.

How do I know? I'm a freaking telepath, remember! Haven't you been paying attention?

"Give me some room," she commanded.

I let go of her and she limped a few steps away. She spread out her beautiful wings and bent her knees like she was about to spring into the air. Actually, that's what she did.

She jumped three or four feet off the ground and beat her wings. She flapped multiple times to try to stay aloft, but it wasn't enough. She fell back to earth and landed on her butt. Not exactly a spectacular landing.

I ran to her side. "How about we just walk?"

She sighed in disappointment and nodded. It looked like we had to get there the old fashioned way ... walking.

Casting out my senses, I knew we had to start walking north. I helped Abbie up and we started limping together in the direction of the lake.

CHAPTER 14

We had been walking less than hour, and I had the feeling that we were getting close. Soon Abbie and I could see the edge of the tree line.

We were about two minutes from the edge of the trees when I stepped on a fallen branch and it snapped in two. Hey, I weigh around ninety pounds, so it wasn't my weight that had snapped it. The cracking sound rang through the trees like a gunshot.

Because the branch had broken so suddenly, Abbie and I were both on our knees. As we helped each other up, we heard the sound of flapping wings. Two huge—and I mean *huge*—deformed-looking birds rose above the trees and flew off in a westerly direction.

We limped the rest of the way to the tree line. Once we got there, we were shocked by what we saw.

Sara and May were kneeling on the ground. Sam was lying on his side facing away from us. Sara was clutching her right arm, blood seeping through her fingers. A reddening bruise marred her left cheek. A slash of red cut across May's forehead and she was holding her right leg tightly to her chest. Her foot was twisted at an awkward angle.

"Are you all okay?" Abbie yelled as we ran to them. Sara gave her a look that said, *Are you kidding me?*

"What happened to Sam?" I asked.

"He got knocked around pretty bad," May replied.

"By what?"

"How about we help him first and ask questions later?" Abbie said commandingly.

She limped over to Sam. I followed closely behind.

He was on his side and curled into a ball. He had a bloody nose and a big lump on the back of his head. His eyes were closed and he was sucking in air like a fish out of water. He had one hand on his stomach and the other between his legs. *I don't think I want to know,* I thought.

"Sam, you okay?" I asked. He mumbled an answer that I didn't understand. "What?"

"No," he moaned. I reached forward to help him, but he stopped me. "No. Just give me a minute."

We gave him some time. I helped May and Sara while Abbie searched for a secure place for us to rest. When I checked on Sam again, he was standing.

"*Now* are you okay?" I asked as I walked over.

"Yeah, my head still hurts though," He gingerly touched the back of his head.

As if on cue, Abbie flew into view and landed a few feet away. "I found the perfect spot."

We followed her about a quarter of a mile away, landing near a huge oak tree that was about thirty feet away from a rock face. An indent in the rocks was deep enough to be considered a cave. The trees around it offered shade and shelter.

I guessed someone had used this as a campsite at one point or another. A rope swing hung from a tree near the lake shore and a small dock jutted into the water. There was even a fire pit near the cave.

"Wow, Abbie, this is beautiful," I said. She gave a wide smile.

We settled into the cave and May sat in the corner to heal us one at a time. She started with Sara, and I sat down next to Sam, who was leaning against the wall.

"So what *did* happen back there?" I asked.

"You wouldn't believe it if I told you," he answered with a sigh. "They were flying warhounds."

I smacked him hard on the arm. "I'm serious, tell the truth."

"Ow! I'm not kidding. It really happened."

"Okay," I said, leaning back. "Do tell."

He smiled. "So after we landed near the lake, we took off our backpacks and jackets. You know, to get comfortable. Suddenly, out of nowhere, these warhounds fell down on top of us." He paused for a breath. "The only difference was that they had wings. They were so funny looking. They looked like Dr. Frankenstein had sewed them on."

He started laughing. I didn't get the joke but I laughed too, even though it hurt with my broken rib.

After we had finished laughing he continued, "There were only two. May and Sara took on this really big one. The one I fought got in a few good hits. I fought back and broke one of his teeth. Speaking of which." He reached into his pocket and pulled out a large, bloody canine tooth. "This is that tooth." He put it back in his pocket.

"Continue with the story please," I asked as nicely as I could.

"Right. Anyway, he got really mad after that and took a swing or two but missed. Then he ... uh ..."

"He kicked Sam where it really hurts, then punched him in the gut," Sara butted in. Her arm had been fixed and Abbie was up next. "Then he picked him up by the shirt and threw him against a tree."

"Thank you, Sara," I said. "I was wondering why he was in that awkward position." I grinned at her.

Sam averted his gaze in embarrassment.

"Jay, you're next," May called.

That's right. I'd almost forgotten about my broken rib. I stumbled over to her.

"So," she asked as I sat down, "where are you hurting?"

"I landed really hard and I think I broke a rib on my left side," I answered.

She shifted to my left side, closed her eyes, and felt around my lower ribcage.

When she opened her eyes, she said, "Yep, it's broken but it's only cracked. What did you land on, rocks?"

"Well, kind of, yeah."

She felt around some more. "This will take a while. I'd say that you should stay with me for about a half an hour and then it should heal overnight."

She spoke so maturely, I almost forgot she was only seven. When I thought about it, it was kind of scary. *Well, doctor's orders, I guess.*

CHAPTER 15

I t was getting late and Sara wasn't back yet. She left to go get more firewood an hour ago. I sat on a rock in front of our cave, worrying. I wanted to go find her but I had to rest. Plus, flying really hurt my cracked rib.

I turned as bushes to my right rustled. Sara wobbled out with a bundle of leaves in her hands. Something was *way* off. She wasn't walking straight. Her usually alert and playful eyes were unfocused, and she had a big grin on her face. It was creepy.

"Sara, you're back," Abbie called, waving.

"Hi, guys," Sara replied. She sounded tired and yet happy at the same time.

"Are you all right?" I asked, even though I could already tell the answer was supposed to be *no*.

"I'm fine," she replied sluggishly. "Look what I found," She held out the bundle of leaves.

"What is it?" Sam asked, getting up from the tree stump he'd been sitting on.

"I don't know, but it smells and tastes delicious. Here, you try some." She handed each of us a big leaf. It smelled sweet and bitter at the same time with a faint twinge of mint. May actually took a bite. She coughed and spat it out.

Sam sniffed it and burst out laughing. Everyone turned to look at him except for Sara, whose attention was on a little yellow butterfly fluttering by.

"What is it?" I asked, wondering if the plant had affected him too.

Between laughs, he said, "She ... found ... a bunch of catnip." He laughed so hard, tears came to his eyes. When he caught his breath, he explained, "Catnip is a plant that normal people sometimes give to their pet cats as treats. The cats get loopy off the stuff if they get too much." He looked at Sara and struggled not to laugh again.

May stood on her tiptoes and felt Sara's forehead. "I'd say this is a big overdose. She has to sleep it off, and she shouldn't eat much either."

"One question," Sam said. "How do we get her to go to sleep and to stay in the cave without her clawing us to shreds?"

I thought a moment and then motioned for everyone to gather around me. Sara paid no attention to us, too intent on pawing at the little butterfly.

"I have an idea, but I've never tried it and I'm not sure how safe it is," I said. "You all know I can read thoughts and get inside people's heads. Well, maybe I can get inside her head and slow her thought process down." I looked at Sara, who was now rolling on her back in the grass. "Well, more than it has already. If I slow her down enough, she should fall asleep."

Sam shrugged, Abbie nodded in agreement, and May started to say something but then agreed.

Honestly, I hated the idea of getting inside someone's mind and shutting them down. It didn't feel right. Even if all I was trying to do was get them to go to sleep, not kill them.

While Sam collected the leftover catnip leaves, I walked over to Sara. She was still on her back, waving her hands in the air as if she was trying to hit something.

"Hey, Sara," I said calmly. "What are you doing?"

She looked at me for a second and then gazed back up at the air again. "I'm trying to catch all of those green butterflies," she said slowly.

I followed her gaze up. Only things up there were the green leaves of the oak tree. No butterflies.

Sam walked up with the catnip in his hands. Behind him were Abbie and May. "Sara, there's more catnip. Do you want the rest?"

She flipped herself over and stood up to take the leaves Sam was holding out to her. When she reached to take them, he dropped the catnip and grabbed her arms. Abbie took hold of her legs, and May helped the two bigger kids pin Sara down.

Sara struggled against their grip. I knelt down by her head and thought, *Forgive me, Sara, for doing this.* I put one hand on either side of her head and closed my eyes to concentrate.

The inside of her head was a hazy, tangled mess. I felt a stinging, searing pain in the back of my head. It wasn't my pain, though. I felt it but it wasn't mine.

I had to focus. Slowly, I worked through her thought processes, making them slow down. I could physically feel her relaxing into a deep sleep.

I untangled my thoughts from hers. I opened my eyes and removed my shaking hands from her head. She was breathing slowly and deeply, while I was feeling light-headed. Sam patted me on the back and told me how proud he was, but I barely heard him. My vision was getting blurry. I felt myself falling backward and then nothing.

CHAPTER 16

I woke up lying in the cave with Sam sitting next to me. His black jacket was under my head.

"How are you feeling?" he asked when he saw my eyes flutter open.

"I've felt better. I've felt worse," I replied. I looked over to the cave entrance. The positions of the shadows told me it was late in the afternoon.

I sat up and had a look around. Sara was still asleep, May and Abbie were playing outside in the sun, and Sam and I were alone together.

"So why'd you pass out earlier?" he asked.

Still a man of many questions, I thought.

"Using my powers like that on Sara not only drained her energy, but mine as well," I answered.

Sam looked over at Sara. "How's she doing?"

I closed my eyes and focused on her. She was still all hazy. "It's not out of her system yet," I replied.

I walked out into the sunlight. Abbie and May were playing tag near the little wooden dock. May was "it." When Abbie ran onto the dock, May did a fast takeoff and tackled her, knocking them both into the water.

I ran to the dock as fast as I could with Sam at my heels. I looked into the water. Both of their heads surfaced.

May laughed. "Tag, you're it!" she shouted, and dove back into the water.

Abbie tried to follow but she popped back up a moment later. "May, get back here, you little cheater! I can't breathe underwater."

I looked at Sam. "A swim does sound pretty good right now."

"Hey, let me show you something," he said with a smile. He spread his jet-black wings wide and flew off the deck. He rose pretty high and then tucked in his wings and dived into the water.

I saw the occasional bubble heading in my direction. I made the silly mistake of getting on my hands and knees and looking over the edge of the dock. He leaped out of the water, grabbed me by the shoulders, and dragged me into the lake.

I surfaced almost instantly, pushing my wet hair out of my eyes just before Sam dunked me again. I surfaced for air but then dove back under before he could force me down.

I grabbed his ankles and yanked on them, letting him flop into the water. Before he could see me, I spread my wings, turned toward the center of the lake, and pushed off. I beat my wings at an angle to speed me forward.

Then I ran into something unseen—Abbie. I surfaced again and she popped up too. "Sorry," she apologized before diving back under.

I was pretty far out and decided to swim back toward shore. I took a deep breath, dove under, and started swimming.

Something shot into the water not three feet from me. Sam's dark silhouette swept closer to me. I tried to swim away but he grabbed me by the shoulders and kissed me right on the lips.

Okay, it wasn't a real kiss, but it was enough to make me release a lot of the air I was holding in.

Sam smiled devilishly and swam away. As my chest tightened from lack of air, I tried to surface but something had tangled itself around my foot and was holding me under. I looked down to see some grass-like stuff wrapped around my ankle. I tried to kick it off, but that just made it worse.

I started to panic, letting more precious air escape my lungs. I looked around but saw nothing that could help me get loose.

My lungs burned for air. My vision blurred, and instinctively I tried to breathe. Water choked me and I started to lose consciousness. I couldn't feel my feet, wings, or hands.

A blurred silhouette entered my vision. It wasn't big, like Sam's, and I knew it wasn't Sara.

I could barely recognize May's anxious face as she came closer. She brandished something in her hand—Sam's pocket knife.

Yes, cut me free. Help me, I thought blankly.

She cut away the plant and pulled strongly upward on one of my arms. We slowly rose to the surface. I wanted to paddle to get there faster but I couldn't move. Cool air blasted my face as was reached the surface, but I couldn't find myself to draw in a breath.

May shouted for help, and Sam and Abbie swam quickly toward us. Sam took one arm and Abbie the other. They pulled me to shore and then dragged my limp body onto the sandy outcrop near the dock.

"May, help her," Sam yelled at May. His voice was muffled and distant.

"I can't," May answered. "There are some things I can't fix."

Sam put his ear to my chest. He lifted his head and started pressing down hard on my chest. I still couldn't breathe. I was fading faster.

He put his ear to my chest again. I was dimly aware of that he'd had a thought, something he could do.

He took hold of my jaw, forced my mouth open, and then pressed his lips to mine and blew air into my mouth. I felt a pop in my throat. He lifted up and I began to cough. He rolled me onto my side and I coughed up a bunch of water.

Abbie and May patted my back. After I had spit up, what seemed like, half the lake, I looked up at Sam with admiration.

I hugged, taking him by surprise. I whispered into his ear, "Thank you. You saved me."

He gave a weak smile and eventually hugged me back.

CHAPTER 17

S am and Abbie helped me over to the base of the big oak tree. As I leaned against the tree's rough trunk, Sam grabbed some sticks and twigs from the pile we'd made and put them in the fire pit. Abbie pulled something out of Sam's backpack and handed it to him. It was the lighter we had taken from the store.

Soon a warm fire was crackling in front of me. Good thing, since I was still shivering. Sam handed me my purple jacket, which I wrapped around me. May passed around the food. Before long, we were roasting lunch meat and hot dogs over the open flame.

Hearing a shuffling sound, I turned to see Sara wobbling out of the cave. I reached out to her with my senses. The catnip was out of her system and she looked well rested.

"You were just going to eat without me?" she asked with her normal playfulness. She sat between Sam and May. Looking at us she asked why we all were wet.

"We went for a swim," I replied.

She turned to me and her eyes grew round with shock. "What happened to you? You look like crap."

"I … uh—"

"Drowned," Sam finished for me. He and I exchanged a quick glance.

"Oh my gosh. Are you okay?" Sara asked.

"I am now," I answered. I exchanged another glance with Sam and then gave Sara a reassuring smile.

"Thanks to Sam," May said before shoving a piece of food in her mouth.

I could feel my cheeks grow hot. This time, I didn't look at him.

Sara sighed. "I guess that's what I get for going all loopy. I'm forced to go to sleep and miss all the excitement. Anything else I missed?"

"Not really," Abbie answered.

I pulled my hot dog out of the fire and took a bite. Sam's gaze seemed to burn my skin.

I scarfed down a second hot dog and excused myself to the cave. It was cold and dark inside. The sun had set not too long ago. I found a small area to lie down and pulled my backpack under my head to use as a pillow.

I had closed my eyes for just a second when I heard footsteps approaching. I sat up as a familiar shape entered the cave. Sam walked over to our pile of backpacks and opened the one May had been carrying. He pulled something out and walked over to me.

He spread a blanket over me. "Here, it's cold in here. This will keep you warm."

I lay back down and turned over. Closing my eyes again, I tried to fall asleep, but more footsteps forced me to sit back up.

Everyone else walked in, tired expressions on their faces. Sam pulled another blanket from the backpack and handed it to Abbie.

"I'm sorry," he said, "but there are only two blankets. On the bright side, the blankets are big enough for two people."

"Yeah, but there are *five* of us," Abbie said. "One of us will be stuck shivering all night."

"It's okay," Sara said. "I don't mind going without a blanket tonight."

"Okay," Sam said. "I guess Abbie and May can share one, and Jay and I can share the other."

"Wait, Sam," I said. "Shouldn't you take watch or something? You know, if the warhounds come back?" I was kind of giving it away that I didn't feel comfortable about sleeping *that* close to Sam.

"I don't mind keeping watch either," Sara said before Sam could speak. "Besides, I've gotten a few more hours of sleep than the rest of you."

Oh, great, I thought. *Thanks for your help, Sara.*

Sam dragged his backpack over and laid down next to me. He curled up under the warm blanket and I did the same. The warmth emanating from his body was comforting and made me feel protected. I turned so my back was facing him.

I had never been this close to him, or most anyone for that matter. I suppressed a shiver and attempted to sleep. *It's been a really long day*, I told myself. *Sara sleep-attacked me, I saved my friend from going splat on the ground, I broke a rib, and I nearly went to a watery grave. That's a lot for one day.*

Not to mention that you used your power to a great extent to help your friend.

I thought that? No, wait. That wasn't me. It was that voice. It still felt familiar and yet a like total stranger. I shivered, hoping the voice wouldn't bother me that night. I was too tired.

I felt Sam turn over and then felt his hand rubbing my back between my wings. Another shiver ran up and down my spine, but in a good way this time. The rhythmic motions soothed and lulled me into a quiet sleep.

CHAPTER 18

A warm stickiness enveloped me. I opened my eyes. Towering trees and a dense fog surrounded me.

I was standing on a leaf-strewn dirt path. Ahead of me, the path wound into the fog. Behind me, it seemed to go on forever.

Jay. A whisper echoed through the trees like the wind. I turned around in a circle to see who was calling me.

Jay. This time it distinctively sounded like Sara's voice. *Jay, come here.*

"Sara," I called out, "where are you?" I started walking in the direction of the voice.

Jay, help me!

I sprinted down the path. All I could hear was the voice echoing in my head and the pounding of my heart. The path led to a clearing, and I stopped.

Jay. The voice sounded like it was only a few feet away from me. I spun around again to find the source of the voice. Nothing was there.

"Sara, where are you? I'm here."

Suddenly the path was gone and the clearing was hemmed in by thick, thorny brambles.

A low growl came from behind me. I turned and saw an enormous black cat that seemed to glow with a hazy red flame. Behind it was Sara, tied up, pale, and weak. The threatening cat stood between us.

"Sara, don't worry. I'll help you."

A tear rolled down her cheek as she whispered, "You can't." The panther-like cat stalked toward me. "I'm so sorry, Jay."

With a mighty roar, the cat lunged at me. It easily tackled me, bowling me over. Its razor-sharp claws raked my side. Blood oozed from the burning wound.

I kicked it off me. It sped away and then turned for another attack. When it launched itself at me, I dodged just in time. It spun again and faced me, lashing its tail. Then almost faster than I could see, it ran at me and dragged its claws across my chest. Another roaring pain shot through me and I cried out in agony. The cat knocked me into a nearby bramble thicket, and the thorns cut my face and arms.

I freed myself and raced back to the center of the clearing. Once more the cat ran at me with incredible speed and agility. Leaping on me, it dug its front claws into my shoulders as its hind claws slashed down my stomach.

I'm going to die.

The cat released me and spread huge black wings. It flew up to a tree branch. I knew what was coming next. I could see it in the cat's eyes. I tried to dodge its attack before it happened, but I couldn't move.

The cat jumped down with its claws out and teeth bared …

I screamed and opened my eyes. Sara was face to face with me, holding me down. "Jay, are you all right?" she asked.

I barely heard her. Ripping my arms free of her grip, I pushed her off me and sent her slamming into the cave wall. I stood up and ran faster than I ever had out of the cave, and into the trees and bushes.

Blinded by the leftover effects of my dream, I didn't see the ravine. I fell in and landed on hard-packed earth hidden beneath a layer of ivy and ferns. The foliage created a small canopy that let in few rays of the rising sun.

I lay there breathing heavily for a long time. When I heard footsteps approaching, I panicked even more. My heart was beating so hard, I thought who—or what—was up there could hear it.

Suddenly, hands reached down and grabbed me by my arms and legs. I thrashed, kicked, and screamed. I did anything to make my captors have a harder time handling me. Still, they dragged me out of the ravine and bound my hands together behind my back. I heard mumbles and shouting, but I couldn't make out any words.

I was dragged back to the campsite and freezing cold water was splashed over my head. Slowly, I stopped fighting as my breathing steadied.

I looked up and realized that my captors were just my friends who wore scared and anxious expressions.

When Sam realized I had calmed down, he untied my hands and tossed the ivy vine he'd used back into the bushes.

"What happened, Jay?" Sara asked.

With a shaky voice, I explained, "It was a dream, a really bad, horrible dream. It was terrifying."

Sam knelt down beside me and wrapped me in a comforting hug, holding me close. I buried myself in his warmth, realizing I was close to tears.

Abbie got onto her knees too and said softly, "Share your dream with me."

"I can't," I answered. "Not without reliving it myself."

"Not like that, I mean. I have another ability I never told you about. By touching someone, I can see their memories and dreams."

I was a little uncomfortable with that. I mean, I'd been inside other people's heads, but I'd never let someone else in mine.

I reluctantly agreed, and Sam held me a little tighter as Abbie took my hand in hers. My dream flew before my eyes, minutes reduced to seconds. The areas where I had been scratched burned all over again.

When it was over for me, Abbie still had her eyes closed. I guessed she was still living it in real time.

Suddenly, she broke away from me with a panicked scream. "Wow," she said, wiping the sweat from her forehead. "That *was* terrifying."

May laid a hand on my shoulder. "Can you share your dream with us?"

"I don't know ..."

"Come on, Jay," Sara said. "You're leaving us out."

"Okay, I'll try it," I said. "But I'm not sure everyone will like it."

Why does this stuff have to happen to me?

CHAPTER 19

We all stood in a small circle. Abbie was to my right, Sam to my left. We all held hands. I still wasn't sure how well this would work.

"Okay, Jay, you know what we have to do?" Abbie asked.

I nodded. She and I closed our eyes and focused on the dream and how it felt from our perspective. I also concentrated on everyone in the circle.

I heard multiple gasps. Opening my eyes, I saw we were standing in the dark forest of my dream. Everyone was there. We let go of one another's hands.

May pointed. "Look, Jay, it's you!"

I turned and sure enough, I was standing on the path. I motioned for everyone to be quiet and listen. A moment later we all heard, *Jay, help me!* There was a *thump* from behind me.

Sara had fainted—the nondream Sara. Sam lifted her up. I knew what happened next in the dream, so I motioned for the others to follow the path.

We got to the clearing just before the brambles closed it off. We all stared in awe at the flaming panther, and then watched in horror as it attacked the dream me. I sat on the ground as every slash of the cat's paws reignited the stinging, burning pain of my wounds.

Soon, it was over and in a bright flash, we were back in the circle. Sara was still out, but Sam and May still held her hands. We released one another and Sara stirred into wakefulness.

"What happened?" she asked groggily.

"We were walking through Jay's dream and you passed out," May said.

"I'm sorry you didn't see it, Sara," I said, "but I don't think I could go through that again."

Sam looked at the brightening sky. "We'd better be moving on."

"Let's eat first," Abbie said added as her stomach growled. "I'm starving."

I smiled and agreed.

We had all eaten and were in the skies once again. Since we had finished off the last of the food, we would have to get more that day.

Not too far ahead was another town. This one was bigger than the last one.

As we flew nearer, I saw a small building with a green-colored roof at the edge of the town. It had a sign in front with those weird shapes called letters on them. Sam had continued to teach me the alphabet, and I recognized a *B*, an *A*, an *N*, and a *K*.

Sam saw that I was trying to read it and said, "The sign says that building is a bank. It's a place where people get money." He paused and then said, "Let's land in the trees over there. I have an idea."

He tilted his wings downward and glided into the sturdy branches of a hickory tree.

We all followed, and I landed in an oak tree not far from Sam's tree. May landed on the branch above me and Abbie and Sara alighted in a nearby evergreen.

"So what's your big idea?" I asked Sam.

He looked toward the bank. "I saw an ATM on the outside of the bank." Seeing our confused expressions, he explained, "It's a machine that spits out money if you give it a specific card. Anyway, my plan is that when the next person comes to use the ATM, we—"

"We're not going to hurt anyone, are we?" Sara interrupted.

"No, but we might do some damage to their car. My plan is that we let them get their money, but before they pull their card out, I'll throw a rock or something at their car to make the car alarm go off. When the person runs over to see what happened to their car, we'll take some of the money from the machine. The person will never miss it."

His idea made me uncomfortable. It felt wrong to take someone else's money, but we really needed it. So we all looked at each other and nodded in agreement.

"What will we do when we get the money?" Abbie asked.

Sam and I said in unison, "We'll buy food."

We stared at each other for a moment. *Had he read my thoughts,* I wondered, *or did I accidentally read his? Or maybe we just had the same idea.*

Then my little voice chimed in, *Great minds think alike.* I answered back, *Shut up. Aren't I allowed to think alone and just to myself sometimes?* The voice didn't answer.

"Okay," Sam said. "If everyone agrees, let's get going."

I know you're probably expecting me to tell you exactly how we got the money and if we got caught. Well, be thankful that I'm sparing you the details. The whole thing went according to plan. We got about four hundred dollars from this bald guy who drives a little blue car.

I don't want to seem like a bad influence, so don't do what we did. It's *wrong.* Stealing is very bad.

Now, where was I? Oh, yeah …

Afterward, we bought food like normal people. Well, kind of. We had to tuck in our wings really tight and cover them with our jackets. Sara wore a hood to hide her cat ears. Sam also bought a book. He didn't tell us why. I had seen books before, back at the DAEL, but they weren't as thin or as colorful.

We still had over three hundred dollars left. After we left the store, we walked around back, stuffed the food into our backpacks, and took off. We found a clearing to land in less than an hour later and had an early lunch. The clearing was secluded with a small stream nearby, so we decided to stay for the rest of the day and for the night.

I walked over to the stream. Finding a rock to sit on, I took off my shoes off and put my feet in the water. I closed my eyes, enjoying the sensation of the cool water washing over my skin. It was a hot day, hot enough to raise a sweat just sitting still.

Sara was catnapping—no pun intended—in the shade of a large maple tree. Abbie and May were playing games and drawing in the dirt. And Sam was … Where was Sam?

"Boo!"

I let out a little scream as Sam scared me off the rock I was sitting on. I landed in the cold stream and glared up at him. He started laughing and I couldn't help but smile. Still, I splashed him back, sending him backing away until he stumbled and landed on his butt.

We both stood up. I stepped out of the stream as he dusted himself off.

"Hey," he said, "do you want to go for a walk? You know, because we're bored and stuff?" He had his hands in his pockets and was acting like it was really hard to ask me. I wondered why.

"Sure," I said.

He led me into the trees away from our camp. We walked in an awkward silence for a minute or two, until he suddenly stopped in front of a large tree with thick, spreading branches. I nearly walked into him.

"Let's rest here in the branches for a while."

He barely had time to finish speaking before I spread my big brown wings and flew onto a sturdy branch. Sam joined me on the same branch, making it sway as he landed on it.

We were both silent again until he said, "So you know how I'm teaching you the alphabet?" I nodded, wondering what he was getting at. He pulled the book he'd bought from his jacket. "I bought this so you can learn to read like I can."

I did not see *that* coming. I smiled and thanked him.

He opened the book to the first page. Written on the paper were many, many letters. Some were familiar, like the letters from both of our names.

"These are all the letters of the alphabet," he said. "In order." He pointed to each one and told me the sound it made, and then read different words from the book. Before we knew it, the sun was setting and the woods were darkening. By that time, the biggest word I could spell was *apple*. It wasn't much, but I was learning.

"I think we should head back," I said. "It's getting late and the others must be worried by now."

Sam agreed. As he jumped down, he brushed against me. I realized then just how closely we'd been sitting together. I pushed the thought away and jumped down.

Just then, I decided to have a little fun. I punched Sam on the arm and said, "Race you back!" I took off running with Sam yelling after me, "No fair. You got a head start."

He and I raced back to the campsite. I skidded to a halt by the fire pit and yelled, "Ha, I won!"

Sam stopped behind me. "Yeah," he panted, "but only because I let you."

We both laughed, but then I noticed we were alone in the clearing. The backpacks were still there but Abbie, May, and Sara weren't.

I looked at Sam. He nodded, and I knew we were thinking the same thing: *let's go find them.*

CHAPTER 20

S am and I took to the skies, hoping to spot them from above. We flew high and looked down into the trees, searching for movement.

While I was looking down instead of where I was flying, I rammed into something head-on. I recoiled quickly, curling my hands into fists, ready for a fight. I relaxed when I realized it was only May with Abbie and Sara close behind her.

May said over the flapping, "You didn't come back for a long time, and we didn't know where you guys were, so we left to look for you, and—"

"May, they get it," Abbie interrupted.

"So where were you guys?" Sara asked.

My stomach growled loudly before I could answer. I smiled. "How about we discuss this over dinner? I'm pretty hungry."

Everyone nodded in agreement. I turned and took the lead back to camp.

I sighed happily. I had a full belly and I was surrounded by my friends. I was lying between Sam and Sara, and Abbie and May were whispering to each other not too far away.

Sara was asleep and so was Sam. I, however, was restless and wide awake. The day was just too short. Sure, I'd had one heck of a morning, but still.

You know things aren't as perfect as you think, that voice said.

What do you mean? I asked.

It didn't answer at first. Everything started to fade and go black, and I heard, *You need to see.* By now I was surrounded by blackness, floating in its darkness.

It's coming, the voice said.

What? What's coming? I asked.

Her end is coming. It's coming fast.

Who's end? What are you talking about? I demanded.

The black disappeared and was replaced by the dark forest from my scary panther dream.

I heard movement in the fallen leaves behind me. I turn, expecting the same black panther, but instead, I see a small, fluffy brown cat with playful green eyes. Sprouting from its back were small creamy-white wings. It sat with its tail wrapped neatly around its paws.

It stood and trotted over to me. It rubbed against my legs, purring, then sat at my feet, playing with my shoelaces. When I reached down to pet it, its purr turned into a deep growl and it pinned its ears back against its head. It lashed out with its claws, scratching my hand before I could pull away.

It ran back to the center of the clearing with its little wings spread wide. Then the cat morphed and grew. Before long the big panther stood in its place, its eyes a searing red.

It crouched, getting ready to pounce, but then it squeezed its eyes shut as if it were in pain. Its growl became a pathetic whimper. Then, in a burst of black smoke, it was gone.

When I woke, someone was gently shaking me. I struggled to open my eyes. A blurry face stood over me. I blinked my eyes into focus to see Sam.

"Good morning," he said. "Hey, we're going to eat breakfast before we leave."

The others were already sitting around the fire, eating. I joined them, and Abbie asked me why I'd slept so long. I finished swallowing the chunk of lunch meat I had in my mouth and cleared my throat.

"Uh, I couldn't sleep well last night. I only really fell asleep a couple hours ago," I said. I could tell they knew I wasn't telling the whole truth, but they dropped the subject.

I finished eating early and started to pack my bag. The idea of leaving gave me an uneasy feeling in the pit of my stomach. Abbie walked up and helped me pack.

"You know, I had another dream last night," she said. "And I know that you had one too." I looked up for a moment.

I glanced at her. "Yes, I did." I straightened up and took one of her hands. Our eyes locked for a moment, and I saw she understood what I meant. I *wanted* to share my dream with her. She closed her eyes.

The dream flashed before my eyes in a second. She opened her eyes a moment later and said, "But ... that's the same dream I had."

I let go of her hand. "Then what does it mean?"

"I honestly don't know," she replied.

I looked back down and continued with my packing. I had been hoping for an answer. Now I was getting a *really* bad feeling.

CHAPTER 21

G ray clouds covered the sky as we flew, leaving an ominous feeling on the wind. I was trying to shift my focus from the feeling and stared down into the trees. Something about them was familiar, but I couldn't figure out what.

"You've been quiet." I flinched as Sam caught up with me and spoke. "Is something wrong?"

"No, not really," I replied. "I was just thinking about how the woods below us look familiar."

"You know, I was thinking the same thing, but don't let it bother you."

We continued on in silence for a while. We could just see another town in the distance when Sara broke the silence, asking if we could land. She was feeling light-headed.

"Sure," Sam and I replied at the same time. I glared at Sam and then glanced at Sara. She looked fine to me. She also looked like she had something on her mind.

We descended into the trees and landed on ground covered in dead leaves. After we'd rested a while, Sara asked if anyone minded if we walked the rest of the way into the town.

"We've been flying so much," she went on, "and we haven't really walked anywhere." Her cat tail twitched with impatience.

None of the others minded and they all nodded in agreement. I didn't like it, but I knew I was outvoted and also agreed. The ominous feeling I'd had earlier returned, stronger than ever.

As we started to walk, I felt someone take my hand. It was Abbie. She looked as worried as I felt.

I have a horrible feeling that something bad is going to happen, I told her telepathically.

I know, so do I, she thought back.

We continued on in strained silence. Now that I knew she felt it too, the feeling sank like a stone in my stomach.

We found an old walking trail and followed it. After about ten minutes of walking, with Sara in the lead, the path led us to a wide clearing. Now things looked *very* familiar, but my mind wouldn't let me remember.

A scream of pain split the air, jolting me from my thoughts. Sara had fallen to her knees and was holding her head in her hands.

"Sara!" I yelled. I turned to May. "May, help her."

The young girl rushed to Sara's side and felt her forehead. "I can't find anything." She had to yell to be heard over Sara's screaming. "She's just in a lot of pain. I can't do anything. You try to help her, Jay!"

Sara was lying on the ground, writhing in pain.

I knelt beside her and held my hand to her head. Instantly, my head was filled with pain and a high-pitched keening. Then I felt like something had punched me in the face. The force of the blow sent me flying back into Sam's arms, but I didn't lose my concentration on Sara.

"No, stop! Stop it, stop it!" Sara cried.

Inside her head, a sinister voice growled, *No. Do it or die. You're meant to. That's why you were created. You are too weak to disobey me!*

I could feel Sara fighting hard against it, but she was weakening.

Either they die or you die. Now, do it," the voice commanded. *Kill them!*

Sara yelled, "No, I won't! I won't do it!"

Fighting me is pointless. Do as you are told and kill them!

She screamed louder as I felt dark energy surge through her.

She's too weak to fight, I thought, *and I can't fight for her.*

"Jay, what's going on?" the others kept asking me.

I couldn't answer. I was too engrossed in Sara's pain, her suffering, her fear. But then another surge of energy forced me from my concentration. I opened my eyes. I pulled away from Sam and knelt beside Sara again.

"Don't do it, Sara!" I yelled. "Don't give up. Fight it, fight it."

"I can't!" she shouted back. She stopped rolling around and lay still on her back. She was panting.

"Don't say that," I told her. "Don't give up. Don't give in." I commanded.

Her whole body went limp. I grabbed her wrist. Her pulse was too fast. Her breath shuddered in and out of her. I couldn't sense any thoughts coming from her. All I could sense was blackness.

Then I felt something shift inside her. Her eyes opened. She pulled her hand from me and pushed me off her with such force, I slammed back into Sam and the two of us rammed against a tree. I thought I heard something crack in my shoulder.

Sara stood up. Her eyes were dark with anger and rage, a look that said, *I'm going to kill you*. Her claws were extended farther than I'd ever seen them.

As Sam and I helped each other to stand up, I reached out to Sara. I could feel it now. She had lost the battle inside her. And, now, she was a prisoner within her own body.

CHAPTER 22

Sara lunged at me. Sam pushed me one way and dodged the other, and Sara rammed into the tree. I ran to the center of the clearing.

Sara whirled around to face me. She was even angrier. She lunged again, catching me this time and raking her claws across my chest. I screamed in pain.

"Abbie, May," I yelled as I shoved Sara off me, "get out of here. Sam and I will handle her."

"No, we're not leaving!" one of them shouted.

I dodged another attack. "Just go, now!"

They finally took off running through the trees. Sara tried to follow, but I ran at her and tackled her.

She pushed me aside and we wrestled, each of us struggling to gain the upper hand. Her strength was powered by her rage, Sara won and slammed me onto my back on the ground. She planted one hand on my chest, her claws piercing my skin. The other hand was raised to deliver the killing blow. I closed my eyes. I didn't want to see it coming.

"No!" Sam yelled, and pulled Sara off me.

I pushed myself up off the ground as Sara and Sam grappled together in close combat.

Sara raked her claws across his face, dangerously close to his eye. He delivered a hard blow to her jaw, but she dragged her sharp claws down his side, splattering blood on the fallen leaves. He lurched back but recovered quickly and launched himself at her, throwing her back against a tree.

Instead of attacking again, Sara spread her wings and flew up to a thick branch of the tree. Watching her, Sam pulled his knife from his pocket and flipped it open. The blade glinting in the light.

Sara jumped off the branch and swooped down at him. At the last moment he stepped aside and slashed at her with the knife, leaving a long, bloody gash down her side. Sara screeched with pain and fury, flying off to land in another tree on the other side of the clearing.

I wanted to rejoin the fight, but something held me back. Sara flew at Sam, swooping low toward and then rising up to land on a branch directly above him. Staying there for mere seconds, she launched herself off the branch, plummeting down, directly at Sam. She kept her wings steady like she wasn't planning on pulling up anytime soon. Sam readied himself, holding the knife with both hands, its blade pointing up at Sara.

With a mighty screech, Sara collided with Sam. Her claws sank into his chest and throat, but then her cry was abruptly cut off.

Together they dropped to the ground, both of them motionless as blood poured from their wounds. I ran to their sides and pushed Sara off Sam. He looked pretty messed up but was still alive. I couldn't see his knife though.

I looked at Sara and found the knife. It was deeply embedded in her chest. Her eyes were wide open and full of pain and fear. Blood dripped from her mouth. She wasn't breathing and I couldn't find a pulse. I pulled the knife from her chest.

"Come on, Sara," I said. "Say something, think something, anything!"

Her eyes were glazing over. Tears pricked my eyes and blurred my vision. Then I heard her final thought: *Tell the others I said good-bye.*

The tears spilled from my eyes, dropping onto her face.

Sara was dead.

I sat there for several minutes, sobbing silently. My friend— my *best* friend—was dead. I remembered all the times, good and bad, that we had shared. Her last minutes played over and over in my head. Her final thought echoed through my mind.

When I finally looked up, May and Abbie had returned. Sam was on his feet but was still bleeding. When I looked at him, instead of feeling comfort and security, I felt hatred and anger and sadness. I could tell the girls were crying as well, but I paid them no attention.

I slowly and shakily got to my feet. Sam took a step forward as if to try to comfort me.

"You!" I yelled as my rage boiled up inside me. "You killed her!" He stepped back, shock spreading over his face. "Murderer!" I shouted. "Murderer!"

"Jay," he said, "if I hadn't, she would have killed us all. She would have *murdered* us all."

"Shut up!" My hands clenched into fists at my sides. I couldn't hold it in any longer. "She was my friend, she was my family, and you killed her!"

Sam's expression changed and he started to tremble. Sinking to his knees, he held his hand to his throat like he couldn't breathe. His mouth opened in a silent scream of pain as small, glowing particles flew off him. I could create things out of nothing, and, apparently, I could also return things to nothing. I could create things and I could also destroy them.

"Jay, stop!" I heard May scream. "You're hurting him."

She tugged at my arms, but not even a warhound could have moved me at that moment. Abbie shouted at me too, but I ignored her as well. Sam had killed my friend, so I would kill him. He started to look transparent, and his howls of agony were weakening.

"You're *killing* him!" May yelled at me.

I was about to finish him off when something hard collided with the back of my head. I heard the skull-cracking *thud* and then everything went black. I was falling, falling into nothingness ...

———•◆•———

Cold darkness surrounded me. I couldn't move. Was I dead too? If so, where was the bright light that was supposed to take me to everlasting happiness?

I opened my eyes. Everything was still black. I tried to focus on my surroundings. I was aware that I was sitting up, propped against something. I could hear the crackle of a fire and the slow breathing of sleeping people.

Just then, my wounds started to throb and burn. I moaned. I heard movement and tensed, ready to fight even though that seemed impossible.

A hand touched my shoulder. "Jay, are you awake?" It was Sam's voice. It wasn't filled with fear or anger, but with concern and … was that admiration?

"Sam?" I croaked out. "Sam, where are we? Why can't I see? Where are the others?" I had so many questions to ask.

"We're still in the clearing. Right now Abbie and May are asleep. And if you haven't noticed, you've been … restrained. And we covered your head with a blanket. Here, let me get that off."

I felt something being pulled away from my face. I blinked, but I was still blind. "Sam, I can't see."

"Yeah, I can tell. Your eyes look different again."

I heard his body shift and then his strong arms wrapped around me. I relaxed a little—and then stiffed when I felt his warm, soft lips press gently against mine. He was kissing me! I couldn't believe it. I couldn't react.

What was he doing? Why wasn't he afraid of me? I had tried to kill when I was last conscious.

The kiss ended and he moved away from me. He helped me lie down on my side and put a backpack under my head. He laid what felt like a blanket over me.

"Go to sleep," he whispered in my ear. He started to say something else, but then he moved away. But I caught the thought he sent out: *I'm sorry.*

———◆———

Bright sunlight woke me the next morning. *Well, I can see again,* I thought as I opened my eyes. The others were awake and staring at me. May and Abbie looked scared and not inclined to come any closer. Sam, however, stood up, walked over, and knelt beside me.

"How are you feeling?" he asked.

I stared wordlessly at him. He reached into his pocket and pulled out the knife.

"Don't, Sam," May said. He looked back at her. She continued, "I mean … she might still be angry with you."

I continued to look up at him. I didn't know how I felt about him. I felt something, but I wasn't sure if it was good or bad.

"It's fine," Sam said to May confidently. "I'm not afraid of her." He cut the vines that bound my ankles and then gently turned me over onto my stomach to release my hands. I sat up and examined the red marks on my wrists.

As tears again filled my eyes, I looked up at Sam and wrapped my arms around his neck. "I'm so sorry," I whispered into his ear.

He hugged me back, thinking, *I forgive you, but will you ever forgive me?*

For last night? I already do.

I mean for yesterday and everything else, he clarified.

I didn't answer. I didn't know the answer.

We pulled apart, and I wiped my eyes on my torn sleeve. Sam helped me to stand and led me closer to the fire. After I'd eaten, he told me that he needed to show me something. He led me to the edge of the clearing. At the base of a tree was a mound of dirt, and, in the trunk of the tree, Sara's name was carved into the bark.

"You buried her," I said blankly. He wrapped his arms around me in a comforting hug, but I pulled away from him and knelt by the grave.

"I'm so sorry I couldn't help you," I whispered, hoping her spirit could hear me. "I hope you forgive me. And please forgive Sam. I'm not sure yet if I can fully forgive him. Sara, wherever you are, I hope you're happy."

Out of the corner of my eye, I saw a spark of bright blue. A blue flower was growing through a tumble of gray stones. I shoved the stones aside and carefully pulled the plant from the ground. Returning to the grave, I planted it in the loose soil.

As tears once more filled my eyes, I stood and walked back to the campsite, Sam at my side.

CHAPTER 23

"Ow!" I tried to move away, but May kept her hand on the wound across my chest.

"It wouldn't hurt so much if you had let me heal it earlier," May said curtly. "Not even Sam squirmed this much and his injuries were worse than yours."

I rolled my eyes and tried my best to sit still.

We were staying at the clearing for another night so I could heal. Already the sun was sinking down on the horizon and we had a bright fire blazing.

"There," May said. "You're done."

I moved away as soon as she spoke, sitting close to Sam and curling up next to the warm fire. After the sleep I'd had the night before, it was good to be warm. It wasn't long before I sank into sleep.

———————◆———————

I was floating and I was freezing, as if someone had sealed me in a block of ice. The black surrounding me was absolutely silent. So silent I couldn't even hear my heart beating or my breathing. My body was so numb and cold, I couldn't feel a pulse. I felt as if I were made of stone.

In the endless blackness, I could see a fleck of white. It was beautiful. It came closer and became clearer. I couldn't believe what—I mean *who* I was seeing. It was Sara! She was wearing a beautiful white dress that seemed to glow like the full moon. Her creamy white wings sparkled like silver.

She smiled. "Hello, Jay." Her voice was gentle and happy. I wanted to say something back, but I couldn't find the words. "I'm so glad to see you." Her tone turned serious. "Jay, I need you to be strong. It isn't your time yet. You still have a difficult road ahead of you."

"You mean to say I'm dying?"

"Sort of." She took one of my hands in hers. "Use some of my energy. You need it." Warmth spread through my body, like a fire melting the ice. She leaned forward and whispered into my ear, "And, Jay, I *do* forgive you, and Sam. You should forgive him too. He did what he had to. Plus, it was my time to go."

She turned away and walked back into the blackness.

"Wait, Sara, don't go," I called after her, but it was too late. She was gone. Now I was no longer floating. I was falling, falling fast and hard.

I blinked my eyes against the morning sunlight. Standing above me were my friends. Their heads were bowed and they were crying. Even Sam, who normally didn't show much emotion, was crying.

"Hey guys, why are you crying?" I mumbled.

They all looked up. Their teary eyes widened in shock, but then filled with relief.

Sam picked me up in a hug so tight, it almost hurt. "It's a miracle," he said. "You're alive. I thought we had lost you."

Abbie and May joined the hug, nearly suffocating me.

"We thought you were ... dead," Abbie cried, hesitating to say the word. "You weren't breathing, and you didn't have a pulse, and you were so cold. May laid a hand on you and said you were ... dead."

"Well, I am alive," I replied.

"W-what happened? How are you still alive?" May asked shakily as if she were talking to a ghost.

I stifled a laugh. "You are going to get quite the story."

CHAPTER 24

A warhound's point of view

He beat his wings strongly but clumsily. They were way too big and hurt like hell. He winced in pain every time they hit an updraft. *Warhounds are not meant to fly,* he thought.

A high-pitched beep in his earpiece told him he was coming up on his target. He signaled to the rest of his team to prepare for landing. The forest below looked exactly like the satellite images the scientists had shown them back at the DAEL.

They managed a not-so-perfect landing in a leaf-strewn clearing. He raised his doglike muzzle to the air and took in the scents. He could smell rain coming, ash, nearby forest animals, and the unforgettable and tantalizing scents of blood and death. Underneath all of it was the smell of his prey: five bird-kids.

He was going to kill the dark one, the one with the silver eyes and the blackbird's wings. He would rip him to shreds for breaking his jaw and tooth.

Another Warhound skidded to a halt in front of him. "No sign of our prey, team leader, sir. There are only traces of their food and their scent. They've flown off again, sir."

The team leader growled with annoyance. This was the third time this had happened, and it was almost as annoying as the problem back at the labs. Hundreds of escaped hybrids were fighting and stealing from the labs. Their small armies kept growing. If this kept up, it wouldn't be long before they outnumbered the warhounds.

From the smells and scents around him, the team leader could tell their prey had been gone at least eight hours. They were getting closer, and soon they would be close enough to capture and kill them.

CHAPTER 25

We were back in the air again. Gee, does this scene seem familiar to you?

Earlier, we had stopped in the town near the clearing to get more food and some new clothes, and we went to a restaurant serving an "all you can eat" buffet. Of course, after two hours or so we'd been kicked out and told never to come back.

We flew for a couple hours, and by the position of the sun, I could tell it was about seven o'clock in the evening.

So far that day, I'd learned that you'll get kicked out of a restaurant if you stay too long and eat too much of their food, clothes are not cheap, and there is a big difference between a town and a city. I'd learned that last one because we were heading straight for our first city.

It had enormously tall buildings and lots of cars running on streets between them. A nasty smell hung over all of it.

The forests below us ended a few miles away from the edge of the city. Well, there went out plan of camping out again. Fortunately, we spotted an empty area near the city's edge. When we landed in a dark alley, though, the buildings were even more intimidatingly huge than I had expected. Even though the area we'd landed in was less populated than the rest of the city, it was still crowded.

Along the back wall of the alley, in the corner, was an empty metal bin five times the size of my cage back at DAEL. It stood several feet away from the wall. Along the side wall was a line of silver trash cans.

I looked up at the sky. Gray clouds still covered it, promising thunderstorms and lots of heavy rainfall.

I felt a tug on my sleeve. May was staring up at me with her big green eyes.

"So are we staying here?" she asked. "I don't like this place. It's noisy and the air smells really bad."

"I know, I feel the same way," I replied, "but there's no other place for us to stay."

I jumped at the sound of metal scraping on stone and pavement. Abbie and Sam were moving the metal bin farther away from the wall. When they'd pushed it far enough, Sam flipped over the two plastic lids, propping them against the brick wall.

"There we go," he said, "shelter for four. We might have to squeeze together a bit and we might get a little wet, but it beats getting completely soaked by the rain."

"Thanks, Sam," I said.

Just after I spoke, a big burst of thunder rolled through the air. Abbie pulled the blankets out of the backpack and handed them to Sam and May. From another backpack she recovered two newer blankets we had just bought. She handed one to me.

Abbie and May crawled into the shelter as the rain began to drizzle down. Sam and I crawled in next. We all curled into our blankets as the rain chilled the air around us.

A few minutes later I gave a wide yawn. Sam wrapped his arm around me and whispered in my ear, "Lie down, you're tired." He pulled me closer and laid my head on his shoulder.

At first I tensed, but then a chilly breeze blew in and I curled up into the warmth of his body. *Did his ... did his heart just skip a beat?*

And that's how we fell asleep, Sam and I leaning against each other and the other two curled up in their warm blankets. But my night was not yet over. Just after I closed my eyes is when things get interesting.

───────◆──────

I was standing in an open plain with springy grasses and the occasional bush. Off to my left was an enormous gorge and to my right was a dark hole.

With a jolt, I realized where I was. I was about a mile outside the DAEL. In a flash, a scene displayed before me: an enormous battle between hybrids and warhounds. The memory played out in a blur—the escape, the battle, the retreat, all of it. Then it all disappeared in a gust of wind and in its place stood Sara. She walked closer, her feet barely rustling the grass. She halted when we were face to face.

Her expression and voice were serious. "Hello Jay. I'm guessing you just saw that, didn't you?" I nodded. "I have two messages for you. The first one I'll keep short and sweet."

She paused. "You remember what happened last night? When your heart stopped beating and you stopped breathing? Well, don't ignore it. It wasn't accident. It's a new ability. Trust me, it will be helpful in the future. You need to learn to control it and to use it to your own will.

"I don't have much time left, so I'll shorten the next one too. You have a new enemy coming that's even worse than the warhounds." I opened my mouth to speak, but she shushed me. "Don't talk, just watch."

I heard a mighty roar from above and gazed up to the sky. Below the clouds were hundreds, maybe even thousands, of those flying warhounds. Then the ground vibrated and an army of hybrids swarmed into the area. Out in front was a huge golden lion. *Alex!* I thought. *Wow, he really took this job seriously. And he wasn't kidding when he said that he'd go back to get the others.*

With a loud roar that seemed to have a metallic ring to it, the warhounds dove down onto the army of hybrids. The lion roared too, a roar so powerful, it sent shockwaves through both sides.

The armies collided and the battle rang out. Both sides were strong, but the warhounds seemed stronger. Blood splattered and stained the ground.

Near me, a warhound burst into crackling flames, and so did the kid it was holding by the throat. The licking flames didn't seem to harm either of them. Then the flames on the warhound went out and in its place stood a warhound made out of *metal*. Its eyes glowed a harsh red and its teeth looked like razor blades.

The metal warhound threw the kid through the air; he landed hard, lifeless. The thing in front of me turned to its next victim—a bird-kid who looked to be my age.

The kid turned to fight, but before he could throw a punch the metal warhound's teeth clamped around his throat. Blood welled up around the deep wound. The warhound ripped its teeth away, tearing the kid's throat open. He fell to the ground limp and bleeding and dead.

This wasn't a dream, this was nightmare. A terrible, horrible, tragic nightmare. And it wasn't over yet.

Alex was taking on a warhound with half of the flesh ripped off its face, exposing the metal underneath. Standing on his hind legs, Alex lashed out with his deadly claws, only to slice through empty air as the warhound dodged the blows. I could tell it was getting bored and Alex was getting tired. It landed a blow across Alex's face, knocking him off his paws.

I looked away. I couldn't watch this. I had never seen so much pain and death and bloodshed happen all at one time.

They're called RUCAs, the voice said. *Robotic Unarmed Canine Assassins. But not only is this their fate, they're coming for you next.*

Everything around me spiraled into blackness, and soon I was swallowed up too.

CHAPTER 26

My eyes burst open and I sat up straight. The rain was pouring down and it was clearly still night. I pulled my blanket tighter around me and curled up closer to Sam. I closed my eyes in attempt to fall back asleep. I couldn't even keep my eyes closed.

I sighed and crawled out of the shelter and into the rain with the blanket still wrapped around me.

I thought I heard something through the rain but ignored it. Closing my eyes, I enjoyed the feeling of the cold rain running down my face.

The sound came again, louder. It sounded like a muffled voice. I heard it a third time, louder still, and it clearly sounded like someone screaming,

"Help! Someone help me! Can anyone hear me?"

I walked to the open end of the alley to see what was going on. The road ahead of me was empty, but it was lit by an overhead light.

The voice called again, but the words were drowned out by a loud roll of thunder. It yelled again, sounding closer.

"Help me! Someone, anyone, help me!"

I peered around the corner.

A tall, lean figure was hobbling down the street, gripping its side. It stumbled every now and then as it kept crying for help. No one answered.

The figure staggered into some trash cans that were on the curb. Both the cans and the person fell to the ground with loud clangs and clatters. I instinctively ran forward to help.

Lying among the cans and trash was a thin beat-up-looking boy around the age of fifteen. His long hair hung over his eyes. He wore a denim jacket and a torn black shirt. He was on the edge of consciousness and was panting in shallow breathes. I knelt down beside him and carefully rolled him onto his back. He winced in pain. I tried to open his jacket so that I could see if something was wrong, but his hand shot out and grabbed my wrist.

"Don't do that," he said weakly through clenched teeth.

"Hey, I'm just trying to help you."

After a moment, he hesitantly loosened his grip. I pulled aside one flap of his jacket. A deep and hideous gash down his left side was bleeding heavily. I gasped and then checked his legs. His jeans were torn and he was bleeding from multiple cuts on his legs.

I grabbed his arm and helped him sit up. He winced again and gripped his right shoulder, which was also bleeding.

I took off my now wet blanket and laid it over his back and then draped one of his arms across my shoulders. After pulling him to his feet, I half dragged him back to the alleyway.

As we neared the makeshift shelter, I called, "Abbie, May, Sam, I need you guys out here."

They stumbled out one by one with tired expressions and blankets wrapped around them. When they saw the injured boy, their fatigue was replaced by surprise and concern.

"Help me get him out of the rain," I said. May and Abbie took him from me and led him into the small shelter.

"Who is that and why did you bring him here?" Sam asked. He sounded angry with me.

I looked right in his silver eyes as I answered. "He was injured and crying out for help, so I thought I might give him some. If I'd left him, he might have bled to his death." Before he could react to what I had said, I walked past him and into the shelter.

The boy was leaning against the wall, holding his jacket tightly closed around him. "Come on," May was pleading. "I need you to take off the jacket so that I can see your injuries. I need you to let me heal it."

"Heal it?" he scoffed. "You're just a kid. What do you know about treating injuries?"

"Hey," Abbie said defensively, "May knows a lot about healing. Now if someone takes the time to help you, you don't argue with their methods of doing things."

I laid a hand on her shoulder in signal for her to calm down.

She sighed and whispered to me, "Why don't you distract him, keep him calm, at least long enough for May to get started?"

"Huh?" I replied dumbly.

"You know, talk to him."

She pushed me toward him. I sighed and sat down beside him.

Now that I was closer to him, I could see the details of his face more clearly. He had long mahogany-red hair that reached past his shoulders. He also had the strangest eyes. His right eye was a dark reddish color and his left eye was the deepest, most beautiful blue I had ever seen.

I hugged my knees close to my chest. Clearing my throat, I asked, "How did this happen to you?" Even my soft voice made him jump.

"W-what?"

"How did this happen to you?"

"I … uh … I got into a fight, and I guess it's pretty clear that I lost. They had guns and knives. There was no way I could have won anyway."

While he talked, May found her chance and held her hand to the wound on his side. He cried out in pain and pushed her away.

"What the heck do you think you're doing?" he said through his teeth. He glared at her with eyes like red and blue chips of ice.

I pulled his hand away from her. "Stop it. Can't you see that she's trying to help you?"

"Help me? What does a little girl like her know about healing?" He tried to pull his hand away from me but I gripped it tighter.

"A lot more than you think," I replied, my tone gentler but still defensive. "Just sit still."

He did, although his body was tense as May laid her hand on the injury again. I let go of his hand as the bleeding stopped and the gash started to scab over. His eyes were huge by the time she removed her hand.

He examined it his healed flesh. "H-how did you … What just—"

"We'll explain later," I said. "Can I ask you what your name is?"

He relaxed a little. "Before I answer that, I have my own questions you need to answer first. Who are you? And should I consider you my captors or my saviors, friends or enemies?"

"*I* think you should think of us as friends. I'm Jay." I pointed to May and then to Abbie and introduced them. "That's May and that's Abbie. And ..." I looked around. "Where's Sam?"

"Keeping watch outside," Abbie said. "And getting cold and wet."

"Is that the tall, dark one I saw?" the boy asked.

I nodded. "Now, your name?"

He hesitated and then said, "My name is Lewis." At that same instant, Sam stepped in. His wet hair was slicked to his head, and his clothes were dripping wet and clung to his skin.

"It's dawn and the rain's let up," he reported. "How's he doing?" I could tell that he really didn't care but was trying to be nice.

May answered him, "I'm almost done with the major ones, and his name is Lewis if you didn't hear."

"No, I heard all of it. So let's get some breakfast."

CHAPTER 27

We were dry, well fed, and enjoying the sunlight. Lewis was all healed up. He had pulled his long hair back and tied it into a ponytail with a dark blue ribbon. Why a ribbon? Beats me.

"Trust me, I'm a freak of nature," he said sourly.

"So are we," Sam replied in a similar tone. "When it comes to freaky, we've seen everything."

"Nothing like me," said Lewis.

I smiled. "Try us. We might just be worse than you. Come on, show us."

"I doubt you could be worse than me, but okay. Don't say I didn't warn you though."

He slowly and nervously shrugged off his jacket and then stretched out full fifteen-foot wings. His feathers were a beautiful russet brown. Everyone gasped except for Sam. That explained why Lewis wouldn't let us take off his jacket.

"See, I told you," he said. He hurriedly pulled in his wings and put his jacket back over them. "I'm a freak, a monstrosity." He turned away.

"No, it's okay," I blurted out. He turned to face me. "Um, let us show you." I pulled off my own jacket and stretched out my wings. His eyes were as round as an owl's. I heard him whisper, "They're beautiful." I motioned to the others to copy me.

In turn, they each showed off their wings—May's fox colored, Abbie's white and black, and Sam's beautiful jet-black wings like the night sky.

Now Lewis' eyes were so wide, I thought they might pop out of his head. I folded my wings back in and covered them again with my jacket. Lewis forced his expression to change so that he looked less shocked. He lowered his gaze.

"We're the same," he said softly. He looked up, cleared his throat, and said, "So if we're like one another, do you have ... powers?"

No one spoke for a minute, and then May said, "Well, you know one of my abilities. I can heal by touch, but I can also breathe underwater."

"That's really cool," Lewis said. He pointed to Abbie. "How about you?"

She spoke hesitantly. "I can make myself invisible with the exception of my two black feathers. I also, in a way, see the future, and I can read people's memories through physical touch."

"Wow. Can you tell me what's in *my* future?" he asked charmingly.

She held a finger to her lips. "Shh, no spoilers."

"Okay then." He glanced at me. "How about you?"

"You're trying to remember my name," I said, "you're very impressed by all of us so far, and you're wondering whether or not the soreness in your shoulder will affect your flying."

Lewis gaped at me. Yeah, mind reading, it'll scare people.

He stammered, "How—how did you ... I mean ... uh, what?"

"I have telepathic abilities," I said. "Now watch this."

I held out my hand and focused. In an instant, a small blue jay had formed in the palm of my hand. It spread its small wing and flew off. Before it got too far, it shattered back into the particles I had made it from. I could sense a bit of uneasiness from Sam but I ignored it. I turned to him and asked him to show Lewis what he could do.

He shook his head. "Not until I see what *he* can do."

"All right," Lewis said, "but watch carefully."

He looked down at the wet concrete he was sitting on. There were small creaking sounds, and the water on the ground around us froze into a sheet of solid ice. May attempted to take a step forward but slipped. Abbie caught her and then slipped herself, leaving them both on the ground. I tried not to laugh as they tried to stand back up, only to slip again.

The ice melted back into water as fast as it froze.

"So you can freeze water," Sam said.

"More than that," Lewis replied in a cocky manner. "I can also freeze solid and living objects."

"Is that it?"

"No."

Lewis glared at Sam for a moment but nothing happened. Then the trash can next to Sam burst into flames, catching on the arm of Sam's black jacket. Sam shouted and waved his arm to put out the flame. Lewis stood and clenched his fist. Instantly, the flames went out.

"Sorry," he said. "I'm still learning to control that one. Now will you show me what you can do?"

Sam grumbled something under his breath. He began to shrink as his clothes and hair shrank into his body and replaced themselves with silky black feathers. His face elongated, nose and mouth hardening into a black beak. His legs grew thin and spindly, ending in bird feet with four clawed toes.

Before long, a large black bird stood in his place. The bird reached about the height of my knees. He gave a loud "Kaw" and took off into the sky.

"Don't worry," I said to Lewis, reading his thoughts again. "He'll be back soon." Sam always came back.

"Can he do anything else?" Lewis asked.

"He can change the color of his hair, eyes, and skin," I answered. "But that's really cool what you can do: controlling and creating fire and ice. That's really cool."

There was a long pause and then Lewis asked what we were doing there, if we were on the run or something.

"Sort of," I said, leaning against the brick wall. "We're running from other hybrids called warhounds who are out to get us to take us back to the hellhole we came from." I thought about my dream the night before—the new enemies, my new ability, the fact that all of the rescued hybrids were going to be killed by these RUCAs. It was all very unnerving. Then I thought about the torturous things that happened before our escape from the DAEL, all of the pain and suffering. Tears gathered in my eyes from the overflow of mixed emotions.

Arms wrapped around me, and I snapped out of it. May and Abbie were hugging me, showing that they shared my pain. I hugged them back. A single tear fell from my eyes, but that single tear was only a fraction of the pain I was feeling.

CHAPTER 28

When the other girls and I separated after a minute, Lewis announced that he wanted to go with us. I stared at him. "What?"

"I want to travel with you if I'm allowed to."

Just after he said that, we heard a fluttering sound over our heads. The large black bird landed at our feet. Its feathers shrank into its skin and its body began to grow. Its wings replaced themselves with arms and hands. Its beak and beady eyes morphed into a familiar human face. Soon, Sam stood before us with his hands in his pockets.

"So what'd I miss?" he asked jokingly. He looked more relaxed and happy than he had been earlier.

Before I could answer him, Lewis said for the third time, "I'd like to travel with you if you'll let me."

Sam stared at him as if he had suggested the craziest, stupidest idea ever.

"I'm serious," Lewis said. "I'd like to go with you."

"Uh, guys, group meeting," Sam called. We all huddled together so Lewis wouldn't overhear, and Sam whispered, "I don't think he should come. I mean, we just met him. I don't know what you think, but I don't trust him."

"Well, I wouldn't mind him coming with us," Abbie said.

"Me neither. I like him," May said.

Everyone turned to me. *Man, I don't like being the center of attention like this.*

"Why are you all looking at me?" I wanted to shrink away from their intense gazes.

"What's your opinion?" Sam asked. "Can he come or should we just tell him no?"

"Uh ... um ... Well, I like him, I think he's nice, but I also know that we shouldn't trust him 100 percent. So ..." *I don't know!*

"Which is it, Jay?" Abbie asked.

Too much pressure! Think, compromise, something. I took a deep breath. It was time to take charge again.

"How about he comes along, and if he shows any signs of turning on us, we throw him out, so to speak?"

Sam gave in. "All right, fine, he can come, but I'm keeping a very close eye on him."

I broke away from the group and walked over to Lewis. "It's been agreed. You can come with us."

To my surprise, he hugged, lifting me off the ground. "Thank you!" He put me back down and said in a calmer voice, "Sorry, I got excited and went a little overboard. I'm just happy that I've finally found others who are like me."

He might be a little too happy to be accompanying you. The voice in my head shocked me a little.

Lewis must have noticed because he studied me with his gorgeous eyes and asked if something was the matter.

I looked away. "No, nothing is wrong." I turned to fetch my bag, but I ran into Sam. I didn't have to read his thoughts because his silvery grey eyes said everything. "Don't be too trusting of him," they told me. "Be cautious around him."

He could see that I got the message and stepped aside for me to pass. *What have I gotten myself into?*

CHAPTER 29

Well, here we are in a familiar scene. After a long day of flying, we had settled on the ground. Thankfully, we had found the woods again. It felt good to have leaves and branches rustling overhead.

The sun had set and we had a roaring fire, thanks to Lewis; and for the first time in ages we had cold water to drink—also thanks to Lewis.

We had eaten and everyone except for me was asleep. I lay awake next to Sam. His deep breathing should have soothed and calmed me, but I was restless. I couldn't think of anything I could do till I was tired enough to sleep. Sam turned over, giving me an idea.

I crawled over to the pile of backpacks and opened the green one that Sam carried. I felt around until I felt the book he had bought. Opening it to the page he had marked with a leaf, I sounded out the words the way he had showed me. I tried to pronounce each word as quietly as possible as to not wake anyone up.

Then I got caught on a long word. I tried my best to pronounce it but I couldn't.

I heard a yawn behind me. I turned to see Sam sitting up and wiping the sleep from his eyes.

"You can't sleep?" he asked hoarsely.

"No."

He moved closer and looked over my shoulder. "You can't pronounce this?" He pointed to the word on the page. I shook my head. "It says *dictionary*. Remember that *tion* makes a *shun* sound." He put a hand on my shoulder. "Let's go somewhere else so that we don't wake the others," he whispered.

I let him lead me into the trees. We stopped in front of one, and I sat down next to Sam on the roots.

"Sam, I can't read the words. It's too dark."

"Make a small ball of light, then we'll be able to see."

I held out my hand and materialized a small light. Sam wrapped one arm around me. His silvery-gray eyes were so soft and gentle as he looked down at me.

Why does my heart pound so hard when I'm near him? I wondered. He opened the book and pointed to the next word. "Let's continue."

———◆———

We'd been reading for more than an hour. My eyes were drooping and so were his. When I started to doze off, Sam shook me awake.

"Come on, just one more word and then we'll head back." He pointed at the word and I gazed at it through half closed eyes.

I yawned out the word—"Love"—and then let my eyes close and my body go limp. I was too tired.

I heard Sam whisper, "And I do you." I didn't know what he meant by that, but he scooped me up in his arms. Cradling me against his chest, he carried me back to the camp.

I let the heavy black curtains of sleep cover me and drag me down into the blackness of a heavenly deep sleep. I slept so soundly that night, I didn't even dream.

I woke up cold the next morning. The grass around me sparkled like glass.

I sat up and noticed that the blanket I had been using was covered with tiny icelike crystals, like the grass.

"Did you do this?" I heard Sam say. I looked around and saw that he was confronting Lewis. "What is this?" Sam yelled, motioning to the ground.

"No, I didn't do this," Lewis said. "It's only frost. Don't tell me you haven't seen frost before?"

I stood and walked up to them. "Why's the ground frozen? What is frost?" I asked.

Lewis answered, "During certain times of the year, it will frost because the weather is cold. You know how when the weather's warm, there's water on the grass in the morning? Well, frost is that water but frozen."

I didn't understand but dropped the subject.

In short order, the others woke up, Lewis relit the fire, we ate breakfast, and we took off into the air. Even though it was chilly, flying kept us warm.

As we traveled, the forest looked thinner than I thought it would be. Snow-capped mountains loomed ahead of us, but I guessed that we would be past them in no time.

We all flew in silence, and I do mean all of us. Not even May and Abbie were talking. I was just thinking about last night.

My heart pounded and raced when I was close to Sam. I also noticed that my heart did the same thing when I was near Lewis. Why did that happen?

Lost in my thoughts, I never knew anything else was in the air with us until something dark and heavy landed on top of me, knocking the breath from me and pushing me down. When I heard a deep growl in my ear, I realized exactly what it was. A flying warhound! It grabbed at my wings, digging its claws into the feathers.

I struggled to flip myself over. Once I'd turned to face it, I threw a quick punch to its face, snapping its head back. That really pissed it off. It hurt my hand but sweet adrenaline dulled the pain.

The warhound lashed out with its teeth and sank its enormous fangs into my shoulder. Blood gushed around its mouth, staining its gray muzzle.

A branch smacked me across my back as we hit the trees. The warhound released its grip on my shoulder when a branch jabbed it in the ribs.

I landed face down in the dirt. I recovered as quickly as possible, running away from where I'd seen the warhound hit. The trees ended abruptly at the edge of a clearing. Sadly, that clearing was a dead end.

Towering above me was a rocky gray cliff. I couldn't climb it, and with my feathers clotted with blood from cuts and scratches, I couldn't fly over it either.

I whirled at the sounds of twigs snapping and bushes rustling, ready to fight. I relaxed a little when I saw it was the other members of my group. They didn't seem to be as happy to see me as I was to see them. I looked up and saw why.

A band of about ten flying warhounds were dropping down on us. One was heading straight for me but collided with Sam when he blocked it.

The one that had attacked me earlier charged at me. I was ready for it, but Lewis tackled it.

Another one had May pinned to the ground. I leaped onto its back, wrapping my arms around its neck. I pulled back and up on its head, forcing it off her. As it straightened and stumbled, I slipped off its back and landed on my butt. May scrambled away. As the warhound tried to follow her, I grabbed one of his big back wings. It whipped its head around to glare at me before pulling its wing away, sending me stumbling back into the cliff.

My head smacked against the stone with a *crack* and I sank to the ground, dazed but unhurt.

I saw Lewis fighting, using moves I had never seen before. Swinging one leg up and around, he kicked a warhound's jaw, snapping its head to the side. Then he turned and punched a warhound that was on top of Abbie, forcing it off her.

I struggled to my feet, using the cliff wall for support. As I started to help Lewis, a warhound stampeded at me at full speed, knocking me back against the cliff with one strong paw planted against my chest.

Before I could even try to fight back, it clamped its teeth onto my throat. This was a new kind of excruciating pain I had never felt before. I could feel my blood seeping into my windpipe. I heard screaming but couldn't make out any words.

Sara's voice echoed in my thoughts. *Jay, I need you to listen. Hang in there a little longer.*

The warhound's grip tightened and then vanished, and I fell to the ground, choking on my own blood.

My whole world spiraled into darkness.

———◆———

I was lying there, floating in the cold blackness. A feeling of euphoria and happiness filled me. *Everything would turn out fine if I just stayed there*, or so I thought.

I felt someone pull me up, their touch warm against my cold skin. They pulled me into a sitting position.

"Jay, we don't have much time, focus," Sara's voice rang out in the emptiness. She snapped her fingers in front of my eyes and I blinked. I looked up at her.

Her hand extended toward me as she helped me to stand on the invisible surface. "What's going on?" I asked. In a flash, it all came rushing back to me.

I turned to her and yelled with urgency, "Sara, I have to get back! The others need me! They're outnumbered and need help! Please take me back!" Sara placed her hands on my shoulders.

"Jay, Jay, calm down. They're fine now, well, mostly. After the warhound let go, it and the other warhounds flew off."

"Sara, I need to go back. Take me back!" I attempted to yell, but only managed a whimper.

"Can you just look at this first?" she asked. I sighed and nodded. She turned me toward a scene that displayed before my eyes.

———◆———

It was in the clearing. I saw myself lying at the base of the stone wall, bleeding heavily from my injuries. The last of the warhounds were leaving. Between two warhounds, hung the dead body of another.

My friends rushed toward my limp body. Sam, the first to reach me, knelt down and picked up my body, holding me close to his chest.

He screamed to May, who came limping up. She laid her hands over my chest and head as tears streamed down her face.

She choked out through her sobs, "It's too late. I'm too late. She's gone."

"No!" Sam cried out. "She can't be. She isn't. Jay isn't dead." Now tears fell from his eyes. "Jay, Jay, wake up. You can't die! I need you. We need you... Please don't die!"

He buried his face in my hair, whispering something to me so softly I couldn't hear what it was. The whole scene brought tears to my eyes, not for myself, but for my friends who suffered.

<hr />

I whispered to my friend while I stared out in front of me, "Am I... am I really dead?"

"That's your choice, Jay." I stared at her. She continued, "You can choose to either go back to them and live on, or come with me and stay dead to them forever." Sara turned away from me and stared blankly into the distant blackness.

Two flecks of white emerged from the darkness as two figures ran closer. One appeared to be a teenage female wearing a flowing white dress, the other a small boy. I stared at them in wonder and shock.

I pushed past Sara running as tears of happiness and grief poured from my eyes. All three of us met together in a group hug: my brother, my sister. I thought I'd lost them forever. I stepped back a moment and looked them over.

My sister's blonde hair flowed down to her knees, her blue eyes sparkling. My younger brother's shaggy blonde hair fell into curls in front of his eyes. Both of their blue jay wings faintly glowed.

"Jay, it's been so long. For this whole time, all we could do was watch," my sister said, her voice filled with beauty and warmth. "You're not the only one with a name now. I'm Melody." She looked down at our brother. "Go ahead, you can tell her."

He looked up at me with big blue eyes, "My name is Jake." I hugged them both again.

"I've missed you both so much," I told them over and over. Words could never explain how much I had missed them.

Sara spoke for the first time in a while, "Jay, we don't have much time left." I looked from her to my siblings.

Melody whispered to me, "I think you should go back. Your friends need you more than we do. Either way, we'll still be with you." I wrapped my arms around her neck.

"Thank you," I whispered back. I let go and knelt down so Jake could hug me, then I stood back up. "I love you both and I've really missed you, but I'm going back. My friends, they're like another family to me."

"Bye Jay," Jake waved goodbye.

"Bye Jake, Melody." I turned to face Sara, "I'm ready to go back now." As she took my hand, my body filled with a sudden warmth. And, just like last time, I felt myself falling, fast and hard.

CHAPTER 30

I coughed and sputtered, choking on the blood that flooded my throat. When I opened my eyes, Sam was staring down at me with absolute joy written across his face. Then May knelt beside me and pressed her hand against my neck. I could feel the wound sealing.

After the dreadful cut was healed, Sam realized I was still choking. He urged me onto my hands and knees and patted my back.

I went into another coughing fit, spitting up blood. That went on for a painful minute until I managed to stop, gasping for sweet air. Then another fit wracked my whole body.

By the time I stopped coughing, I'd coughed up a scary amount of blood—and had thrown up most of my breakfast.

While May moved to help the others, I laid down, dizzy from the loss of blood. Sam sat next to me.

"Before you woke up, just now, May told me you were dead," he said, staring off into the trees.

"What?" I glanced up at him.

He continued as if I hadn't spoken. "I didn't want to believe it. I even cried for you. Eventually though, I started to believe her. You really scared me back there. I just saw that warhound

132

attack you, and from the wound it made, I thought you might die from it."

He paused and gave a little laugh. "I can't believe I actually killed him. The same warhound that kicked my butt last time was here. I slammed him up against the wall a couple times until I heard a loud *crack*. I let go and he fell to the ground, dead. That's when I saw that other one attack you."

He looked down at me and patted my head. "Please try not to scare me like that again."

I smiled. "I'll try."

He always tried to hide his emotions, so I had to answer that way. This was the first time he'd ever said anything so heartfelt. I shifted under the blanket and closed my eyes. I fell asleep like that, with Sam stroking my head, humming to himself.

———◆———

I woke up slowly. When I finally sat up and glanced around, I was instantly alert. Lewis was poised to strike Abbie, who was standing in a defensive position.

Before I even realized it, I was up and running toward them. I tackled him and we both fell to the ground, with me landing on top of him.

"What the heck do you think you're doing?" I yelled. He struggled under me as I tried to pin him.

"Jay, stop it, he wasn't doing anything wrong," Abbie said, pulling me off him.

"You're telling me to stop? He was trying to hit you."

Lewis got up and dusted himself off. "I was showing her some fighting and defensive moves. You know, if the warhounds ever come back." I frowned, eyeing him nervously. "I could show you some too."

"Uh, sure, I—I guess," I answered. I was a little sore, but I figured I'd be fine.

"Okay, now watch closely."

———◆———

Lewis was bent over his knees panting. I was too. We had been sparring and so far the score was three to one. Sadly, he was winning. I'd find a way to get back at him later.

As soon as he regained his breath, he said, "Okay, now I'm going to use some more dangerous, more lethal moves. I'll go easy on you, though."

I gulped. The others were watching, and Sam looked worried.

Lewis threw a punch that I easily dodged. That was a huge mistake.

He turned quickly and kicked out one of my knees, forcing me into a kneeling position. He raised his hand to deliver a final, lethal blow. *He won't do it. He won't kill me*, I thought.

Suddenly Sam was beside me, knocking Lewis away. "You idiot!" he yelled. "You were going to hit her with full force. That would have killed her."

I had never seen Sam that mad before. It almost scared me. I slowly stood up.

Lewis pushed Sam back. "No. I would never try to kill her or any of you."

"Really? Then what was that?" Before Lewis could reply, Sam grabbed my wrist and pulled me away, leading me into the trees.

As soon as we were well away from camp, he dropped my hand and spun to face me. "How, Jay?" he shouted, throwing his hands in the air. "How can you trust him like that? How can you look at him with so much trust?"

I winced. It was strange, him yelling at me. He never raised his voice at me.

When I didn't answer, he continued, "He could have killed you, and I bet he would have."

I stalked up to him and stared him dead in the eye. "What is your problem, Sam? Why are you acting so hostile toward Lewis?"

He took a slow, deep breath. "What's *my* problem?" he said softly. "Shouldn't you know already, little miss mind reader?"

I was taken aback by his comment. Sam was blocking me, not allowing me to read his thoughts.

He grabbed my hand and pressed it against the side of his head. "Tell me, Jay," he said calmly. "Tell me my emotions. Tell me what my feelings are toward you." His eyes softened, and he allowed me into his head.

Even when I closed my eyes, I could go no further than his thoughts, and even those were difficult to read. I opened my eyes and whimpered, "I can't."

He threw my hand away and pushed past me. "Of course," he muttered as he stormed away.

What was that about?

CHAPTER 31

W e decided to spend the night where we were, although we moved away from the clearing and farther into the trees as to not be spotted from the skies. As usual, I couldn't sleep.

I lay there staring up at the stars through the branches, thinking about that day—seeing my dead family, dying and living to tell about it, and that intense moment with Sam. And I wondered how I could use this strange new power of mine, how I could learn to control it.

Listen to your heartbeat, Sara's voice said in my head. *Feel it.*

I could feel it, pulsing in my chest, my wrists, my neck.

Now imagine it slowing, your breathing slowing with it, she whispered to me. I closed my eyes, feeling them grow heavy as I focused. *Now imagine them both completely stopping.*

A sudden cold rushed over me, and for a moment I couldn't feel anything. Then I felt myself standing.

I blinked open my eyes to see Sara walking toward me from the blackness. "Good job, Jay." She continued before I could say anything, "Jay, sometimes it won't be me here. Sometimes it will be Melody or Jake meeting you here."

"Okay, Sara, I get it. I'd like to ask you a question though. I need some advice."

"What is it, Jay?"

"Do you know what's going on between Sam and Lewis?"

"I know your feelings toward Lewis, and so does Sam. You like him, maybe a little more than a friend, and Sam really doesn't like that, how you trust him the way you do."

"But why does Sam act so strange around me?"

"How you don't know shows how blind you can really be," she said tartly.

I sighed. I wasn't going to get many answers here. "Okay, how do I get back now?"

She smiled, clearly happy to be off the subject. "Take my hand and think about the rhythm of a heartbeat."

As she held my hand, my whole body was filled with warmth. It was like a hot fire melting the ice. I could hear my heart pounding in my ears. I could feel the powerful beat in my chest and the cold air filling my lungs. Then I felt as if I was falling backward over a cliff, the normal sense of falling, but this time I didn't panic.

My eyes fluttered open, and I saw a blurred face above me. "Sam?"

The figure shook its head. "No, it's Lewis."

As my vision cleared, I could see that his different-colored eyes were calm and his long hair fell loosely onto his shoulders. My head was in his lap, and he held my hand in his.

"How do you do it?" he asked. "How do you die and yet still live to see the next day?"

I was a little shocked by his asking. "I—I don't know. I can't explain it," I lied.

He squeezed my hand. "Your heart's beating really fast. What's the matter? Are you afraid of something?"

"No. Nothing's wrong," I lied again.

"If that's the case," he said, his expression blank, "just go back to sleep then."

How could I? After what had just happened, I'd be lucky to even get a wink of sleep that night. I wasn't tired.

I moved away from him and curled into my blanket even though I wanted to stay close to him. *Maybe Sara is right. Maybe I do ... like him.*

Lewis leaned over and kissed my forehead. Suddenly I was exhausted, tired enough to sleep for a week. Before I even realized it, I was sound asleep.

CHAPTER 32

We finished off the last of our food for breakfast and took off not completely satisfied. We robbed another guy of about three hundred dollars once we hit a small town, but he wouldn't miss it. The dude had a ton left. And it was for a good cause: feeding hungry bird-kids.

As we left the town, I realized how many more signs and other stuff I could read. I also realized that the mountains stretched much farther than I'd thought.

The snow below us piled up in drifts and mounds. Our breaths came out in billows of steam. Even as we flew, I shivered in the cold mountain air. I zipped up my new thicker, not bloodstained coat.

Noticing Lewis was flying at the back of the group, I fell back to join him. "Do you want to explain what happened last night?" I asked.

He looked at me with the same expressionless gaze. "I apologize. I suppose I should have told you earlier."

"About what?"

"It's a strange ability I have, but it's more like a curse. Sometimes, through physical touch, I can drain another living thing's energy and take that energy into myself. I'm still trying to control it." He turned his gaze away. "What about you? What about the fact that you died last night and yet you're still here, living and breathing?"

"It's something I'm still learning about," I replied. "Why didn't you tell us before?"

He sighed. "I was afraid I might scare you too much and you wouldn't let me come along. What about you? Why haven't *you* told anyone?"

"A similar reason," I answered. "But I'll tell them when the time is right, so keep quiet about it."

I realized I had been edging closer to him and pushed myself away with a simple flap of my wings. After a few minutes of silence, I turned my attention to the forest below. Not too far ahead, a thin stream of smoke rose from between the trees. As we drew near, I saw it came from a small cabin. A truck was parked in front and a winding dirt road led up to it.

Two older men were sitting on the porch. One looked up and started shouting, pointing up at us. His friend followed his gaze and then ran into the house. He returned with a long sticklike weapon that I had learned was a gun. Raising the gun, he took aim at us. A loud sound exploded in the air, followed by a high-pitched whistle as the bullet whizzed by.

"They're shooting at us!" Sam shouted. "We've got to pick up the pace! Let's go, let's go!"

Instantly, we all put on a burst of speed. More shots rang out, and Sam shouted in pain as one grazed his leg. More bullets zipped by, and one bang seemed louder than the rest. That's probably because that's the shot that hit me.

I felt it rip through my left wing. I cried out and tried to continue flying. All I have to say is that there is a reason why flying creatures have *two* wings instead of just one.

"Guys, I'm hit!" I yelled as I started to plummet.

I crashed into the trees. Cracking sounds followed my descent, but I couldn't distinguish the snapping of branches from the snapping of bone. When I hit the ground, I simply lay there in the snow, curled into a ball of excruciating pain. I heard the distant roar of an engine. The shooters' truck, I guessed.

I struggled to my feet, only to fall again as the pain intensified in my right leg. I rolled up my pant leg and was shocked to see bone poking through the flesh of my shin. Blood poured from the wound, reddening the snow. Blood dripped into my eyes and down my face from a cut on my head. The roar of the truck was getting louder.

I whipped my head around, looking for something that might help me. I couldn't walk, I couldn't fly. What could I do?

The very least I could do was hide my wings so the men wouldn't see them when they found me. Slowly and painfully, I pulled my wings through the slits in the back of my coat, and then I rolled my pant leg back down over my injury.

The truck was very close now. The sound of the engine clicked off, and I heard doors open and close. The men spoke to each other and then went stomping off into the trees. From the sound of it, they were both moving away from me. For now.

I heard rustling in nearby foliage and I tensed. *Did they bring friends to help? Will they find me?*

A bush rustled and shook, and I jumped as a large gray rabbit bounded out of it. It raced past me and disappeared into the trees.

I sighed and laughed silently at myself for being so scared of a small animal. I hushed up instantly when I heard more rustling in the same bush.

This time, a small person stumbled out. Or should I say, a small bird-kid. May smiled and turned, running back the way she had come.

"May, wait!" I called after her. "I need help." I clapped my hand over my mouth, remembering the two hunters out there.

May ran back with the other three close behind. She tried to pull me up, saying, "Come on. We have to go. We can't let those men find us."

I pulled my arm away. "I can't walk and I can't fly. I was shot in the wing. That's why I'm down here. And then I badly injured my leg in the crash. I can't move."

We all stiffened when we heard a stick snap.

"Everybody," Sam whispered urgently, "hide your wings. The hunters are coming. Quickly!"

The two men strode out of the trees, their guns in hand. They both stopped dead in their tracks when they saw us. One gasped and dropped his gun, and both of them were gaping at something just beyond me.

I turned and saw what. May hadn't apparently heard what Sam said. Her tawny wings stood out like a beacon against the trees and snow.

The first man fell to his knees and did an odd thing with his hand, touching his forehead, heart, and both shoulders, and then clasped his hands together.

The other hunter struggled to form words. "W-who are you? W-what are y-you? Why—why are you here?"

The first one cried, "An angel, Devon. Angels is what they are." Tears streamed down his face.

Sam picked me up, careful not to touch my injured wing, and cradled me against his chest. "My friend here is injured because of you and we're leaving to get help for her." He opened his own wings.

The other man fell to his knees, folding his hands. "Good Lord, we've shot an angel. Will the Lord ever forgive us for harming his child?"

Both men were crying, begging for forgiveness.

I didn't know this *lord* they spoke of, but it felt right to say, "He forgives you."

Those simple words made them so happy. They thanked us and thanked us. They offered us help, food, and shelter, but we had to tell them no.

After a while they left, saying, "Such a shame to die so young. We pray for you."

I had absolutely no idea what they were talking about.

CHAPTER 33

W e trekked through the trees and snow. Abbie and Lewis flew overhead, looking for any sort of shelter. They relayed messages down to me telepathically and I passed them on to Sam and May.

Hey, I think I see something, Abbie thought to me.

That's great, what is it? I replied. I shifted in Sam's arms. May had done enough healing so that I wasn't in agony any longer, but the pain was still intense.

Hold on. I think it's a small building. It's about four miles from where we are.

"Abbie thinks she may have spotted a house," I said aloud. *How long would it take for us to walk the rest of the way?*

About an hour or two at this rate, Lewis answered.

In what direction? I asked.

It's northeast from where you guys are, Abbie answered.

My voice croaked a little as I spoke. "Sam, turn northeast. There's shelter about an hour or two away."

He looked down at me. "Are you going to make it okay."

"I'll be fine."

He looked back up and turned in the direction of the house.

We continued for about thirty minutes with May beside us. Suddenly, Sam stopped and heaved an aggravated sigh.

"This is taking way too long. I'm going to try flying the rest of the way."

I gazed up at him dizzily. He had that determined look on his face, and I knew I wouldn't be able to convince him otherwise. I wasn't even going to try. I was too tired to argue with him.

I closed my eyes as he spread his enormous black wings and broke into a fast run. A branch whizzed by my face and Sam winced as one scratched his cheek. I was jostled around a bit, but that didn't last long.

Soon his powerful, beating wings carried us high into the crisp mountain air. May easily caught up to us. Abbie and Lewis said they'd wait for us at the house.

Sam spotted the small wooden building almost immediately and put on a burst of speed. My eyes fluttered open as his angled downward for our decent. The landing was rough, and I fell ungracefully from his arms, landing on my broken leg. I cried out loudly. No, I wasn't being a baby. That really hurt. Have you ever broken a leg that badly?

Sam pushed himself up and trudged through the snow to me. "Sorry about that."

The cabin was about fifty feet from us. Smoke rose steadily from the stone chimney. It wasn't very big, but it was big enough for five bird-kids to hide for the night.

With May preceding us up the steps and onto the porch, Sam carried me to the cabin. Abbie and Lewis flung open the door and helped me inside. Abbie told me to sit in a chair near the stone fireplace.

I glanced around the cabin. In the far corner was a small open kitchen with a stove, refrigerator, and many cabinets. Off to the other side was a staircase that led to a second story loft. We were in the living room. It had a fur rug, a long couch, and two chairs. Everyone was shivering, trying to get warm by the fire.

I closed my eyes and allowed my mind to wander. Random questions flashed through my head.

How were the warhounds finding us so easily? Why were things so strange between Sam, Lewis, and me? Why hadn't I heard from the little voice in a while? Who or what was the voice anyway?

Then, through all those worrying thoughts, I heard someone singing. The voice rose and fell in a rhythmic and soothing hum. As I focused on the voice, I saw a blurry image of a woman staring down at me. I couldn't make out any of the details of her face but I was aware of the sensation of being held.

Some muffled words from the song she was singing came through.

> For one so small, you seem so strong.
> My arms will hold you, keep you safe and warm.
> This bond between us can't be broken.
> I will be here, don't you cry.

This all happened within a few seconds, but that one vision had enough emotion built into it that tears filled my eyes.

My heart tightened with a strong sense of grief and loss.

I opened my eyes again. Sam was staring at me with the gentlest of gazes. His little half smile made my heart melt.

A mouth-watering smell drew my gaze away from him. Lewis was standing in the kitchen, stirring something in a large pot on the stove. As I watched, he took some bowls down from a cabinet. With the spoon, he filled each bowl and then carried the steaming bowls out to us on a tray. Moments later, he was back with a handful of spoons. He passed a bowl and spoon to each of us.

I held the bowl and looked at the liquid in it, wondering exactly what it was. It was brown and had pieces of meat and vegetables floating in it.

"It's only soup," Sam explained. "It's okay to eat." He shoveled a spoonful into his mouth to show me.

I copied him. My eyes widened at the taste. It was amazing, much better than lunch meat and hot dogs over a fire. I shoved more into my mouth, savoring the taste. As the soup revived me, I became aware of the pain in my injured wing. I leaned forward to take some pressure off it, but I'd forgotten about my broken leg. I put too much weight on it and cried out, nearly spilling my food. I squeezed my eyes closed, trying to block the pain out.

Instantly, my friends were surrounding me, asking what was wrong. "My leg, my wing, it hurts," I choked out. Lewis took the bowl from me as May told the others what to do.

They helped me onto the floor, lying me on my stomach. Someone eased my jacket off and gently spread my bloodied wing. Glancing over my shoulder, I saw the brown and black feathers were stained red.

After a moment's examination, May scolded, "Why didn't you tell me earlier?"

"I thought it was pretty obvious why I fell," I retorted. "And I *did* tell you." The position I was in was no help to my leg. If anything, it was making it hurt more.

She murmured something to herself and continued looking at the injury through the feathers. "Jay, you may need to see this."

I glanced over, and my eyes widened at the sight of her fingers fitting through my wing where there was supposed to be bone. The bullet hadn't grazed me as I'd thought. It had gone completely through.

"This is going to be extremely hard to fix." With the look of concentration, she looked much older than seven. "I'm going to come back to it to work with it further. I need to see her leg now."

They all helped turn me over and sit up, so that I was leaning against the chair I had been sitting in. She rolled up my bloodstained pant leg.

The bone still poked through the skin. Abbie gasped loudly, covering her mouth with her hands.

"I'm going to have to realign it but it's going to hurt ... a lot," May said.

Oh, crap, this is going to hurt like hell.

Sam took my hand in his. He thought to me, *Squeeze it as hard as you have to when the pain comes.* I smiled at the gesture.

Abbie was trembling, a terrified expression on her face. "Abbie, can you get me some fresh water?" I asked her. I didn't need it, but it gave her an excuse to move away and do something else.

"Are you ready for this?" May asked.

"As I'll ever be," I answered. She started to pull on my leg while pushing down on the disconnected bone. I screamed and gripped Sam's hand as hard as I could. He grunted in pain.

I heard a sickening cracking sound over Sam's screaming.

He pulled his hand away. "I think you did it a little too hard. Actually, I think you may have broken my hand."

"Sorry. That just really hurt," I whimpered.

Jay, I have an idea. Lewis' thoughts forced themselves into my head. *You might not like it, but it's something.*

What?

You're going to have to die.

WHAT!

Not like that. Like what I saw last night.

I don't know …

It's the best way and you know it. They're going to have to learn about it eventually anyway.

I sighed. "All right."

Abbie reentered the room and handed me the water bottle. I set it aside.

"You all know," I began, "that I've … died and I'm still here. Well, I've found that it wasn't just a freak accident. It's a new but strange ability. It's a dangerous one, yes, but it's something that's also protective."

"Why bring this up now?" Sam asked.

"Because it might spare me the pain," I answered.

I saw Sam thinking it over, and May was doing the same. May said that it sounded all right to her, but Sam remained silent for a moment.

"You said that it can be dangerous," he pointed out. "What exactly did you mean by that?"

149

"I'm still trying to figure it out myself, and I'm not sure when or if I'll wake back up."

"It sounds a little risky. Are you sure about this?"

"Yes, I'm sure," I answered quickly. Without waiting for his reply, I closed my eyes and began to slow my heartbeat. I opened my eyes when I felt my pulse finally stop and I saw the usual black plain.

There was one problem though, No one was there with me to help me get back to earth.

CHAPTER 34

Something wasn't right. Wasn't Sara supposed to meet me there? I spun around in search of … well, anything. Now I was a little scared.

A panting sound from behind me made me jump. I turned only to nearly run into my sibling.

My brother stood before me, his long blond curls falling in front of his shining blue eyes. He was bent over at his knees, trying to catch his breath.

After a moment, he straightened up and stared at me. "I'm sorry. You took us off guard and I had to really rush to get here. This was really unexpected."

I was shocked at his vocabulary. He died when he was seven, and I couldn't even talk then, let alone him.

"Sorry, Jake," I apologized. "As you probably saw, I got hurt. But I didn't expect to see you here. I was hoping—"

"To see Sara instead of me," he interrupted. "We need to wait a couple of minutes before you can go back."

"Why's that?" I asked.

"They're still fixing your injuries and I wanted to tell you something." I leaned closer. "I don't like Lewis. You need to be careful of him. You shouldn't trust him as much as you do."

I didn't know how to respond to that. We stood there in silence for a few minutes, until I saw his eyes lose their focus, leaving him with a confused expression. He shook his head as if to clear it.

"Jay, it's safe to go back now." He took my hand. "I really need you to focus or it won't work. I'm not as strong as Sara and Melody."

Not long after I closed my eyes and imagined my heart beating again, I felt the now familiar sense of falling.

It felt like I had been falling for much longer than the last time, but I was finally back on earth and very much alive. When I woke up, I was lying in a bed with May asleep in another bed. Abbie was sitting on the end of my bed.

She must have heard me gasp as I drew in that first breath, because she leaped up and ran down the stairs to the living room.

I was lying on my back with my right wing stretched out. The sheets that covered me kept me warm.

Many sets of footsteps sounded on the stairs as the others ran up to the second floor. Everyone crowded around my bed.

I was peppered with questions until I asked for quiet. "How long have I been out?" I asked.

"About two hours," Abbie answered.

"Why's May asleep?"

"With how much she used her powers," Sam answered, "it really wore her out."

"Is my wing fixed yet?" I tried to move it only to wince at its soreness. Looking at it, I could see it had stopped bleeding but the big hole was still there.

"Not quite," Abbie answered. "On the bright side, she's almost done with your leg."

I rolled my eyes and then yawned.

"Come on, guys," Sam said. "Let's let her rest. It's late."

Abbie crawled into bed with May while the boys went back downstairs. A small fireplace sat at one end of the loft. It easily lit and warmed the room. For a moment I watched the light of the flickering flames on the walls. It wasn't too long before I fell into a pleasant sleep.

———————◆◆———————

I dreamed of the vision I'd had earlier. A woman whose face was just out of focus stared down at me while singing that sweet song. But while I was listening to the words of the song, a malevolent voice started talking in my head, drowning out the song.

"We'll take them when I say, but do not harm them. We'll just keep them running until they tire out. Then we'll capture them when they can no longer fight."

The voice sent shivers down my spine, alerting me to a sense of impending danger.

I tried to fall asleep again but it was no use. I sat up and glanced around the room.

Lewis was asleep on the floor, using a balled-up blanket as a pillow, and May and Abbie were sleeping in the other bed. Since my wing didn't hurt much and my leg was only a little sore, I decided to go downstairs and check on Sam. I pushed off the covers and forced myself out of the bed. I limped my way over to and down the stairs.

As I reached the final step, I looked out the window at the bottom of the stairs. Dawn was not far off. Stars were fading in the sky even as I watched. In that milky light I could see Sam asleep on the long couch. His knife was in his hand and lying beside him was something made of wood.

The fire in the fireplace was almost out. I limped over to the pile of wood and threw the last of the logs onto the dying fire, and then I hobbled over to Sam's side to check on him. He was breathing deeply, occasionally releasing a light snore as he slept. The wooden thing looked like a long branch that forked into a *Y* at one end. The bark and splinters had been carved away, most likely by Sam's knife.

I sat on the floor and leaned against the couch, resting my head next to Sam's warm hand. Closing my eyes, I tried to relax, tried to shake this strange feeling that something bad was about to happen.

Whispered voices filled in my head:

"I'm tired of waiting, I'm going in now," one voice said in a deep growl.

"No, only at my command. Our time will be soon, I promise," another said with a faint metallic hum embedded in its voice.

I opened my eyes again as an image of an enormous tiger with glowing multicolored eyes flashed in my mind.

I slowly realized that Sam was stroking my hair. Turning my head, I saw he was looking at me, his silver eyes reflecting the color of winter clouds.

"You have such a worried face," he said. "Whatever it is, it'll be fine."

I didn't know how to react but I relaxed a little. I understand that Sam had strong feelings toward me. I just couldn't tell what they were yet.

———————◆◆———————

The crackling fire was growing dim again, sparks flying up as a log collapsed onto the glowing embers.

We were eating the last scraps of the soup while May searched outside for more wood. I'd used a brush I'd found to comb through my knotted hair. Abbie was attempting to do the same with her long tangled hair.

Apparently, the wooden thing Sam had made was a crutch for me to lean on while I was walking. Lewis didn't seem too impressed with the gift, but I reddened at the kind gesture.

I still had that sense of impending danger. No matter how much I tried to ignore it, I knew I couldn't stop it.

I was deep in thought, running my fingers over the smooth wood of my gift. I looked down as my fingers hit a rough edge. Sam had carved a heart shape into the wood with the letter *S* in the middle.

We all jumped when we heard heavy footsteps on the front porch.

"Come out, come out, little ones," a deep voice called. "I know you're in there and I'm coming in after you."

The door burst open, the metal hinges snapping off the door frame. A small winged warhound stood in the doorway, one paw clamped around May's neck as it held her in the air. She kicked and struggled to no avail.

The warhound smiled, revealing two rows of shining razor-like metal teeth. Its eyes glittered and glowed a harsh red.

I leaped to my feet, completely ignoring the soreness in my leg, my eyes wide in recognition. *Oh God, a RUCA. Not here, not now!*

Two other warhounds joined it. I could see that these were the originals. Something about the way they moved, the way their pointed ears pricked at the slightest sound.

The RUCA threw May at Lewis, slamming both of them into the back wall. Sam instinctively stepped between the rest of us and our attackers, but the RUCA easily slapped him aside. One warhound moved in on him as the other ran at Lewis and May. The metal warhound turned toward me and Abbie.

I whacked it across the face with my crutch, scraping away some of its false fur, revealing some of the shining metal underneath.

It quickly caught my arm, sending a jolt of electricity coursing through my body as the monster lifted me off my feet and flung me to the other side of the room.

While my mind was still scrambled from the shock, Sam scooped me up in his arms and ran out the door, into the snow. I gripped the crutch tightly in my hand. Looking back at the house I could see the other bird-kids running after us. The warhounds followed them out onto the porch but didn't stop any of us. We all took off into the sky and flew away from the cabin.

I gazed back down at the wooden building. None of our attackers were flying after us. Instead, they were running back into the woods.

What will we do now? I thought. *How long can we run from them? How long before they finally catch us?*

CHAPTER 35

My teeth were chattering and I was shivering terribly in the icy mountain wind. My coat, as well as all of the backpacks, had been left behind at the house. Sam's body heat was warming me slightly, but even he looked like he was going to freeze over. We were falling behind, the others occasionally glancing back to check on us.

"Jay?" Sam finally said without looking down at me. "Can you ask the others to land? I need a rest."

With my ever so useful telepathic ability, I asked them to land. Soon we were shivering in the snow while Lewis built a small fire.

The sun was sliding down toward the horizon, the temperature slowly dropping with it.

Sam took off his heavy coat and draped it over my shoulders, saying his jacket was warm enough for now. After we'd rested and gotten warm, he suggested we walk a little farther while we still had some daylight left. It was best, he figured, to get as far away as possible from the warhounds and whatever that other thing was.

I pushed myself up and I tucked the crutch under my arm, putting half of my weight on it and holding my injured foot up off the ground.

While the others were arguing between walking and flying, I started walking off into the trees. When they realized I'd left, they quickly caught up. I laughed a little. It made me feel good to take the lead again instead of having to be carried. I hated feeling completely useless.

◆

Already it was a long night. Shivering, hungry, we huddled around a small fire. It was almost impossible to sleep. We'd pushed away as much snow as we could, but we were still lying on a thin layer of white. The moon's and the fire's light reflected on the glistening snow. I was shivering as I lay next to Abbie and May. My small purple jacket wasn't enough to keep the cold out or the heat in.

Sam had kept insisting I take his coat as a blanket until I convinced him to wear it while he stood watch.

I closed my eyes in an attempt to fall asleep and then opened them again at the sound of crunching snow. Sam was crouched down in a defensive position, staring into the woods. I looked over to see what he'd seen.

At the edge of the trees, barely discernible in the faint glow of the fire, stood a large gray dog, its pointed ears pricked, its bright blue eyes fixed on us yet somehow exuding gentleness.

It slowly walked into the light as Sam and I watched it carefully. When it was still several yards away, it threw its head back and howled. The sound was low and beautiful.

My eyes grew heavy as I watched Sam drop to the ground, instantly asleep. I couldn't keep my eyes open either.

———◆———

I don't know what had happened or why, but it was the best night's sleep I'd ever had.

When I woke up, the fire was big and warm as if someone had been tending to it all night, there were paw prints all over our small camp, and I was covered in a thick woolen blanket.

A dead deer lay at the edge of the trees, obviously killed by a strong bite to the throat. The meat was still warm and fresh, but there was no sign of the large dog.

It was well past dawn and the temperature was still pretty cold. I looked at the freshly killed deer and my stomach growled loudly.

I was almost tempted to eat the whole thing raw, but I knew that the others had to eat. Plus, I wanted to stay under my warm blanket.

———◆———

When we were all awake, everyone had questions but no one had answers. Sam and I described what we'd seen last night while we ate the deer—after we used Sam's knife to cut it and cooked it, duh. Afterward, we all looked like bloodthirsty monsters, our hands and lips stained red with the animal's blood.

After a moment's laugh, we washed our hands and faces in the snow and warmed up by the fire. As we sat there, I got a sense that the warhounds were stalking closer to us. We took off as soon as possible with me wrapped in the blanket and Sam carrying me.

As we flew off I saw I'd been right about the warhounds. They ran into the camp, glaring up at us but not following us.

After a half an hour's flight, Sam reluctantly passed me over to Lewis. About another hour later, we landed at my request.

I was tired of feeling useless and other people doing things for me. After we touched down, I asked May to work on my wing more. She still couldn't seal the hole in the bone.

Irritated, I stood anyway and ran, ignoring the pain in my leg and spreading my wings out to full length. Against their pleading, I attempted a takeoff.

Somehow I managed to get a few feet off the ground before crashing to the snow. I almost started to cry, not because I was hurt—I wasn't—but because I felt absolutely weak, powerless, and useless. I hated it.

So I was carried again through the air. Around noon, I smelled a familiar sour scent in the air. We were nearing the end of the mountains and were quickly approaching a city.

CHAPTER 36

As we walked between the towering buildings of the city, we got some shocked glances, some sad looks, and some strange stares as we passed.

Well, let's see. You're going about your everyday life when you see five kids who look about as thin as the dead, and like they slept in a tree and fell out when they woke up. One is limping along with a branch as a crutch, wearing an old wool blanket as a coat, and another is only seven years old. How would you react?

Would you stop and buy them food, or give them money so they could find a place to stay? Nope, people just walked on by. Not even a "Do you kids need any help?"

Earlier we had landed outside of the city, deciding to walk through instead of flying over. I question how clearly we were thinking at that moment.

You wouldn't believe how many times we were shoved aside, pointed at, pushed around, and how many times I was knocked to the ground and had to stop the boys from beating up the person who did it, whether it was an accident or on purpose.

Some of you out there might be saying, 'it's just like high school.' Well, it's much bigger than high school.

We were halfway across the city when the sun sank below the horizon and the harsh streetlights drove us into an empty alley. So there we were, five lonely, hungry, homeless bird-kids with nothing to eat and nowhere warm to sleep. We relied on each other for warmth, but none of us slept well with all the noise of the city around us.

I think at one point in the night, Lewis got up and left for a while, but I wasn't very sure.

———◆———

I had only one dream that night. I could hardly remember it, but I'd dreamed about the tiger with the multicolored eyes fighting an unexpected opponent.

A large black raven attacked the big cat from above, scratching and pecking at its eyes while the tiger swatted at it, its lethal claws extended.

I woke up to May tending to my wing. She said it was more important to fix my wing than to fix my leg. The wound closed a little more, but there was still a good-sized hole.

We continued to walk through the city, trying to get to the other side while we avoided slipping on frozen puddles or tripping on trash that had been thrown to the ground. As we walked down a less crowded street, I caught a strange smell on the rancid wind.

I stopped. "Hey, do you smell that?" The others stopped and turned to me. "It smells kind of rotten, and I mean more than the rest of this place."

"Yeah, I smell it too," Sam answered.

"Well, I don't smell anything," Lewis scoffed. "Let's just keep going."

He turned and kept walking, his hands shoved into his pockets.

"Wait, I think it's coming from this way," Abbie said. She turned down another street and into an alley. We followed quickly with Lewis walking slowly behind.

She stopped just short of the entrance to the dead-end alley, staring in horror. Walking up behind her, I soon found out why.

Near the end of the dead end alley was a pile. After I took a step closer, I saw exactly what it was—four or five young women, dead.

They looked as if nothing had happened, as if they had just fallen asleep there. They had no visible injuries, there was no blood.

"Hey kids, what are you doing?" A man's deep voice took us by surprise.

I turned and saw that the man was a police officer wearing a black uniform. He looked over our heads at the dead women and then looked down at us, his expression serious.

"Okay, I need you to stay calm and come with me," he said gently. Something about him made me suspicious. "I have some friends who can help you. They need to ask you some questions and then they can help find your folks."

I quickly scanned his thoughts and realized what his intentions were. He was going to shove us into the back of his police car and take us to the police station, keeping us there until someone claimed us. And the someone who would claim us, once the police issued a report that we'd been found, was DAEL scientists.

Sam and Lewis stepped between the officer and the rest of us. "We're not going anywhere," Sam said defensively. "Not with you, not with anyone."

The man looked surprised by his defiance. "Son, I need you and your friends to come with me peacefully and cooperatively, or else we'll have trouble."

"We've already told you our answer," Lewis said, crossing his arms over his chest.

The officer spoke into his radio, keeping his eyes on us, and then said to us, "Come along now or I'll make you. I will be resolved to use force if you are unwilling to cooperate."

He had no sooner finished speaking when we could hear an approaching police siren.

"I don't think so," Sam said, and rushed at the officer, tackling him. "Come on!" he shouted to us. I could hear the wailing sirens of the police car and I knew he could to.

Lewis grabbed May and followed Sam while Abbie and I ran behind him. Fear dulled the soreness in my leg as I ran. As we fled down the street, I glanced back. The police car stopped in front of the alleyway and the officer jumped inside. Instantly the car was after us, its lights flashing and siren blaring.

Lewis took the lead and turned sharply to the right down another street. We were nearing the outskirts of the city, and I didn't know if that was a good thing or a bad thing. We ran across the street and down another street. Car horns blared as we ran in front of the moving cars.

Near the end of the street was a building that looked like it could fall down at any minute. Lewis ran inside it. I ran in after everybody else and slammed the door shut.

I sank to the floor, panting from the hard run. I heard the police car speed past the ramshackle building.

At that moment, I was both happy about and hating the fact that I was genetically enhanced. I was able to run faster than normal people, and I was much stronger. But if I weren't a bird-kid, I wouldn't be in this mess in the first place.

CHAPTER 37

*G*reat, *just great,* I thought. *Now we have the DAEL scientists, warhounds, RUCAs, and the police after us.* I sighed and leaned against a wall. I wasn't sure how it could get any worse, but I guess I shouldn't have asked myself that. Things could always get worse.

We ended up staying in that rotting building for the rest of the day and were planning on staying the night there. Yet another cold, hungry night in a noisy, polluted city. I missed the trees and the ability to see the stars overhead. At least it was warmer in that building than it was outside.

Lewis was asleep on the floor and May and Abbie were talking to each other in hushed voices.

"What's on your mind?" Sam asked. He'd been lying on his back, staring up at the ceiling, but now he sat up.

His question took me by surprise, and I sighed. "A lot of things."

"Hey, back at the cabin in the mountains, when that thing and the two warhounds attacked, you acted like you'd seen that thing before. What is it?"

I glanced around the room at the others. No one was listening. "A RUCA," I answered.

166

"A what?"

"A RUCA," I repeated. "It's like a metal warhound that will stop at nothing to kill its target. I've seen them in a dream." I thought back on the dream I'd received, what felt like, so long ago. "I'd never seen anything that could kill so mercilessly and without remorse. I'd never seen so much blood spilled at one time."

"And not only that, but now we have human authorities after us to."

"Yeah." I sighed again and then lay down on the dusty floor. "Good night, Sam."

"'Night, Jay."

I missed moments like this. Nights when you can go to sleep saying a simple good night to someone you care about, knowing that they're all right and that you'll see them again when you wake.

———◆———

The ground trembled beneath me as a mighty growl reverberated through the air. My eyes shot open and instantly watered in the rising dust around me.

The others quickly woke up too, and we all stood and stared out the nearest window. Arrayed before the building were numerous bright yellow metal monsters, all rumbling and growling with men climbing in and out of them. Nearest the building was a square with a long metal neck extending high into the air. Dangling from it by a long cable was an enormous ball that looked like it was made out of rock.

As we watched the ball started moving, swinging on its cable, aiming directly for the front wall of the building.

"Run!" I yelled.

We ran down the hallway toward the front door as the first contact was made. With a deafening roar, beams snapped, chunks of plaster fell off walls, and windows shattered. The whole place was about to cave in.

Sam and Lewis made it out the door first. Not a second after I burst from the building, the whole front of the house collapsed.

I screamed. Abbie and May hadn't made it out in time. The last of the building fell but none of the workers seemed to notice the three kids running from the collapsing building.

I fell to my knees, my sobs overwhelming me. Sam knelt beside me and held me close.

After a minute, I realized nothing was moving any longer. All of the machines had stopped. Looking around, I saw men lying on the ground or slumped behind the wheels of their big vehicles. Even Lewis was asleep. As I stared around me, trying to figure out what had happened, I was aware of the echo of a low sound fading away.

I shook Lewis awake and the three of us scrambled over to the pile of rubble. Digging through it, we called out Abbie's and May's names. A dark gray dog was sniffing around the pile too, but I hardly paid attention to it.

Together, we moved broken beams, splintered wood, and chunks of plaster and bricks, without finding them. I'd almost given up when I heard a loud bark.

The big dog was staring at us with its bright blue eyes. It barked again and then howled at us to come. As I stumbled over the debris toward it, it backed away.

Reaching the spot where it had stood, I pushed away the rubble and brick. As I removed a large piece of drywall,

I revealed Abbie's dust-covered face. I yelled to the boys to hurry over and help me.

The boys lifted a broken wall and I dragged her out. She was unconscious but alive, thank God.

The dog was barking again and digging at some plaster and brick a few feet away. It reached its head into the small hole and lifted out the small, twisted form of May. She coughed against the dust that hung in the air.

I ran over to get her, and again the dog backed away. I realized it was the same dog Sam and I had seen in the mountains, the same one who'd left us the deer and the blanket.

It turned and ran off. "Hey, wait!" I called after it, but it was already gone.

The workers were starting to wake up, so we had to go. I carried May in my arms, her small arms wrapped around my neck. Sam carried Abbie—who was still unconscious—and Lewis carried what we could salvage: a fistful of money we'd taken from some of the workers.

We found an old motel and rented the cheapest room they had. We could only stay the night with the fifty dollars we gave them, and we had to leave at the noon the next day.

The room had only one bed and a small couch. In the bathroom the shower leaked and the hot water faucet in the sink was broken. Abbie and May were asleep on the bed while the two boys sat on the couch staring each other down. The more time they spent together, the less they liked each other. I could practically see them throwing daggers at each other.

I ignored them and sat on the floor, trying to unravel the mysteries going through my mind. How did the warhounds keep finding us? What was with that dog and why was it following us?

I didn't get any further in my thinking, since my little problem flared up again. It was bound to happen again, and it was better when I was on the ground than when I was in the air. My vision shut itself down and I was blind again.

I heard a small shuffling sound and asked, "What's going on? What's happening?" This time, I hadn't freaked out. I guessed I was getting used to it.

"Nothing's wrong, Jay," Lewis said. "May just shifted in her sleep. Didn't you see her move?"

"No," I answered.

"I get it," Sam said. "Don't worry, Jay. It'll just pass like the last episodes."

"What? What will pass?" Lewis asked.

I sighed, "Sometimes I have episodes when my vision shuts off and I'm temporarily blind, but it passes and my sight comes back."

I heard more shuffling and shifting, followed by a small yawn. I figured May had woken up. After that, no one said or did anything for about twenty minutes. Eventually I heard some faint grunting sounds and more movement, but then silence again. A few minutes later, I could hear Abbie finally waking up.

May told her to lie still for a moment longer. For a while, all I could hear was the dripping of the shower faucet and the sounds of people breathing, and then Abbie spoke in a hoarse voice.

"Can someone tell me where we are?"

May quickly explained what had happened.

While she was talking, my vision started coming back. I could see that May's and Abbie's wounds were almost completely healed, and that Lewis had left the room. He was sitting on the small balcony, lost in thought.

Abbie and May had nervous expressions as they whispered with their heads close together. They separated and Abbie said softly, "I don't know about this. I feel kind of bad for doing this."

"Come on," May said, "we have to do this. It's better for all of us if we tell them."

Abbie agreed, and May asked us to join them on the bed. "Abbie and I have something to say." She shouldered her friend, telling her to go on. Abbie shook her head, saying that she didn't want to say it. May sighed and said, "Abbie and I are leaving the group."

I gasped. "Why?"

"We believe the warhounds are after only you and not us, and that it's too dangerous for us to stay. Everywhere we turn, there's something after us. You guys are treating this like a child's story and that if we keep running, we'll find our happily ever after. You may not know it, but you're slowly cutting us from the picture. You act like we're a group of three when we're really five." Tears filled May's eyes and her voice cracked when she continued. "We're leaving because we have no reason to stay. We're already almost out of the picture and it won't make much of a difference if we leave." She stopped for a moment and then said seriously, "We leave at dawn. We'll say our good-byes then."

I couldn't believe what I was hearing, but there was some truth in what she was saying. Abbie held her as an older sister would to comfort her younger sister. Both of them were crying, no doubt afraid of what tomorrow would bring. And honestly, I was too.

CHAPTER 38

We all walked out back behind the motel as the sun began to shine over the horizon. We all hugged good-bye, and Abbie, May and I cried a little. We gave Abbie and May the last bit of money we had left, about fifteen dollars. It wasn't much but maybe they could buy a small meal or a warm blanket to sleep under when they reached the next town.

I knew, as they turned to fly away, that I wouldn't be able to convince them to stay even if I tried. Hot tears flowed down my face as they spread their wings. Abbie's white and black wings glowed in the growing light, her waist-length hair flowing in the faint breeze. May's tawny wings turned copper in the sun's golden rays.

With one final good-bye, they ran and pushed off the ground, gaining height with each beat of their powerful wings. It looked like a scene from a movie as they flew off in the direction of the rising sun.

Leaning on Lewis' strong body, I limped back inside. I'd never felt so much physical and emotional pain, except for when Sara died. Once we'd reached the room, I flopped down onto the bed.

Something white flashed in the corner of my eye. It was one of Abbie's feathers sticking out from under a pillow. I pulled it out and rubbed it along my hand and between my fingers.

My heart and body ached. I closed my eyes as I heard that little voice. *Everyone has a place in this vast world, and apparently theirs isn't with you*

———◆——

Someone knocked on our door, reminding us that we had to leave. We gathered what little we had left and walked out of the room.

I limped alongside the boys, my heart pounding inexplicably, as usual. The plan was to walk the rest of the way out of the city and fly a little bit from there. We'd figure out the rest later.

We were walking down a sidewalk, and I was playing with the feather in my hand, when we heard a scream from behind us. We all turned and ran toward the sound. The scream came again, and I traced it to an empty lot surrounded by a tall wooden fence.

I found an opening in the fence and slipped through, the boys right behind me.

In the empty lot, cornered into the wooden fence, was a girl with long brown hair, a pair of torn jeans, an old white t-shirt, a black waist long jacket, and amazing blue eyes. Facing her were the two warhounds and the RUCA.

"Jay," she yelled. "Help me!"

I had no idea how she knew my name, but I rushed forward to help.

The attackers turned to glare at me. As they did, the girl morphed into a large gray dog and hurled herself at the nearest warhound, biting down hard on its throat. Sam and Lewis launched themselves at the RUCA.

Blood gushed up around the dog's mouth as the warhounds fell to the ground. She raised her head, releasing her grip. Blood covered her muzzle, and she looked all the more terrifying. I was happy I was on her side.

The warhound managed to push her off with its last effort, slamming her into the wooden fence and forcing her back into her human state. She pulled out a large stone knife from her belt.

I ran at the other warhound and jumped onto its back, making it stumble backward as I pulled at its enormous wings. It reached back over its shoulder, trying to pull me off.

I caught a glimpse of the girl as she ran at it and sank her knife into its heart.

It gave a last mighty roar as it fell to the ground dead, with me still on its back. *Two down, one to go.*

Sam was on the ground, his body spasming uncontrollably. I guessed the RUCA had just shocked him. Lewis was grappling with the monster, but the RUCA was too powerful. The girl turned into a dog again and ran at the mechanical monster. She leaped onto it, biting and tearing at its metal throat, tearing away some of the false flesh.

It easily threw her and Lewis away, roared, and took off into the sky. From the other side of the fence we heard shouts and screams as some normal people saw the beast fly away on metal and feathered wings.

I pulled myself out from under the dead warhound's body and stared at the panting dog. Sure enough, it was the same dog I'd seen twice before.

CHAPTER 39

May's point of view

May soared effortlessly through the sky, breathing in the freezing winter air. The wind made her eyes water. It hadn't been more than two hours since they'd left the others. Her heart ached at the thought of them.

Abbie flew beside her, lost in her own thoughts. May leaned in closer and bumped her with the tips of her left wing.

"Ow!" Abbie exclaimed. "What was that for?"

"Nothing. I was just checking to see if you're all right. Is something wrong?" May asked, brushing some of her long brown hair from her eyes.

"No. I mean … I'm just wondering if we did the right thing by leaving them," she said, dropping her gaze to the trees below.

"I think we did," May answered. "We had to. Remember, they're after *them*, not us. We just need to find a safe place to stay till this blows over."

Abbie didn't respond.

The silence stretched out for a long time before Abbie said, "Do you mind if we land? I need a short rest."

"No, it's fine. Let's meet in that gap in the trees over there." She tilted her wings forward and rocketed to the targeted area.

At the last second, she pulled up and put her feet out in front of her, making sure her knees were bent. She hit the ground running and slowed to a stop.

Abbie landed in a nearby tree and leapt down, landing skillfully on her feet. She glanced around nervously as if expecting something to happen.

"Are you sure you're all right?" May asked. "You're acting kind of jumpy."

Abbie nodded. "Yes, I'm fine. I wish we had some water, though. I'm getting really thirsty."

"I wish we had some food. I'm starving."

They sat under a tree near a small clearing, but quickly jumped at the sounds of movement. Two deer bounded through the trees and were quickly out of sight.

Abbie laughed. "I guess we're both a little jumpy right now."

They laughed and agreed a short nap was in order.

May jumped up a while later, waking Abbie as well. She sensed danger.

A warhound stumbled into the open with a gun in its hairy paw, grumbling something about the team sending the little guy to find lunch. It took him a moment, but he soon spotted the two bird-kids.

"I knew I smelled something good over this way and look at what I found," it said. He quickly raised the gun and aimed at May.

Abbie shoved May aside as he pulled the trigger. When the little girl looked up, Abbie's eyes were wide and blood soaked her white shirt from the bullet hole in her chest. She remained standing for a moment and then, as if in slow motion, fell to the ground.

The warhound looked stunned, as if it couldn't believe it had actually pulled the trigger. It stared at both of them, perhaps thinking he'd somehow managed to shoot them both, since Abbie's blood had splattered onto May. He ran back into the trees, probably to get the rest of the team, May figured. As soon as he was out of sight, she crawled over to Abbie.

She shook her friend, fearing the worst. She turned her over, reaching to heal the wound that had pierced her heart. Abbie reached up and weakly grabbed May's hand.

"May, you need to run. Run fast, run far. Fly away if you can. Just leave me and get away from here."

Tears welled in May's eyes. "No! I'm not leaving you here to die. Just let me fix this—"

"No, it's too late. I know what's happening, I know what will happen. I've seen it so many times before. I've just got to stop it from happening to you too. Now run!" she ordered.

Instead of doing as she was told, May heaved her dying friend onto her shoulders and moved as fast as she could through the trees. She finally found a large oak tree to hide behind.

"May, I can't let you do this, I can't let you stay. You'll get yourself killed." She pushed May away from her as she lay against the tree's trunk. "Go, they're coming. I'll do my best to keep them busy. You know what's going to happen as well as I do. Now just go. Do it for me."

May hesitantly stood, her body racked with sobs.

Abbie smiled weakly. "No, please. Don't cry for me. I know what will happen. I'll be fine."

May knew that wasn't the truth. Still, she turned and flew up through the branches of the tree as her friend struggled to her feet, leaning against the tree for support. She hobbled back out into the open as the warhounds thundered through the trees. May looked back as she rose high above the ground.

Abbie didn't even attempt to run. The small warhound raised the shotgun and pulled the trigger, hitting its target in the head, killing her instantly. The shot rang out and echoed in May's ears as she flew away.

Soon she was out of range of the warhounds and their gun, tears streaming down her face.

Where do I go now? I have nowhere left to turn, nowhere to go. I'm all alone now.

She shook her head. *No, I still have one place left. I don't like it much, but how many other options do I have left?* She adjusted her course and headed back in the direction from which she had come.

CHAPTER 40

"Y-you're the dog," I said shakily as the girl changed back into her human form. "The one we saw in the mountains and—and at the wrecked building. The one who helped us."

"Dog?" She looked confused and then she laughed. "You seriously think that I'm just some huge dog? No, no, I'm a wolf. Most people who see me usually get it right off the bat and scream, 'Run, wolf.'"

"Well, we're not like most people," Sam said.

"I'll say." She laughed again. "You guys can fly." She must have seen our shock that she knew what we were, because she glanced around and said, "Look, let me show you."

She shrugged off her jacket, revealing enormous black wings, the feathers tipped silver and flecked with a gold color. She hurriedly pulled her coat back on. "See, I'm just like you."

Police sirens sounded in the distance. I motioned for us to leave and fast. We didn't need another game of chase with the authorities today.

As we ran out of the opening in the fence, Lewis stopped and glared at the bodies of the dead warhounds. There was a small spark and they were soon in flames.

We ran away from the fire and the rising smoke. The girl took the lead, saying, "Quick, follow me." We ran together through blocks of houses, down narrow alleyways, and between buildings. Soon, we were running alongside a road that led out of the city.

We slowed down and walked across an empty field to the beginning of a tree line. We found another road that ran through the trees and walked along it as we talked.

"That was awesome of you guys back there," the wolf-bird-girl said. "That was an epic fight. And that was really brave, Jay."

"What?" I said, glancing over at her.

"The way you rode that warhound like a wild bull. It takes real courage to do something crazy like that."

"How do you know us anyway?" Lewis asked. "Who are you?" He glared at her suspiciously as if waiting for her to pull out her knife and slit his throat.

"My name is Katie. While I was living in the mountains, I saw you flying overhead. I followed you and watched from a distance because I hadn't seen any others like me in a long while. I even know your names." She pointed to each of us in turn. "Jay, Lewis, Sam, and ... Wait, where are the other two?"

"Others?" I said blankly. It still hurt to think of Abbie and May leaving us.

"Yeah, there were two other girls with you, Abbie and May."

"They left," Sam answered shortly. "They went off on their own."

"Aw, that's too bad."

We walked in silence, until Katie noticed I'd fallen behind due to my limping. She asked if my leg was bothering me.

"No, it's fine, I can walk on my own."

She walked up to me and laid her hands on my shoulders, making me stop. "Jay, I can tell that's a lie," she said seriously. She motioned for me to sit on a fallen log. "Roll up your pant leg please."

I reluctantly sat down and did as instructed. She knelt at my feet and rubbed her hand up and down my leg, her touch warm and soft. The pain melted away.

I shifted as her touch began to tickle. I couldn't keep a wide smile from spreading across my face, and then I couldn't help but laugh. It was like her touch spread a strange giddiness throughout my body.

The boys just sat there, looking at me with confused expressions as I laughed even harder. They glanced at each other and then back at me.

I could hardly breathe, I was laughing so hard. Even when Katie stopped and stood, I continued to laugh till tears came to my eyes.

Sam stepped in front of her. "What just happened? What did you do to her?" He continued to stare at me as I fell backward off the log, landing on my back, still laughing.

"Nothing really, it's just another gift I have," Katie explained. "I can temporarily block the feeling of pain and speed up the healing process. As you can see, if I do it enough it makes a person feel super happy and they start laughing."

She rubbed Sam's back and he started to relax, his eyelids drooping a little. A small smile crept across his face. A moment later he was rolling on the ground, laughing with me. Lewis just leaned against a tree, his arms crossed at his chest.

After catching Lewis by surprise, we were all laughing. Once I caught my breath, I crawled up behind Katie and tickled her.

Between laughs she said, "No, stop! I'm ticklish! Stop!"

It took a long time before we stopped laughing and caught our breaths. I could tell, even though we hadn't agreed to it yet, that Katie would be staying with us and things were going to be interesting.

CHAPTER 41

May's point of view

May landed on the top of a small house. She was on the outskirts of the city she'd just been in. She sat at the base of the house's chimney, her folded wings pressed against the cold brick, her legs pulled up to her chest and her chin resting on her knees. She had the feeling her friends were still within the city limits.

Words could hardly describe how she felt—anguish, grief, anger—but it was more like a strange jumbled mixture.

Her eyes stung from crying. She squinted as the warm sun shone on her face. She felt like crying again as another wave of grief washed over her, but she bit back her tears and stood. She folded her wings into her coat and easily jumped down from the second-story roof.

As soon as her feet hit the ground, she glanced around to check that no one had seen her. She headed toward the motel they'd stayed at, hoping her friends were still there.

On the way she'd passed the demolished building. The brightly colored trucks were clearing away the remnants of the building.

Once she reached the motel, she easily slipped past the front desk and up the stairs. She stopped in front of the room they'd stayed in, scripting out in her head how she would talk to them. She knocked.

A young man answered. His dark brown hair was a shaggy mess and dark shadows circled his green eyes.

May jumped back in surprise. "Oh, I'm so sorry. I must have the wrong room," she said as sweetly and innocently as possible.

He smiled and closed the door. May ran down the hall to the stairs. They weren't there. She was sure she had the right room and they weren't there.

She raced down the stairs and out the front door. If they weren't there, where were they?

———◆———

May had been searching the area for over two hours. She sat down, exhausted, on a wooden bench in a small park. Slumping forward, she rested her head in her hands as she watched the people walk by. A few kids played in the nearby playground as their parents watched them like hawks.

A part of her wanted to go over and play in the sunshine like a normal child, but she wasn't normal. She wasn't even completely human. She knew she had to find her friends, and soon.

At the thought of her friends, tears pricked her eyes. What if she never found them? What if she found them and they sent her away because they were mad that she'd run away?

Soon, she was crying from worry and loss again. For a moment she heard nothing but her own sobs, and then she heard the sound of footsteps coming closer. She looked up to see a kind-looking woman staring at her.

"Are you all right, sweetie?" the woman asked. "Are you lost?" May sniffled and nodded. "Can't you find your family?" May shook her head.

The woman knelt down so that she was eye level with her. "What's your name, sweetheart?"

"M-May," she answered.

"Well, May, how about I help you find your family?" she asked, taking May's hand. May nodded, wiping her tears away with her sleeve.

The woman had dark blonde hair that fell over her shoulders and vibrant blue eyes. May thought she was very beautiful.

"You look tired," the woman said. "What if I call my son over and you come back to the house with us for a snack and a rest, then we'll find your family? How does that sound?"

May smiled at the kind gesture. "Thank you."

CHAPTER 42

"**S**o where are you from?" Sam asked Katie, throwing another couple of sticks onto the fire.

Katie shrugged. "I don't know. The first thing I remember is being in this scary hellhole of a science lab called the DAEL."

"Really?" I leaned forward in interest. "Us too. Well, we don't really know about Lewis." I glanced over at Lewis who was lying on his back, his multicolored eyes focused on the stars.

We'd moved northeast by foot, farther into the trees. When the sun began to set, we settled into a small area where the trees thinned but the branches weaved heavily overhead. Katie had skillfully hunted and killed a few rabbits, and we'd wolfed them down as if we'd never eaten before. Now we were deep in conversation.

"You were in DAEL?" Katie said. "How'd you get away? How long have you been out?"

"*How* isn't important," I answered, "but we've been out for a couple of weeks or so."

"I've been out for at least two months."

My eyes widened in surprise, my mouth gaping for a moment. "Two months? We'd heard of some others like us who'd escaped before us. Was that you?"

"Maybe, I made it out with a few others, but now I'm the only one left." She pulled her legs up to her chest, resting her chin on her knees.

"What happened?" Sam asked gently.

"They followed us, the warhounds. They hunted each of us down one by one. There were four of us. There was Zero, my closest friend, Blue, Fawn, and myself.

"Blue, he loved to work with his hands, and with a small collection of paper clips, he managed to pick the locks on our cages. Zero, being the strongest of us, pulled the grate off the air vent in the room. Fawn, who had a strange effect on electronics, short-circuited the cameras in the room.

"I used my nose and led us outside, where we easily flew over the fence and were out. However, we did get caught on camera and we soon had warhounds at our heels.

"We flew west, but that only led us to populated areas and a really big body of water that we couldn't see the end of. Only a day or two after we hid ourselves in a cave along the beach, warhounds showed up. Blue, Zero, and I escaped, but Fawn was killed." She stopped and stared into the fire as if it held the answers as to why any of this had happened.

Lewis sat up and joined in on the conversation. "How exactly can you change into a wolf like you do? It doesn't seem possible."

I glanced at him in surprise. Had he forgotten that Sam could change into a large raven?

Katie looked up. "I don't really know but I think that it's a result of untangling human DNA and reassembling it in a different way. I've found that when a certain time comes, we can unlock our true powers."

"How do you know this?" Lewis asked. "Have you done it?" His body tensed as he waited for her answer. He was clearly excited by the idea of unlocking his own true powers.

"No," she answered, "but I've witnessed it. It happened to Zero. He could make balls of blue fire with his hands, and when he threw them, they became deadly weapons."

"How is it done?" Lewis asked eagerly. "How do you unlock such a power?"

She shook her head. "I don't know. Most hybrids died before it happened. I guess Zero was just one of those few who did it. He loved his new power. But it drove him to the point of madness, and when that happened, he made one fatal mistake and was killed.

"After that, it was only me and Blue. I loved him deeply. I loved his dark eyes, his gray feathers, and his black hair. We would laugh together when he made a joke to lighten my spirits. We would share meals and would keep each other warm as they nights got colder."

She paused, tears welling in her eyes. "The same night that he told me that he loved me back, the warhounds attacked again. Blue stood over me as I lay beaten on the ground. He acted as my shield. He yelled for me to run and to get away. He said, 'No matter what, keep running till you're safe and hidden. And always remember that I love you.'"

I hugged her as she cried.

"I—I ran. I ran away. I let him die. I let him get killed ..."

Tears welled in my own eyes at this sad story. The worst part was that it felt both nightmarish and real at the same time.

CHAPTER 43

May's point of view

May was already on her third hot dog and the woman was peppering her with questions. She and her son had tried to convince her to take off her coat but she refused, afraid of what might happen if they saw her wings.

"So, May, where do you live?" the woman asked.

"With my friends," May answered between mouthfuls of food.

"I asked *where* you live," the woman repeated, the slightest irritation tingeing her voice.

"I said with my friends. We don't stay in one place for very long."

"What about your family, your parents?"

"My friends are my family, almost like brothers and sisters. We don't have parents." She spoke without the slightest bit of sadness.

"So you're all orphans?"

"I don't know what you mean."

The woman sighed and pinched the bridge of her nose. She changed the subject.

"Do you know how we can contact your family? I mean, your friends?"

"It's okay, I can find them myself."

"They'll be getting worried, won't they? Maybe we can call them and have them pick you up."

May pondered that and then said, "I don't think they could hear you from this far away."

The woman laughed. "No, no, I meant over the phone."

"Oh," May said. She shook her head. "No, they don't have a phone."

The woman seemed surprised. "How else will they find you?" she asked.

May stood, swallowing the last of the food even though she wanted to eat more. "Thank you for the food, ma'am, but I need to leave and find my friends."

May turned to go, but the woman called after her. "Wait! You can't go. It's too dark out. Why don't you stay here and maybe we can search in the morning?"

May considered it a moment but didn't wish to risk it. "No, I really should go now."

The woman continued to insist, though, and May finally agreed. The woman showed her to a guest room in the back of the small apartment. She said it used to be Brandon's—her eldest son's—before he moved out.

The woman offered to give her a large T-shirt for a night shirt, but she refused it. She settled into the large bed in her clothes and coat and easily fell asleep on the soft mattress. It was much more comfortable than a leaf-strewn forest floor.

That night she dreamed that everyone was together and happy. Even Abbie and Sara were there and smiling, laughing with everyone. They were all so happy and having fun. She missed them.

In one corner, however, where Lewis stood, was an enormous black shadow that threatened to swallow him whole.

———◆———

May woke about an hour past dawn and knew that most of the people in the building would soon be waking for the day.

She reluctantly crawled out of the bed and over to the window. As she opened it, the bedroom door swung open. The woman stood in the doorway, her blonde hair messy from sleep.

The woman's blue eyes were as wide as an owl's as she stared at May's wings fitting through the slits in the back of her coat.

Before she could scream or cry or pray, May dove out the open window. She spread her tawny wings and turned sharply to avoid crashing into another building.

The woman stood awestruck in the room, staring out the window as the bird-girl flew away. The single feather on the floor and the messed-up bed were the only signs that the girl had been there.

CHAPTER 44

I ran as fast as I could, my heart pounding in my chest, my breathing ragged and uneven. The ground passed under me in a blur. The tiger was gaining and the angry raven flew right behind it, trying to nip at its waving tail.

A cliff jutted out just ahead of me. *Great, I can fly away. Tigers can't fly.* I poured on the speed and leaped off the edge. I tried to spread my wings but there was one little problem: they weren't there.

As I plummeted down, the wind tossed my hair back and made my eyes water. Instead of rocky ground below me, blackness rushed up to meet me.

Suddenly, I stopped falling and started floating. The black plane stretched out in front of me as I stood on its sleek surface. Abbie stood in front of me, haloed in a white glow. She was dressed in white and her hair was combed out, and her black and white wings were folded against her back.

She stepped forward and wrapped me in a warm hug. "It's so good to see you again, Jay."

I couldn't react. Did this mean she was …?

She stepped back. "You don't have to believe it yet, but you'll get it soon enough."

She continued to back away, and then turned and ran. I broke out of my stunned silence and took off after her, yelling, "Wait, Abbie, wait!"

It wasn't long before she was completely out of sight and I stopped running.

"Hello, Jay."

The voice came from behind me and made me jump. I spun and came face to face with my older sister.

I yelped and fell back, landing on the black surface. "Melody, don't do that. You scared me!"

"Sorry," she said, holding her hand out for me to take. "I just really needed to talk to you, and I couldn't wait till you came to visit us."

As she helped me up, I asked, "What's so important that you had to scare me in my sleep?"

She rolled her eyes. "A warning. You are under the tiger's spell and only the raven can stop it. Beware of the tiger's hypnotic eyes."

"What is that supposed to mean? When will you stop talking to me in riddles?"

"One: you'll figure it out yourself, two: when you finally get it. But I have something else to tell you." She crossed her arms over her chest. I copied her position, waiting to hear it.

"I have a mission for you. You're getting close and you're already beginning to remember." She paused for effect. "I need you to find our birth mother."

I cocked an eyebrow. "What?"

"I need you to find our mom. Don't you remember the song at all?" As soon as she said that, the image of the woman's blurred face flashed in my mind again.

When I blinked it away, Melody had her back to me. She rocked herself back and forth, singing the song quietly.

> For one so small, you seem so strong.
> My arms will hold you, keep you safe, and warm.
> This bond between us can't be broken
> I will be here, don't you cry.

I walked up to her and sang along with the words that seemed to come so naturally.

> This bond between us can't be broken
> I'll always be here, don't you cry.

We stopped singing and she looked at me seriously. "Don't worry, Jay. You'll know her when you see her."

She gave me a quick hug, turned, and walked away. I made no move to follow her as the blackness swallowed her ...

———◆———

I blinked against the bright sunlight that shone through the trees. Something had woken me. A moment later I realized that *something* was a cold and wet nose pressed against my ear and the sound of a dog panting.

I sat up quickly, realizing what it was, and rubbed the wetness off my ear. "Katie, don't do that. That's not how you wake people up."

I turned to glare at her but she was on her back laughing, still morphing from wolf to human, her wolf tail thumping heavily on the ground.

"Why'd you do that?" I asked.

She sat up, wiping a happy tear from her face and trying to stop laughing. "Because it's time to get up."

I looked up. It was only an hour or two after dawn.

"So what song were you singing?" she asked.

"What?"

"In your sleep you were singing. Very quietly but I could hear it. What song is it?"

"It's nothing." I pretended to yawn. "Hey, when are we eating and when are we leaving?"

She seemed annoyed that I'd changed the subject but answered, "We'll be eating soon and I think we'll be leaving afterward."

She morphed back into a wolf and loped off into the trees, not seeming to mind that she stepped on Lewis as she left.

CHAPTER 45

About an hour later we were stuffed with roasted bird and rabbit. Lewis was tying his long mahogany hair into its usual ponytail and Katie was lying on her back, basking in the sunlight.

I opened and closed my injured wing, testing its soreness. It actually didn't hurt much. I slowly made flapping motions. It felt as good as new, but it still had a bullet-sized hole blown through it.

Sam, who'd been watching me, stood and followed me as I walked off into the trees. It took about five or ten minutes, but we eventually found a break in the trees and an open field. Perfect.

I stopped and opened my wings full length. Sam followed close behind. I sensed he was going to tell me to stop, but I was already running.

The tall grasses rushed past me in a green-yellow blur as my feet pounded across the field. *One push, one beat, that's all it takes. It's now or never.*

I beat down with my wings as hard as I could. My feet left the ground for a second, more or less, before touching down again.

I pushed again and, while my feet were off the ground, pushed again, gaining a foot more off the ground.

I kept beating, pushing harder with my injured wing to keep balanced, gaining height with each push.

I could feel the blood coursing through my wings, the muscles flexing, the tingle of my feathers as the wind whistled through them.

Soon enough, I was high above the trees. I tried banking right to go back, but that's where things went wrong.

As I turned, my balance went completely uneven and I began to spiral downward. I tried to regain my balance to stay aloft, but it was like trying to grip water.

In an incredibly fast blur of black, Sam flew beneath me and caught me by the hand. He pulled me closer and held me against him as he headed back down to the field.

He did his best to land us gently, but that didn't go as planned either. We hit the ground hard and went tumbling heads over tails.

He somehow landed on top of me and it took some effort for me to push him off. After we dusted ourselves off, he scolded, "I told you not to do it." I rolled my eyes at him and stuck my tongue out at him playfully.

As we walked back toward the camp, Sam asked, "So how'd it feel to fly again? You know, before nearly crashing." He shouldered me off balance.

I shoved him back playfully. "Great, until I tried to turn." Suddenly, I stopped, thinking I'd heard something, but I dismissed it and kept walking.

Then it came again, a little louder and clearer. Sam looked back at me when I stopped again. "Everything okay?"

"Uh, yeah, I'm fine," I answered, and continued walking. The sound came again, this time loud enough to make both of us to stop.

It sounded like someone yelling, "Jaaaaaaay!" Then again, "Jaaaaaaay!" I turned, trying to find who was calling me.

Before I saw anything, a large flying mass slammed into me, knocking me to the ground and sending me skidding back a good eight feet across the grass. It clung to me with an amazing grip.

I was about to try to beat it off me when I realized it wasn't an *it*. It was May. Her small arms wrapped tightly around my neck, she was crying into my shoulder, her hot tears soaking my jacket. She kept saying my name over and over as if I'd been lost for the longest time and she was so relieved to find me.

"I'm sorry. I'm sorry. I'm so sorry," she kept saying.

I sat up straight and hugged her, patting her hair.

Sam sat beside us. "May, what are you doing back here? Why did you come back? Is something wrong?"

She gazed at us, her green eyes dim. I looked around, expecting to see Abbie walking toward us, proving my fearful thoughts wrong. She wasn't there.

"Where is Abbie?" I asked.

May squeezed her eyes shut. Burying her face in my jacket, she cried even harder.

Tears gathered in my own eyes when I realized it was true. My dream had been right. Abbie was gone.

———◆———

I carried May back in my arms, feeling more exhausted than I'd ever been. Lewis and Katie were surprised to see us in tears and Sam walking behind us in a stunned silence.

We got May calm enough to tell us what had happened. I was relieved she had suffered for only a short time. Or maybe longer, because she'd know her death was coming. She might have lost her life, but she'd saved another. For a short while we sat in mournful silence.

"Wait, why were you out there in the first place?" Lewis asked, eyeing Sam and me suspiciously.

I felt myself redden under his gaze. "I was testing my wing," I replied. "Flying."

"And?"

"It was the same result as the last time, only a little better."

May touched my wounded wing. "Only a little better, but it's still healing," she said. After a moment, I felt the normal tingly sensation of her healing power.

Katie crawled over. "May I help?"

May turned to stare at her as if she'd just realized she was there.

"May, this is Katie," I said. "She's kind of like a healer too."

May reluctantly moved aside and allowed Katie to help, although she kept an eye on her.

The feeling in my wing intensified, turning from a tingly sensation to an overwhelming numbness. I felt strangely light-headed, like I could pass out at any moment.

I must have at one point, because when I opened my eyes Lewis was steadying me from behind. I thought I felt my heart skip a beat at his touch. Sam stood by, leaning against a tree, glaring at him.

When I looked over at my wing, I was astounded. The hole had nearly completely sealed itself. May and Katie looked winded and exhausted. To speak in scientific terms, Katie must have used herself as a catalyst to speed up the healing process that May created. See, I've learned a thing or two.

I gazed up at the sky. It was about an hour past high noon. Obviously, we wouldn't travel far this day. Especially since I still couldn't feel my right wing and I just felt like sleeping. I pulled away from Lewis and lay down on my side.

Things can only get easier from here, right? I thought. *As soon as my wing is fully healed, we'll be back in the skies, moving faster than ever. We'll be farther away from the warhounds, the RUCAs, and the DAEL.*

I was such a fool for thinking like that, because we all know it never works that way.

CHAPTER 46

As predicted, after I awoke, my wing was as good as new, or at least good enough. During the flight, I flew as smoothly as ever, but someone was always behind me to catch me in case I fell.

The trees thinned out below, eventually giving way to open prairie and grassland. The occasional tiny grove of trees dotted the plain. The trees had long ago lost their leaves and the grass was beginning to yellow and turn brown.

By dusk—which was coming sooner and sooner every day—we were all tired, so we landed for the night. We were going to sleep under the stars, in the open.

It was kind of scary being in the open. If the RUCAs flew overhead, we'd be spotted immediately.

I lay between Lewis and Katie, which alleviated some of my fears. Katie laid her coat over me like a blanket before changing to a wolf. She was curled up on my right. My heart pounded hard as Lewis lay behind me, his back pressed to mine.

I thought to Katie, *Do you mind if I ask you a strange question?*

She rolled over to face me, her furry ears pricked to listen.

What does it mean when your heart beats really hard around a certain person? I thought nervously. *Every time I'm near Lewis, my heart automatically goes into hyperdrive.*

It means that you like him, she replied. She sat up so that we were eye level with each other.

Well, yeah, we're friends. Aren't friends supposed to like each other?

She shook her furry head. *I mean more than that, I mean that you* like *him, the way me and Blue liked each other.* She lay back down and rolled away from me.

When Katie had talked about Blue, she hadn't said they just liked each other. She had said they loved each other. Did this mean that I *loved* Lewis? I curled into a ball, still thinking about it as I let my consciousness slip.

———◆———

I was running in a grassy green field with Lewis running playfully behind me. The sun shone brightly, warm on my bare skin. I laughed as he tried to catch me. When I looked back at him, though, the whole scene slowed down.

For a moment, it switched to the strange-eyed tiger chasing me, but then it was with Lewis again.

The two different scenes continued to flicker back and forth until they seemed to blur together. The little voice spoke: *Remember your sister's words. You are under the tiger's spell and only the raven can stop it. Beware the tiger's hypnotic eyes.*

Then it all clicked. Well, sort of.

Lewis was the tiger and I was under his spell. What the heck did that mean? If Lewis was the tiger, then who was the raven?

Moments later the tiger lay on top of me, having pinned me to the ground. Its eyes were full of fury and hatred, and a growl rumbled deep in its throat. An icy feeling clawed at my heart. Only one question, however, struck my mind: *Why do I have such vivid dreams and why do they keep happening?*

I woke slowly to find the sun just breaking over the horizon. Katie and May were still sound asleep, but the boys were awake and alert.

Sam was poking at the kindling atop last night's embers while Lewis stood scanning the horizon. When they noticed that I'd woken Sam smiled and greeted me. Lewis simply looked at me from the corner of his eye, gave the slightest nod, and turned his gaze back to the distance.

Even with that millisecond of eye contact, my heart was already thudding heavily in my chest.

Katie stirred next to me. She slowly got up onto her four paws and leaned back in a stretch, yawning widely.

"Hey, Katie," I said as she slowly morphed back to her human form. "Are you going to hunt this morning?"

She rubbed the sleep from her eyes. "I could try but, it would be kind of pointless. All of the birds are heading south, the rabbits and prairie dogs have already gone into their burrows, and there are no deer that I can smell."

I looked back at Lewis, who seemed to be listening intently to something. I listened carefully for what he could be hearing but heard nothing.

He sighed to himself, turned, and walked over to me. Leaning down, he whispered in my ear, "May I talk with you a moment? Somewhere where the others can't hear."

"Uh, sure," I replied, pushing myself up to follow him. I swore that if he got any closer, my heart would explode.

Lewis draped his arm across my shoulders and led me away from the others. I looked back at Sam. He was staring after us, his eyes full of anger.

We walked in silence across the windswept plain. On the crest of a hill that rose ahead of us was a grove of trees.

Once we were in the shelter of the trees, Lewis let go and spun to face me. He opened his mouth to speak but I interrupted him. "Before you say anything, close your eyes."

What the heck am I doing? I wondered. I felt as if I wasn't in control of my actions.

He looked at me questioningly but then closed his eyes. I stood on tiptoes and laid my hands on his shoulders.

What am I doing? No, stop.

I closed my own eyes and quickly pressed my lips to his. Warm, soft. He tensed but then quickly relaxed.

When I pulled away, his face showed no emotion at all. As if he had no emotions to begin with. His red and blue eyes just stared at me blankly.

"This has worked more brilliantly than I'd imagined," he said. The slightest smile crept across his face. "I brought you out here to talk, but I see there is even more to explain."

He reached into his denim jacket and pulled out something that completely shocked me, nearly making my heart stop as I saw it. In his hand was a pistol. He raised it, aiming directly for my head.

CHAPTER 47

My first reaction: petrified with fear. My first instinctive decision: get the hell out of there! I turned and ran for my life.

I got only a few feet before I fell to the ground, unable to move my left foot. I looked back. It was frozen to the ground, covered in a thick layer of ice. An instant later, my other foot was also iced to the ground.

I tried screaming for help. "Sam! Kat—" The words literally froze on my lips as Lewis cupped his hand over my mouth, wrapping a sheet of ice around my mouth.

I tried to flail my arms around to make as much noise as possible in the fallen leaves. Lewis, however, grabbed my arms and froze them together behind my back, using the ice like handcuffs.

He planted a knee in my back, nearly crushing my wings. "You didn't think you were the only one who plays mind games, did you?" he said, holding the gun to my head. "I *made* you like me to keep you from being suspicious. And no, I'm not a victim of the DAEL, I work for them. I'm their most valuable and powerful weapon."

He cocked the gun. "Enjoy your *real* death, Jay."

I heard a loud yell and then Lewis was no longer holding me down. Looking up, I saw Sam had tackled Lewis, knocking him off me. The gun fired, not hitting its intended target but an innocent tree, sending a shower of splinters into the air.

The boys wrestled on the ground, rolling back and forth in the fallen leaves, each straining for advantage. When they smashed into a tree, they split apart. Sam had a bloodied nose, a split lip, and the gun in his hand.

He cocked the gun and took aim. "You're a traitor, Lewis," he yelled. "A traitor!"

Lewis pushed back his denim jacket to reveal two more guns on his belt. He pulled one out and aimed it at me, still trapped by his ice. "How can I be a traitor if I was never on your side to begin with?"

Sam looked as if he was about to pull the trigger, but Lewis just shook his head. "You pull that trigger and the girl gets a bullet through her skull."

A low growl came from behind Lewis, and a large gray wolf leaped out of the bushes with a stone dagger held in its jaws. Katie jumped up at Lewis and buried the blade into the side of his neck.

Blood spurted from the wound and he staggered back. Sam found his chance. He fired the gun three times, each time hitting his target square in the chest.

Lewis leaned against a tree for a moment, looking from his bleeding wounds to Sam and the gray wolf that stood beside him. Then he straightened and reached for the knife in his throat. Gripping the hilt, he pulled it out. Blood sprayed out onto the leaves.

I thought he would fall dead, but the exact opposite happened. The gaping wound in his neck sealed, quickly and completely. The same thing happened with the bullet holes. The only signs that he'd been shot were the holes in his shirt and the blood that stained it.

He laughed. "You can't kill me that easily."

Katie growled and launched herself at him, ready to tear him apart. He simply stepped out of the way and, as she ran past, drove her own blade into her side. Sam lifted the gun again to shoot, but nearly dropped it when a fire started behind him and quickly spread around him and me in a wide circle, enveloping us in a wall of heat. The wall parted enough to allow Lewis in before closing again behind him. Sam held the gun confidently as he aimed for our new enemy's head.

Lewis threw his head back in a laugh that sent chills up my spine. "Go ahead and shoot, raven-boy. You can't hurt me. But if you do fire, you'll be killing your precious Blue Jay. She's not exactly bulletproof."

I struggled against the ice, hoping the flames had started to melt it, but Lewis kicked me hard in the side. All the air left my lungs and tears welled in my eyes.

Lewis looked up through the trees at the sky. "It looks like my mission is just about done. Remember, we'll hunt you down, one by one if necessary. You're all dead birds flying."

He spread his enormous mahogany wings, the tips of his feathers barely touching the flames. With powerful thrusts of his wings, he was airborne, dousing the flames around us with the gusts of air he created. As he rose above the trees, he yelled down, "Oh, and Sam. I've got a little present for you."

He pulled the third gun from his belt, aimed, and fired twice before flying away in a burst of speed.

His first shot hit the ground only inches from my head. Another ferocious bang split the air. This time, the bullet struck Sam in the stomach and came out his lower back, splattering his blood on the leaves and the trees.

He fell to his knees, gripping his stomach. I silently called his name, terrified that he was going to die right in front of me. He moved, scrambling in the dirt for something. I couldn't figure out what he was doing until his fingers pried a large rock from the ground.

Leaving a trail of blood, he crawled over to my side. Holding the rock in both hands, he lifted it over his head and then brought it down on my arms, breaking the ice that bound them.

He tried to do the same thing with my legs but I stopped him, using my telepathy since I couldn't speak. *Stop. Find May and get yourself help. Don't waste your energy on me.*

"No," he said, continuing to bash at the ice. "I'm doing this so that you can get May to come and help us." After a hard hit, he managed to free my left leg.

It might be too late by the time we get back. She can't fly as fast as I can.

"Then take Katie to May and come back for me," he yelled, freeing my other foot. "She's hurt more than me."

He pushed me to my feet, urging me toward the injured wolf. Blood clotted her dark fur. Her eyes were beginning to dim and her breaths were coming in gasps and whimpers.

With as much strength as I could muster, I dragged Katie out of the grove of trees and took off with her hanging in my arms. As my breathing became heated and deeper, it melted the thin layer of ice that covered my mouth.

Within a minute, I was landing—as gracefully as one can land when carrying extra weight—in front of May.

She scrambled up to us. "What happened? Where's Sam? And Lewis?"

"Can't talk, got to get back, help her," I panted before turning around and taking flight again.

Even before I landed, I saw Sam was lying face down, not moving. I ran up to him and shook him hard, tears streaming from my eyes. "Sam, wake up!"

He was hardly breathing and his heartbeat was frighteningly slow. I flipped him onto his back. He was unconscious, pale, and still losing blood. He didn't have a lot of time left.

I couldn't carry him in flight, since he was too heavy, so I closed my wings and heaved him onto my back. And I ran. I ran as fast as I could. I ran faster than I'd ever run in my whole life.

We were only yards away from May and Katie when Sam began to cough and sputter. I slowed down and laid him on the ground.

His eyes were open and glassy. "Jay," he said, his voice raspy, "it's so beautiful, it's incredible. Don't you see it?"

I followed his gaze to see nothing. "No, Sam, I don't see it. What is it?"

"A beautiful light," he whispered. "Should I go, Jay? Should I go join Abbie and Sara?"

Tears blurred my vision and I held him closer to me. No, I couldn't lose another one.

"No," I cried. "No, Sam, don't leave, don't go, don't die! Just hang in there a little longer."

"But I don't have much longer, do I?"

"Shut up! Don't say that! May, Katie, get over here! Hurry!"

May came running with Katie, in human form, hobbling after her. As they set to work, pulling his shirt off, I closed my eyes and thought, *Melody, Sara, Jake, Abbie, help him. Don't let him die, oh, don't take him away. Keep him with us, I beg you.*

When I opened my eyes again, Sam's wound was almost completely healed. He still remained motionless, silent. His eyes were a dull gray, not their usual beautiful silver. I couldn't see him breathing. I laid a hand on his chest. I couldn't feel a heartbeat either.

I leaned down and whispered into his ear, "Come back to me, Sam. Come back."

The light seemed to return to his eyes. His body spasmed, and he gasped in a breath of air. His heart pounded heavily.

He looked around at the three of us until his gaze landed on me. "I've come back, Jay. And I'm here to stay." His eyes closed as he slipped from consciousness again, this time, into a healing sleep.

CHAPTER 48

L ewis' words echoed in my head: *Go ahead, raven-boy ...*

That's it! I thought. *Lewis was the tiger and Sam was the raven that freed me from his spell.* My cheeks flushed with embarrassment at the thought of the kiss I'd shared with Lewis and how I'd been fooled by his telepathic ability.

I was sitting beside Sam, waiting for him to wake up. *Thank you, my friends in heaven.* May and Katie had gone off, May to scout the area and Katie, I hoped, to find some food. The temperature was beginning to drop again as the sun slipped down in the western sky.

My mind started to drift, and I unthinkingly hummed the song to myself. The song itself seemed to call everyone together.

May appeared first. She was uninjured. A good sign. Katie trotted along behind her, a scrawny rabbit dangling from her jaws. And Sam roused from his sleep.

I stopped singing and helped him to sit up. Katie dropped the freshly killed rabbit on his lap and backed away, as if to tell him that it was all his.

We gathered around the fire and tried to come up with a plan, while Sam ate as much meat as he could from the tiny rabbit.

"There's a small town about a fifteen minute's flight away," May reported. "Do you think you could make it that far, Sam?"

He nodded. "If necessary, we can stop along the way, but I think we can make it." He was still pale seemed a bit light-headed, but I was happy that he was feeling better.

I raised my head to stare at the sky. It was mostly clear, but clouds were gathering heavily in the northwest, promising snow.

I was shivering already and dreaded how much colder it would be in the air. Sam tossed the leftover fur and bones—and other things I don't wish to describe—into what was left of the fire.

He stood shakily and slowly stretched out his enormous black wings. "Let's get going while the weather is still fair and there's still daylight," he said.

The last sparks of the fire blew out like a birthday candle as we took off into the sky, leaving only flecks of blood and a pile of smoldering ash.

The wind had picked up and it was hard to fly in such cold, but we made it to the town. At first we had flown over huge fenced fields and tiny farmhouses that were at least a mile apart from one another. Then dirt roads turned to gravel roads and those eventually gave way to paved roads that led straight to town.

A fountain stood in the center square with a small school off to the side. There was one grocery store, one gas station, and sixty or seventy houses.

We walked along the roads until we found a gap between two buildings where we could stay sheltered from the wind and maybe most of the later snow.

Leaning against one of the buildings, we huddled together. Katie had morphed again and given me her jacket. She pressed against me to help warm me up before a sniffling Sam took over, and Katie curled around May instead.

Despite the freezing air. I had almost fallen asleep when I heard a woman cry, "My goodness, you poor things. You look nearly starved to death!"

We all looked up to see a short woman with graying hair wearing a thick coat and an older man wearing his own winter coat and cap.

They walked closer to us, the man saying, "Leave them alone, Joanne. They're none of our business."

She smacked him on the arm.

"Now, Jasper, it's not courteous to leave a child in need," she scolded. She looked down at us. "You kids don't go anywhere. We're going to bring you something nice."

She turned and left with the man following behind her, grumbling to himself.

What happened next really confused me. The couple returned twenty minutes later carrying a bundle of coats and blankets, containers of food, and a steaming thermos. We each drank a little from the thermos—except for Katie—while they watched. The liquid was warm and tasted extremely sweet. It warmed me from the inside out.

We swathed ourselves in the blankets and wolfed down what little food was in the containers. I can't tell you what the food tasted or looked like because it was gone *that* fast.

The woman smiled as she watched us eat. The man had stormed off, grumbling to himself. It took forever, but the woman finally left too. We were warm, fed, and had somewhat better shelter for the night.

I was clothed in a man's winter coat that was probably three sizes too big. May wore a coat that reached her knees. Katie, who was still in her wolf form, was wrapped in a thick quilt. Sam also wrapped himself in a blanket, savoring its warmth.

Using the largest blanket the woman had given us, we covered ourselves completely as we lay down, making a tent of warmth. And that's how we slept, curled up upon one another under the blanket. It was the warmest night we would get through in a while.

I woke shivering with something heavy on top of me. I pushed up against it, feeling its weight. I pushed again till the blanket flipped off us.

The brightness all around us temporarily blinded me. The sky was mostly clear and the sun shone strong, but already clouds were gathering. The others rose, gasping at the sight around us. The world was covered in a thick blanket of white snow that glistened and glittered in the brilliant sunlight.

Before any of us could speak, I heard a crunching sound in the snow that was coming closer. I stood, not knowing who or what it was.

The woman who had helped us the night before appeared between the two buildings. She was back with more containers and another thermos.

She smiled. "Well, I'm glad you're still here."

She handed us the container and thermos. I opened the thermos and used its lid as a bowl. I poured the steaming brown liquid into it and allowed Katie to lap at it happily. After we'd eaten every scrap of food, the woman collected the containers and thermos and simply left.

CHAPTER 49

I t was even colder in the air as we flew from the town. Our new coats kept us warmer, and it was easier to fly when our body temperatures were warmer. We of course had modified the new coats as we had all the others, by cutting two long slits down the back.

My breath billowed out in front of me as we flew. Snowflakes were falling lightly again and they stung my eyes. Still, it wasn't long before we flew ahead of the clouds and were in bright sunlight again. We took a short break around noon, hoping to get some food but had no such luck. So we flew off again, our stomachs growling in protest.

It didn't feel like long before the sun had set and the stars began to twinkle high above. On the horizon was the glow of another city or town.

We forced ourselves to land for the night, even though we could have gone much farther. We were forced to lie huddled together in the snow without a fire. We were, again, on an open prairie without a single tree in sight.

I snuggled between May and Sam with May curling into my warmth. I tried my best to keep my eyes shut, but I was finding it difficult to fall asleep. A strange feeling was bubbling inside of me as I thought of the long chain of events that had led up to now. Tears welled in my eyes at the overwhelming senses of stress, pain, suffering, and grief.

The tears rolled down my cheek as a light snow drifted down on us. Sam rolled over to face me. He wiped the tears from my eyes.

"Hey, hey, don't cry," he whispered. "It's okay. What's wrong?"

He's always so nice to me.

"N-nothing," I sniffled, trying to calm down. "I—It's n-nothing."

"Please don't lie to me. I find it hard to live with myself when you do. It can't be nothing if it's making you this upset." He brushed a loose strand of hair from my eyes. "What is it?" He pulled me closer to comfort me.

I began to cry harder. "It's everything." I buried my face into his shoulder, not wanting him to see me like this. "It's just everything. The chasing, the fighting, the death, just everything."

"You wish we never left the DAEL?"

"Of course not." I looked back up. "You know we had to leave. It was torture to be alive there and death came only as a blessing."

"Well, I can't fix everything but I can make you a promise," he said calmly. "I will endure everything along with you. Even if every day is a living hell, I'll stand by you until I can fight no longer."

"Thank you." I closed my eyes and lay in his embrace. He stroked my hair until I drifted into sleep.

———•◆•———

This dream was not so much a dream as it was images flashing in my mind. As soon as I tried to focus on the one in front of me, another took its place. Then they slowed down dramatically and I could make them out.

The first was the same blurred image of the woman gazing down at me as she hummed the song to me. The next was an image of the woman and a smaller person looking at me, the woman with love and the little girl with curiosity. It was just as blurred as the first picture.

The final image was a little clearer. I stared down at a baby boy in little blue airplane pajamas, his eyes bright as he smiled up at me.

I didn't know what to make of these strange images, but then the woman's voice wove through my thoughts: *I'm here, Jay. Come find me.*

Then I realized that *the* voice I'd been hearing was actually *her* voice.

Yes, Jay, it's me. Come and find me. I need to see you. I will protect you.

I didn't know what to think.

Then she yelled urgently, *Jay, run! Leave! Danger! Get away from the danger, quickly!*

I jolted awake, sitting up so quickly I made myself dizzy. I whipped my head around, gazing over the snow-covered plain. I couldn't see any trouble.

Clouds covered the sky, tinting everything gray. The air was freezing, but there was no wind to make it colder on the ground. It would, however, be twice as cold while flying. Everyone looked okay. Still asleep but okay. Then a loud grumble startled me. It sounded close.

The sound came again, but I laughed softly when I realized it was only my stomach growling in protest against my hunger.

Then it came to me with a jolt, making me smack my forehead with my palm. *How could I be such an idiot?*

I held out my hand and focused. *Food*, I thought. *Make some kind of food.* All that happened was a small spark flashing right above my hand.

"Huh?" I tilted my head in confusion. "What was that?"

I tried again. Another spark, nothing more. I growled, frustrated, and tried something else. Only another spark. Again. Spark. Another time, another spark.

While I was grumbling to myself and trying to get it right, my friends roused from their sleep. They all stared through half-closed eyes in puzzlement, but I paid no attention. Sam was the first to speak.

"Uh, Jay, what are you doing?"

"I'm trying to make us something to eat," I muttered, "but my stupid power isn't working right."

I tried again, concentrating hard. Just a bigger spark. I growled loudly in my frustration.

May laid a hand on my shoulder. "Just calm down a little. Take a rest maybe."

I sighed, pushing her hand away.

Katie, who had morphed back to her human form, raised her hand and started waving it above her head. "Hello? Anyone? I'm really confused over here."

Sam quickly explained my ability, making sure that it wouldn't end in a story. He clearly didn't want to tell about how I nearly killed him with the same power.

"Oh, I see." She nodded. "We get stuck with some of the strangest powers, don't we? Well, maybe it's the cold or maybe it's because you haven't used it in a while."

"I don't know." I took a deep breath and held my hand out again. After a moment's wait, another fiery spark flashed. "Oh, come on!"

Sam laid a hand on my arm. "It's okay, Jay. It's only one more day. I think we'll be fine."

"Yeah, but if it keeps up, we'll starve to death. So what's the plan? We fly to the next town and keep moving?"

"I guess so," Katie said.

The woman's ominous words echoed in my mind, making me want to leave all the sooner. I stood up and stretched my wings out.

"Hey, what's the big hurry?" Sam asked, looking up at me with confusion.

"It's nothing. I ... uh, just feel a little uneasy." I shifted from one foot to the other to add emphasis.

"Well, if you're uncomfortable with staying," Sam said, "we'll leave. You've got to give us a little time to get ready though."

I waited impatiently for them to dust off the snow and spread their wings. I was the first to start running.

Hurry, Jay, hurry, the woman said in my head. *Get away. There is danger coming very fast.*

I know, I know, I thought as my feet left the ground. *I'm going.* That's when my bad luck started.

My vision gave out and I halted in midair, hovering. I did my best to lower myself gently to the ground by gradually slowing my beating wings.

Once my feet touched down, Sam scared me by asking from above me, "What's going on? What happened? Why are you stopping?" He landed next to me, his feet crunching in the snow.

I heard Katie and May land as well. "What's going on now?" Katie asked. "I thought we were leaving."

I didn't have to say anything because Sam said, "She's blind. She can't see. And she can't fly if she can't see. Just wait, it'll pass."

"How can you tell?" Katie asked Sam. She spoke in a whisper, but I could still hear her.

"Look at her eyes, they look different. You see?"

That's when I heard it, far off and distant. The drone of machines. I realized what the familiar sound was. It was the sound of approaching RUCAs, and from what I could hear, a lot of them.

CHAPTER 50

"**G**uys, we have to leave, now!" I shouted as the sound grew stronger.

"What's wrong? We have to wait for you to be able to see," Katie said.

"Don't you hear them? They're getting closer. We have to leave now or we're going to get killed!"

"Hear what? Who is *them*?" Sam asked.

"The RUCAs, the RUCAs! Can't you hear them coming?" I was nearly in tears by now.

"I don't he—" May stopped midsentence.

Someone grabbed me and slung me over his—her? its?—shoulder.

I panicked, not knowing who it was. My kicking foot connected with something solid.

"Ow, Jay, quit it. I'm trying to help."

It was Sam. I stopped struggling, allowing him to carry me away. But then something hit us, knocking us to the ground, and I went tumbling away from him. The blow knocked my vision back, though.

I flipped over to see Sam fighting a RUCA, dodging its blows. The RUCA's false fur was a sickly brown, soaked because of the surrounding snow and the warm metal beneath.

May was running from another while Katie was attacking one in her wolf form, until two more fell on her.

As I stood, ready to join the fight, I heard a loud metallic roar. Six more flew above me, diving down to attack. The first one tackled me, plowing me into the snow. Closing its claws around my neck, it pulled me up and held me suspended from the ground.

A huge course of electricity flowed through my body, and then the beast threw me a good five feet, leaving me stunned and spasming on the ground. Even my thoughts were scrambled from the shock.

Two more fell on me, cutting my skin with their metal claws. I struggled against them, but it was in vain. When the first one tried to join in by shoving another aside, I was able to fight my way free. I kicked the last one off me and ran—and immediately found myself trapped between two groups of three.

The voice suddenly called to me. *Jump as high as you can and fly straight up.* I crouched down and jumped up as hard as I could. Quickly, I unfurled my wings and pushed hard, flying up. It seemed to take our robotic enemies a second to realize that I'd flown away.

Now, go for the neck, the back of the neck, the voice commanded. *Dive down and strike the back of their necks.*

Why? I asked.

It's their weakest point. Now go!

I twisted my body around and dove straight down. I was nearly on top of one when I rotated so that my feet were thrust

223

out in front of me like a hawk's talons. They collided heavily with the back of the RUCA's neck.

I heard a satisfying *crack* as I landed on the ground. The monster stood like a statue for a moment before falling forward and crashing to the ground, motionless.

That was it! The mystery of how to destroy these things was solved. Now we at least had a fighting chance.

The other RUCAs rushed me, and I had to be fast. Using the skills that Lewis had taught me, I dodged a blow from one, using its forward momentum to make it crash into the others coming up from behind me.

As another charged at me, I leaped and delivered a roundhouse kick to the side of its neck. Its head snapped unnaturally to the side and it slumped to the ground, the harsh red light disappearing from its evil eyes.

Nearby, May was trying to pull one RUCA off Sam by tugging at its wings. I ran up to them and delivered a heavy blow to its neck. I heard two cracks that time, simultaneously. One was the RUCA's neck breaking. The other was my arm breaking on the hard metal.

I gripped my broken arm as I shouted, "Break their necks. It's the only thing that kills them!"

A moment later two more tackled me to the ground. My head connected with something hard. A rock hidden beneath the snow maybe.

I blacked out for a moment but quickly came back around to find Sam slamming his arm down on a RUCA's neck. The other already lay motionless.

I pressed my hand to the side of my head and then pulled it back to look at it. Blood.

Katie was fending off five in her human form, her knife in hand. Her jeans were shredded and bloody and one sleeve of her large coat was missing. Sam pulled me up, asking if I was okay. I nodded, and together we ran to help Katie.

In the end, all but one of the RUCAs were "dead." I have no other word to describe it. The last one flew away in retreat.

———◆———

Against our pain, we flew away. We skipped the next town, afraid the RUCAs might find us if we stayed there. The next few towns seemed to blend one into the other. It would be nearly impossible to find a place to land without being spotted if we tried staying there.

We veered north to search for the farms and fields again so that we could rest. The search took a while, but we found a place that was perfect—a large metal barn with pastures surrounding it. A few animals dotted the fields, held in by white fences.

We landed in the field closest to the barn. I didn't think the animals would tell their owners about the arrival of four strange birds.

These beasts were huge. They all had hard feet and long faces. They looked almost like deer but bigger and more muscular and without antlers. Long hair ran the lengths of their necks and dangled and swished behind them in thick tails.

There were also other animals that were bigger, but shorter and slower. They only had a tuft of hair on the end of their tails, and some even had horns sprouting from their heads. These creatures came in all sorts of colors too. They were black, brown, white, gray, russet, and a couple had multiple colors.

Sam must have seen my curiosity because he pointed to the deerlike creatures and said, "Those are horses. Some people will ride on their backs because the horses can run fast. And those"—he pointed to the shorter, bulky animals—"are cows. They provide milk for people. People also slaughter them for their meat."

We ran to the fence that enclosed the field and crawled under it. We were only feet from the barn. No one seemed to be coming. We yanked open the barn doors. No one was inside either. We were, however, greeted by more animals.

The horses were in what looked like cages, but they could stick their heads out to stare at us. I didn't understand what it was with humans putting animals and other humans in cages. It seemed cruel, and we should know.

We split up and looked for places to hide. "What about up here?" May asked, pointing at a ladder that led up to an open hatch on the ceiling.

Sam climbed the ladder and disappeared into the space. His head popped back into sight. "It's a hay loft. It's dark, big, and there's hay for us to lie on. Good job, May."

She beamed proudly.

Sam pulled May up. Katie climbed up and I followed, taking one last look before entering the dark loft.

CHAPTER 51

We huddled in the back corner of the loft, lying in the hay as Katie and May took turns working on our injuries. While May tended to Sam and me, Katie dealt with her own cuts. Between the two of them, they quickly healed my broken arm, the gash on the side of my head, and my other minor cuts and scrapes.

We didn't say a word, or really even move or make a sound for that matter, for fear the humans would enter the barn and find us.

Hours later, we did hear someone walk into the barn. Footsteps creaked on the ladder and the hatch was closed, eliminating any light that could find its way in. Darkness. Silence.

We could faintly hear the humans talking below us, but they were soon gone. We waited a while longer, but no one returned.

I stood and stretched before lying back down. The others seemed relaxed as well. Katie actually pulled off one of her coats because it was so warm in our hiding place.

"My guess is that it's nighttime," Sam said. "We could keep going and get even farther away from *them*."

"No," Katie argued. "We can't pass up this opportunity. We're warm and if we go down, we'll be well fed."

"We won't kill any of the animals," Sam said. "Not for food, not for anything. The owners will get suspicious and worried if even one is missing. Then they'd be sure to find us."

Katie huffed out a breath, crossing her arms over her chest. I agreed with Sam.

"He's right," I said. "We can't kill here. But Katie is also right. We should stay, at least for tonight."

They both sighed. I turned to get May's input, but found her fast asleep, snoring lightly.

"Okay, we'll stay," Sam finally agreed. "But I still feel uncomfortable being so close to our last location."

He rolled away from us and closed his eyes. Katie did the same and fell right to sleep. I moved closer to Sam and shut my eyes. I didn't sleep, but managed a light doze. After a while, I'm not sure how long, I felt movement beside me in the hay.

I peak through nearly closed eyes to see Sam's silhouette sneaking away over the hay. He moved silently, as if he were a shadow.

I crawled after him, trying to be just as silent. He slowly flipped open the hatch and slid down the ladder. I paused for a few seconds before following. The door at one end of the barn was slightly open. I ran to it in time to see Sam running away.

I stepped out of the barn as he flew off into the clear blackness of the star-filled sky. What was he doing? Was he running away? No, he wouldn't do that. But I needed an explanation.

I took off after him, beating my wings at an angle to gain extra speed. The cold wind made my eyes start watering, and I closed them as I pushed harder.

I suddenly slammed into something solid. My breath whooshed from me as I started to fall. Opening my eyes I saw Sam falling too. We both tried to regain our balance, but to no avail. The freezing wind twisted us around as we fell. I finally managed to open my wings to catch myself, but it wasn't soon enough.

I hit the ground with a sickening *thud* and lay there stunned. Sam landed beside me a moment later, crashing onto his shoulder and most likely dislocating it. He stood almost instantly, tensing for a fight. When he spotted me, he reached down and grabbed my shoulder, his other fist pulled back, ready to slug me. When he realized it was me, he knelt down next to me in the snow and asked if I was all right.

I stared up at him. I didn't answer because I couldn't. I slowly regained feeling in my body, but the first thing I felt was pain. I sat up carefully so as to not cause any further damage to my—most likely—broken bones.

"Why did you do that, Jay?" he asked, laying his hand on my back. "You could have killed us. Why did you follow me?"

"Why were you leaving in the first place? Are you running away?"

"No, Jay," he answered. "I just needed some fresh air."

I smiled and quoted him. "Please, Sam, don't lie to me. I find it hard to live with myself when you do." His weak return smile told me he remembered. "Please, just tell me the truth."

"I ... I needed to clear my head," he said. "I've got a lot on my mind." He stood and turned away.

I stood as well. "Maybe I can help. Why don't you tell me?" He diverted his gaze, avoiding eye contact. "Come on, tell me. It might lift something off your chest."

He sighed, giving in. "This whole thing is so stressful, so emotional for everyone. We don't know where our next meal will come from, whether or not we'll get attacked again, or whether one of us will fall dead." He paused a moment, shifting his gaze to the stars overhead. "I'm trying to be strong for all of you. Not shedding a tear when you cry. But this is taking a heavy toll on me too. Being on the run isn't easy. And I feel useless. I have no real powers like you or Katie or May. I have nothing useful to offer. All I can do is turn into a black bird and change the color of my hair and eyes. What's the use in that? I have nothing to help or fight with."

His fists clenched at his sides. "The DAEL," he growled. "If it weren't for them, we wouldn't be in this mess in the first place." He bowed his head, squeezing his eyes shut, tears coming soon after.

This was one of the few times I'd ever seen him cry. The other times were the first two times I died. But these weren't tears of sadness and grief. These were tears of anger, rage, and mental pain.

Something began to glow. I looked down to see that it was his fists, his hands. They were glowing a blinding bright blue.

"Uh, Sam?" I was staring wide eyed at his hands, but he didn't notice.

"They did this!" he shouted. I backed away at the intensity in his voice. "They did this. They took me from my parents, my family. They locked me in a cage! They turned me into *this*! And they've tortured me up to now."

He raised his fist, as if to strike down an unseen enemy, and threw the punch.

The light that haloed his hands transferred into the punch and left his hand, traveling farther than the punch itself. The light traveled on till it struck a fence that exploded on impact.

Sam stood motionless, obviously stunned at what he'd just done. He stared at his hands, acknowledging their glow for the first time. "W-what just happened?"

I stared at the damaged fence and the upturned earth around it. "I think you just gained a new power."

CHAPTER 52

S am raised his uninjured arm and arched it as if he were throwing a ball. The light followed the arch and continued on as a glowing downward curve until it sliced through another portion of the fence.

"Wow." He smiled. "This is so cool." He tried another time, swinging his good arm around sideways, creating a sideways arching blade of light that traveled quite a ways before hitting something.

Sam began to look a little faint, and the light in his hands dimmed and flickered. I draped his uninjured arm over my shoulders before he collapsed. His hands went completely out.

"I'm just guessing here," he said, "but I don't think I should be doing that too much. It's pretty draining."

We limped back to the barn. Sam couldn't stop smiling the whole way there.

I helped him climb the ladder and we crawled over the hay to the others. Both Katie and May were still asleep.

I shook Katie awake. "Could you do a quick healing job for us?"

She yawned and stretched. When I indicated Sam, she crawled over to him and felt his hurt arm.

"It's not broken, just popped out of place." She looked at him. "This is going to hurt but try not to yell."

She held the palm of her hand against the top of his shoulder. Sam nodded and took a deep breath.

She suddenly pulled his arm while pushing on his shoulder till we heard a *crack*. He grunted and pulled away, swearing under his breath.

I removed my jackets and told Katie that I felt most pain in my right arm and side. She got to work and by the time she was done, I was silently giggling even though it slightly hurt due to my *five* cracked ribs.

"So how did you get so banged up in the first place?" she asked.

Sam told her about the crash. Katie sighed, shaking her head. "Did anything else happen? Because I'm having a hard time believing you two just went for a midnight flight, crashed, and came back all beat up."

"I am too," May added. Obviously, she'd woken up.

I turned to Sam and asked him telepathically, *Do you want to tell them? Do you feel well enough to show them too?*

He answered silently, *Yeah, I will.* He straightened and announced, "I've finally gained a new power."

Katie and May congratulated him and then immediately asked for details and a demonstration.

"Well, Jay and I were talking," he began. "Then I got kind of upset."

Kind of?

"And I lost control of my emotions and … That's it."

A short pause. "Well, show us," May said. She was nearly trembling with excitement.

"I'll try, but I'm not sure I know how to work it yet."

233

"Wait," I said. "Shouldn't we do this outside? I've seen what damage it can do."

He thought a moment. "What if I only turn them on but don't use it?" he suggested.

I was a little uncomfortable with that but shrugged in agreement.

His eyebrows knitted together as he concentrated. His hands blinked on a second or two later. The three of us stared in awe.

"If I swing my arm really fast, it creates a blade of light that keeps going until it hits something. And the same thing happens if I throw a punch. It's very draining though."

"From the sound of it," Katie said, "it sounds like the power came only when you released your emotions. Maybe the light is a mental or psychic energy that was buried in your emotions and is now taking a physical form."

I only understood half of what she said, but I nodded in agreement anyway.

Sam started looking light-headed again. The lights in his hands went out again, leaving us in darkness. He fell back on the hay and was instantly asleep.

May yawned. "I think that's a good idea. Let's go to sleep." She and Katie curled up in the hay and were both asleep in minutes.

I rolled over and tried to follow their example.

CHAPTER 53

I couldn't sleep. I'd lain awake for at least an hour, so I decided to try to force myself to sleep by dying another false death. I slowed my breathing drastically, and my heart slowed with it. I closed my eyes and felt the coldness of death fill me.

When I opened my eyes, I was in the black plain. I watched as a distant white fleck came closer and became my sister.

I smiled. "Hello, Melody."

She seemed both confused and aggravated at the same time. "Hello, Jay. Why did you come here when you didn't need to? You could have just stayed awake." She frowned sourly.

"I also need an explanation," I answered. "Why isn't my power working correctly?"

"It's merely focusing and concentrating itself," she explained. She began to pace nervously. "You're getting closer, Jay. So close. You just need to alter your course a little. Start heading northeast. You need to find our mom. She is your only salvation for the future."

As I made that mental note, she grabbed my hand and I instantly felt warm. Then I felt the usual sense of falling.

My eyes opened and I sat up. *Why did she send me back so fast?* I thought almost angrily. And what did she mean by my powers were being concentrated? I held out my hand and tried to materialize a simple bird. What a horrible idea.

If you don't see the problem, let me refresh your memory. We were in a *hay* loft and every time I materialized something, the result was a *fiery spark*. Last I checked, *hay* and *fiery* don't mix well.

The spark seemed to jump from my hand to the hay I was sitting on. I yelped and jumped as the hay burst into flames. I yelled for the others to get up. They were instantly alert and terrified. The fire was spreading so quickly that the flames already blocked our path to the only exit.

Without hesitation, Sam flicked on his hands. He faced the metal wall behind us and swung his arm forward. The light sliced a big hole into the wall, allowing us an escape route. We leaped from the burning loft to the ground below. I turned, hearing the horses inside crying out in fear.

Sam was bent over his knees, trying to regain his energy, but he saw the determined look on my face. "No, Jay," he said. "Don't go back in—"

I'd already taken off running. I pulled open the doors, and smoke quickly rolled out. Flames were already licking at the wooden beams. I ran to the first cage and fumbled with the sliding bolt lock until it opened. The panicking gray horse bolted out the doors.

I moved from one to the other, each time releasing another terrified horse. There were still so many to open though.

A falling beam nearly hit me as I unlocked another one.

I had just released what I thought was the last one when a portion of the loft above me collapsed. Burning wood landed on me, pinning me down, singeing my clothes and skin. A gash on my forehead bled into my eyes.

Dazed, I stared as a small cat dashed across the barn, smoke streaming from its fur. It stopped to stare at me with big green eyes and meow pleadingly before bounding away.

I coughed on the smoke that filled my lungs. *Sara*, I thought. *Was that Sara? Or was it a sign from her?* I gazed through the burning rubble at the last remaining stall door, closed.

I tried but couldn't pull myself free. Tears streamed down my ash-covered face, tears from the smoke and the realization that I could really die here.

The weight was suddenly lifted off me. I looked up through the smoke to see Sam standing over me. He was straining to hold the rubble and the beam just long enough for me to crawl out.

He dropped it and grabbed my arm. "Let's go. This place is going to collapse at any minute." I pulled away from him. "What're you doing?"

I coughed. "I have to save the rest! I can't let anything die for my stupid mistake."

I ran to the last door, leaping over fallen debris and dodging falling chunks of ceiling. When I touched the metal lock, I instantly pulled away. It was scalding hot. I glanced inside the stall.

There were two in this one. A large bay horse and a spindly-looking baby horse.

From the corner of my eye, I saw Sam's lights flick on. "Get out of the way!" he yelled.

I jumped aside as a blinding flash of white blew past me, demolishing the door. A shower of splinters covered the walkway.

In the stall the horse had backed into the corner, showing the whites of its eyes. The baby one, however, remained lying down as if it couldn't walk.

I leaned down and picked up the little one. Its mother flattened her ears at me. I wanted to send calming thoughts to her, but I didn't know how to telepathically communicate with a horse.

Sam ran in and grabbed the straps that wrapped around her muzzle and head. He pulled the stubborn horse from the crumbling stall while I followed with the baby in my arms. The smoke burned my lungs and eyes as I sprinted across the barn. The heat was nearly unbearable. The dancing orange and yellow flames were everywhere. I could hear the roar of the fire, the pounding of my heart in my ears, and the shrill cries of the horses outside.

Sam, the horses, and I burst from the flames, smoke and ash streaming from our coats and hair. The first thing I saw was a man and a woman, no doubt the owners of the farm.

The woman was on her knees, crying, while the man stood behind her with a hand resting on her shaking shoulder. Both stared at us in awe.

I stepped forward, but then stopped when the man raised a shotgun and pointed it at me. We stared at each other as I walked slowly forward and laid the small animal beside the woman. It breathed a sigh of relief as it lay on solid ground. Its mother walked over and sniffed him, checking to see that her baby was all right, as any good mother would do.

The owners looked from the animals to me, and the man hesitantly lowered the gun.

I bowed my head and said, "I'm so sorry this has happened. All of the animals that were inside are out now. I'm glad that no one got badly hurt." I walked past them, patting the mother horse's neck as I passed. And then I ran with Sam at my heels.

Smoke continued to rise as black clouds, but the sky was already changing color, awaiting the new dawn. We took off at the same time. Sam explained that May and Katie would be waiting just north of the collapsed barn. The cold bit even harder at our flushed skin, but it soothed some of my burns.

We soon caught up with the others. I took the lead and turned us to the northeast as my sister had instructed. *I sure hope you are right about this, Melody.*

I felt like I was getting closer to something great. I just couldn't tell what it was yet.

———◆———

The wind drastically picked up after we crossed a huge muddy river that seemed to stretch on forever to the north and south. We couldn't find a place to land because the area was so crowded.

I was nearly trembling with anticipation and anxiousness. With every passing mile we were getting closer and closer to whatever I was seeking. I flinched as something swatted the back of my head. Katie flew directly above me, glaring down at me.

"I've been calling your name, Jay," she yelled down.

"I'm sorry. This wind is really loud," I shouted back up.

"Is something wrong? You're acting a little jumpy. It's getting hard to fly in this wind."

"I know. I'm fine, though."

She nodded and fell back slightly.

On my own again, I allowed my mind to wander, putting my body on autopilot, so to speak. Without realizing it, I began drifting downward. When I snapped back to the real world, I was flying far below the others. That was when my bad luck continued.

I tilted my wings and tried to fly back up to them, but I'd forgotten to calculate the power of the wind. The moment I tilted up, the wind blew my wings back, nearly popping them out of place.

I flailed around, desperately trying to gain balance, but it made things worse. The wind twisted and spun me around as I spiraled out of control toward the ground.

I yelled for help, but my words were snatched away by the wind.

As I spiraled, I saw the blurred shapes of tall buildings not too far away. Fortunately, it looked like I was about to crash into a small grove of trees, not one of those buildings. I attempted to turn myself around so that I would land on my side instead of my head. It was too late, though, and I crashed headfirst into the trees.

CHAPTER 54

I blinked my eyes into focus as the lights in the room were flicked off. A beautiful woman with long blonde hair and sparkling blue eyes laid me in my bed and pulled the blankets up to my chin.

She leaned down and kissed my forehead. "Good night, my little girl. I love you."

I smiled back. "I love you too, Mommy. 'Night, 'night."

She smiled lovingly and straightened. "I have to go check on your brother," she said. "Now go to sleep. We have a big day tomorrow."

I rolled over and pretended to sleep even though I was wide awake. *Yay!* I thought as she left the room. *I'm going to be four tomorrow! It's going to be my birthday!*

I don't know how long I lay there staring up at the gold stars and moon hand painted on my ceiling as I thought about my birthday. I was too excited to sleep.

A sudden crash startled me, and I heard my mom screaming out in the hallway. I flung myself out of bed and peeked through the crack in the door. The window at the end of the hall had been shattered and two large men wearing black stood in the hall. I could hear my mother crying. One of the men held a little bundle in his arms. My baby brother! The other man held the struggling body of my older sister.

A third man, who'd come from farther down the hall, saw me spying and flung open my door. He grabbed me before I could move away. I kicked and screamed and struggled all I could, but he was much stronger than I was.

When he lifted me from the ground and carried me into the hall, I saw Mom running after us. The man that held my brother kicked her away, slamming her into the wall. That didn't stop her. She came at us again, and the man raised a gun. Still, she grabbed his arm, but he shook her off. The men shouted something I couldn't understand, and then the one who held me pulled a thick sack over my head.

I couldn't see it but I could feel it. I was being taken from my home, my family, and my mother.

———————————

I opened my eyes and was nearly blinded by the bright sunlight. What had that vision been? A memory only now coming back?

My heart began to run on adrenaline as I saw three faces looking down at me. Who were they? Where was I? What had happened?

I screamed and swiftly stood up, staring wildly at the unfamiliar figures. The last thing I remembered was being in my cage at the DAEL with Sara.

Blood dripped into my eyes as I studied the three strangers. One was a girl with long brown hair and striking blue eyes. Another was a little girl with long dark brown hair and bright green eyes. The last one, however, terrified me. He was tall and thin with black hair that fell over his silver eyes. He wore a lot of black and stared at me strangely.

Who were these people? The tall dark one took a step forward, and I took one back.

"Jay? It's only us. Calm down," he said in a soothing tone.

I tensed as he took another step closer. "Who are you? How do you know my name? Where is Sara?"

Looks of confusion crossed their faces.

"Jay, it's us, remember?" the little girl said. "Sara's been gone for a long time now."

What was she talking about? Sara was *dead*? I tried to flash my wings, hoping to scare them off, but I couldn't move them. I looked at my back.

My lab clothes were gone and I was, instead, wearing something thick and heavy that held my wings against my back. I had no other choice—I turned tail and ran. Twigs and leaves scratched at my face but I didn't care. I heard them pursuing me.

I burst from the trees and ran alongside rows of buildings and wide strips of hard black stuff. The buildings grew bigger and bigger around me as I ran on. My shoes pounded heavily on the hard ground. The others followed closely, shouting my name. I kept running. I had to lose them somehow.

I ducked behind buildings and around corners, but they followed like shadows. As soon as I pulled ahead, I hid in a crowd of people to confuse them and then turned around a corner. I immediately ran into someone.

The woman I'd bumped into dropped her books and papers. I looked up at her and was shocked into immobility.

The same blue eyes. The same blonde hair. The same person as my dream. It was my mother.

I instantly hugged her and began crying. "Help me. Help me, Mom! They're following me!"

"I'm afraid you've mistaken me for someone else," she said calmly in that oh, so familiar voice. "Who's following you?"

"No, I'm not mistaken. You're my mom. I remember now." Just as I said that those three came charging around the corner. I hid behind the woman, whispering, "Help me."

The tall boy said, "Jay, what are you doing? Why did you run from us?"

The woman took charge. "Why were you chasing this girl? Can't you see she's terrified?"

"She's our friend and we're trying to help her, but she doesn't seem to remember us," the boy explained.

"Do you kids have any parents I can contact?" the woman asked.

"No, ma'am," he answered politely. "We have no parents." He slowly walked forward toward the woman and me. He said gently, "Jay, it's me, Sam. Don't you remember me?"

I shook my head. "I—I don't know you. I don't know where I am."

"Do you need to go to the hospital?" the woman asked me. "You've got a bad cut on your head."

"No," the boy answered. "It wouldn't be a good idea."

A hospital? What's that? I thought.

The woman seemed to ponder the situation. She pulled something out of her pocket and I backed away.

"Will you stay here a moment while I speak to someone over the phone?" she asked. She pushed a few buttons on her device and held it to the side of her face.

The two girls who stood behind the boy didn't seem to know what to do, but they weren't leaving either.

The woman began to talk to herself as if she were talking to someone else. After a few minutes, she put the device away and said to us, "Come with me. I think I can help you for the time being."

She began to walk away and I quickly followed, still afraid of the three people who claimed to be my friends.

———◆———

We followed the woman to a tall building. She led us inside and ushered us into a small metal room. The doors slid closed, and my heart fluttered with anxiety as the room seemed to move. When the doors opened again, the outside was completely different. I was mystified by this, struggling to figure out how it was even possible.

The woman led us down a hallway to a room that had a large bed against the wall. I sat on the bed and the woman went into a smaller room, returning with a thick piece of cloth that she pressed to my head wound. She then used a wet cloth to clean my face of soot and blood. When she pronounced me clean, she said she would get bandages for my head.

While she was gone, the others tried to refresh my memory. The girl with the blue eyes transformed, to my surprise, into a gray wolf. The boy made his hands glow a bright blue and then transformed into a black bird.

When my mom came back, we were all sitting on the bed, the other three talking to me about who they were. Nothing they said made me remember anything.

The woman placed the bandage securely over my head wound and every time I spoke to her, I addressed her as Mom.

"Why do you call me Mom?" she asked. "I can't possibly be your mother."

"Because you *are* my mom," I said. "I remember *that*."

The woman sighed. "I had children, yes," she said sadly. She pulled a booklet from her bag. "But they were all taken from me." She opened the booklet to show us photos of two little girls with curly blonde hair and a baby boy. "These are my daughters and my son."

"If they were taken," said the wolf girl, "then there's a possibility they're still alive, right?"

"Yes, but it's highly unlikely," the woman replied, staring at the pictures with love and grief. "They were taken many years ago. Nearly ten ..." Her voice trailed off.

"I remember," Sam said, "that I was taken from my parents at a young age."

My mom stared at him in surprise. "Then you *do* have parents?" she asked.

"I don't remember them at all, though. I can't even remember my last name. It's a miracle that I can remember my first."

I stared at the pictures before pointing to two of them. "My little brother and my older sister."

"That is my eldest daughter and my six-month-old son," the woman said after a moment. "How did you know that?"

"You're my mom." I pointed to the middle picture. "And that's me."

She looked from me to the picture, and then to the mirror on the wall as if comparing us.

She shook her head as if to clear it and changed the subject. "You all need to rest. Why don't you go to sleep? You can have the bed if you'll fit." She stood and walked out of the room, taking her bag with her.

I slid under the covers of the bed and was joined by the other three. The boy lay to my right and the girl with the bright blue eyes to my left. The little girl lay near the end of the bed, the only place she'd fit.

When the two girls fell asleep, the boy, Sam, leaned over and kissed my forehead. "Good night, Jay. We'll try again tomorrow. I hope that if you remember anything, you at least remember me."

It took me almost an hour to fall asleep but I eventually did. I was almost afraid of what the next day would bring.

CHAPTER 55

I shifted restlessly in my seat as the engines came to life with a hideous keening sound. I was in newly bought clothes and my hair was combed out. The other three, who I still didn't remember, sat next to me and my mom.

We were on an airplane leaving the place where we were—a city called Chicago—and heading for a place called Montana. Yes, I realize the irony of a bunch of bird-kids on an airplane, thank you.

Mom had stayed up all night making phone calls, and she told us she'd managed to convince them to give her five plane tickets to her home state. She didn't explain who "them" was. And don't ask how we got through security without being found out. It's a secret. And it really confused me anyway.

I was terrified when the plane took off. My ears popped with the changing pressure. The others looked just as scared as I was. We were strapped into seats with our wings held to our backs. There was no way out without getting caught.

The plane trip took forever, and when we landed, I'd never been happier to be on the ground. I was also on constant alert because, according to Sam, we were hundreds of miles closer to the DAEL.

When we left the airport, we stepped into a cold day filled with ice and snow. Mom led us to a place she called a parking garage. It was filled with those big metal things called cars.

We stopped in front of one. It was a sleek black and as tall as I was. Mom threw her bags into the back and told us to get in.

She and Sam sat in the front seats while the rest of us were squished into the back seat. Katie had to help me put the seatbelt on.

We drove for almost two hours from the city of Bozeman, through country back roads, to our destination hidden among the trees.

It was a large wooden building that Michelle—that's Mom's name—called a cabin. She strode up to the door and unlocked it.

We were welcomed by a bark as a dog trotted up to the front door, her tail wagging. She sniffed at us each in turn. When she came to me and Mom, she barked happily and licked my hand.

"This is Nicky," Michelle said. "She's a miniature German shepherd." Michelle glanced at me. "She doesn't normally do that to strangers."

As I walked into the cabin, I saw a small kitchen to my left and a living room to my right. A dining room was on the other side of the kitchen. Almost directly in front of us was a staircase that led to the second floor.

"There are four bedrooms upstairs: my bedroom and three others. The couch in the living room folds out into a bed if necessary. I occasionally have family and friends over to visit."

I slowly ascended the stairs and found myself at the head of a hallway lined with five doors. I opened the first one to my right and stepped in.

I was shocked when I stared up at the ceiling. It was dark blue with little gold stars and a crescent moon. This was *my* room!

A different bed was tucked into the corner where my old bed used to be. No curtains covered the window and a thin layer of dust coated everything.

Michelle walked in behind me. I said in a shocked whisper, "This is my room."

"You can stay in this room if you'd like," she said. "But I'd have to make the bed first."

"No," I replied. "I remember. This was my room before ... before I was taken."

"Yes, my second daughter stayed in here," the woman whispered as if to herself. She bowed her head and left the room, leaving me alone.

———————

I explored the rest of the upstairs. The room across from mine apparently had been my sister's room. The top half of the walls were white while the bottom half was covered with flowers painted in bright colors. The ceiling looked like the daytime sky with clouds dotting the blue. The room next to it was my mom's room. She didn't want me going in there, so I moved on.

The room next to mine was similar to mine. It had blue walls and the night sky painted on the ceiling. It had been my little brother's bedroom, I realized, but it now had a bigger bed, not a crib.

The room at the end of the hall was a bathroom filled with the normal stuff.

The others came up and claimed their rooms. May and Katie were going to share my sister's room and Sam laid claim to the one next to mine. Katie didn't want to sleep in a girlie room, but May didn't want to sleep alone.

By the end of the day, we'd remade the beds and dusted the rooms. Michelle gave Katie, Sam, and me sweatpants and T-shirts to sleep in, and May got an oversized T-shirt to use as a nightgown. After we all said good night, I turned out the light in my room and crawled into bed. I pulled the blankets up to my chin and rolled onto my side so I didn't hurt my wings.

My door was flung open and the light came on. I rolled out of bed. The other three walked in, May in front, dragging Sam behind her.

"Jay," she said, "we've thought of a way to bring your memory back." She stood on tiptoe and whispered something into Sam's ear.

"Wait, we never agreed to that," he argued. "That might shock her a little too badly. We don't know what will happen."

"Sam's right, May," Katie said. "We can't do that to her."

"He's right, we *don't* know what will happen," May said. "But we *have* to do it."

They exchanged anxious looks, but then Sam sighed and said he'd do it. "Jay, come a little closer please."

I took a few hesitant steps toward him.

"Now, pay close attention to me," he instructed.

I focused on his face as he took a deep breath. From the roots of his hair, his black hair changed to a dark mahogany red color. His eyes changed too. One eye became dark red and the other a deep blue.

The result terrified me. I cupped my hand over my mouth as a name echoed in my mind. *Lewis.*

It all came rushing back, flashing through my mind as if it were a movie stuck on fast forward. The escape, Sara's death, Lewis, my first death, Katie, all of it. It came to me with such a force that I fell backward, landing hard on my back.

They stood over me, my friends, and for a moment, I saw what they saw. Me lying on the floor, my eyes as wide as an owl's, the pupils contracting to specks floating in pools of hazel.

I blinked, and they sighed in relief. Sam's hair and eyes faded to their original colors as I sat up.

Michelle came running into the room. "What happened? I heard a loud bang and you weren't in your rooms."

"It's okay, I just fell," I said, rubbing the back of my head. "I'm fine, better than fine actually." Katie pulled me to my feet.

"What do you mean by that?" the woman asked.

"I remember now. My memory is back." I smiled and then glanced at the others. "Why don't you guys go back to bed? I'll be fine." I gave each a hug as they left.

The woman watched my friends leave before helping me back into bed. "I'm happy that you got your memory back, but you need to rest now."

She turned to leave, but I grabbed her wrist. "Wait. Why don't you believe me? That I'm your daughter?"

"Maybe it's because I don't want to believe it. I saw this coming, in a dream. But I knew it was too good to be true. You may look like me and claim to be my child, but I don't believe you are." She tried to pull away but I held on tight.

Melody's voice echoed through my head. *Sing her the song, Jay. She'll know it's true. She'll believe you then.*

I closed my eyes and began to sing the lyrics that had been following me for so long.

> For one so small, you seem so strong.
> My arms will hold you, keep you safe, and warm.
> This bond between us can't be broken
> I will be here, don't you cry.

I didn't even finish the song before Michelle was crying. She hugged me. "How do you know that song? It must be true. You really *are* my little girl."

I hugged her back, simply saying, "I remember, Mom, I remember. And I still and always will love you."

CHAPTER 56

Clearly, the backtracking confused our enemy, because we went a whole week without being attacked. Yes, a whole week. I'd had three blind incidents, however.

Once my mom finally accepted the fact that I was her daughter, I of course had to show her who exactly I was. She was bound to find out eventually anyway. We'd been there several days when I pulled her into my room with Nicky trailing behind us. I closed the door as quietly as I could.

"The others will kill me when they find out about this," I said. "Promise me you won't freak out."

"I promise," she replied. "Nicky do you promise too?" The dog cocked her head, making us laugh.

"Okay." I unzipped my jacket and shrugged it off, unfurling my wings till they touched the walls. She gasped and backed up against the bed, abruptly sitting down.

It's okay Mom, I thought to her. *This is real. This is really happening.*

"It's impossible," she said, shaken. "But, how?"

Evil people who torture the innocent for their own personal gain, I said telepathically. *Sam, May, and Katie are like this too.*

The wings, I mean. We each have different gifts that allow the impossible to be possible. You must keep this a secret between just us.

I folded my wings back in and pulled my jacket back on. Even out of something so serious, she tried to make a joke. "I'm guessing that's why I've found feathers in your beds and why you won't take off those coats."

I laughed a little, even though it wasn't very funny. "Yeah. Do you want to talk to the others about this?"

She shook her head. "Maybe later. This is a lot for even me to take in. But what exactly did you mean by 'gifts'?" she asked as she stood.

"We have supernatural abilities," I explained, "like how I communicated with you through thought. The others can do some pretty amazing things."

"Oh."

She apparently couldn't think of anything else to say, because she just shook her head and headed toward her room. I walked down the stairs, preparing myself for the scolding I was about to receive.

"You what?" Sam yelled when I found him and told him what I'd done.

"I showed her my wings," I repeated. *I thought I was pretty clear the first time.*

He smacked his forehead with the palm of his hand dramatically. "Thanks, you may have just put us at risk again."

"By telling *one person*? My *mom*?"

He sighed. "I'm sorry. I don't know. We've been on the run for over a month now and we haven't been attacked in a week. I'm just on edge, like they'll be on top of us at any minute."

"I understand," I said. "But I felt like I had to show her. She would've found out soon enough anyway."

"I know." He leaned against the kitchen wall. "But I can't help feeling that she's hiding something from us. And that something bad is about to happen."

We turned at the sounds of footsteps coming down the stairs. Mom poked her head around the corner. "Where are May and Katie? I'm ready to see now."

———◆———

Sam sliced through another tree, sending it crashing to the ground. He bent over his knees, out of breath.

Mom stood nearby, awestruck, taking in every detail. She laughed as she saw Katie and Nicky play wrestling in a blur of gray and brown fur.

We were in the back acreage of the property, showing her our powers. I was on my hands and knees, staring into the murky pond May had disappeared into five minutes earlier. We'd shown her all of our powers except for Katie's sleeping spell song and my deaths and resurrections. I think she could live without seeing those.

She walked up to me and asked, "Can you really fly? You know, with the wings and all?"

"Uh, yeah," I answered. "How else could we get to Chicago from the west coast in three weeks? We couldn't just walk there."

She laughed. "I guess you're right. Could you please show me?"

Minutes later, she was watching us rise, dive, and bank through the air through a pair of binoculars. Soon enough, the sun began to sink beyond the horizon and we headed inside. The days were getting even shorter now with the impending winter.

We ate a delicious dinner and headed for bed. Before I crawled into bed, Mom said, "You keep telling me that you remember me being your mother and having a brother and sister. Do you know what happened to them?"

"Yes, I know," I said sadly.

"So what happened?" she asked. I diverted my gaze and shook my head. She needed no other explanation. "I see. Good night, Jay."

"Good night Mom," I whispered as she left the room, turning out the light.

She knew now. My siblings had gone through the same tortures I'd endured, but they hadn't survived.

CHAPTER 57

As the next few days went slowly by, my agitation became greater and more noticeable. My blindness attacks happened more frequently. A recurring nightmare haunted me, leaving me screaming as I woke.

The RUCAs come. They break into the house and slaughter my friends and mother. They tie me up, leaving me in the puddles of my friends' and mother's blood. Then they set the house aflame and watch me slowly burn to death, with big crooked grins on their malevolent faces.

My mother hung a dream catcher on my bed's headboard. It didn't help at all.

During random times of the day, images of Lewis pointing a gun at me would flash in my mind. I was half tempted to hide in my room with the lights off like someone who'd gone completely insane. Nicky had never left my side. I guess she sensed my agitation.

One day when Katie and I were sparring in the backyard, another wave of images flooded my mind, scenes of slaughter and massacre.

I watched from behind metal bars as the others were killed, and then Lewis held his gun to my head. The sound of gunshots filled my ears and I saw a lifeless body lying on a tile floor. Blood splattered her clothes and the floor around her. Blood ran down her face and something was wrapped tightly around her neck.

That was when I realized it was me, dead. Not coming back.

My head cleared and I found myself pinned under Katie's weight. She laughed. "Looks like I win again."

Tears filled my eyes, and her smile swiftly turned to a frown. "Hey, I'm sorry. I shouldn't boast. Did you get hurt?" She got off me, and I shook my head. She pulled me closer. "What's wrong? You've been getting upset a lot lately. Has something been bothering you?"

I said nothing and just sat there as she tried to comfort me. *I sense something coming,* I thought. *It scares me.*

That night I twisted and turned in my bed as I was cursed by another dream. This one was different.

A warhound chased me through the scientists' maze. Everywhere I turned, dead ends led to walls of fire. Inside of the fires, my friends and family were being burned alive. Sam, Sara, Abbie, Katie, May, Melody, Jake, and Mom. All of them dying. All of them reaching out to me, pleading to me to save them.

I found one path that didn't lead to a dead end engulfed by flames, but my exit was soon blocked by a warhound with glinting red eyes. It stalked slowly toward me, a crooked grin on its ugly gray muzzle. As it got closer, it morphed, growling smaller and less furry with every step. The fur seemed to roll off it and dissipate like smoke. When it was only feet from me, it had completely transformed into the familiar figure of my worst enemy whom I used to love so deeply. Lewis stared at me with his hypnotic eyes.

He raised his gun, his finger on the trigger. "Enjoy your real death, Jay," he said emotionlessly. "This one is eternal."

The screams of pain from my loved ones echoed in my ears as he pulled the trigger.

———————◆◆———————

I woke up in a sweat, breathing heavily with my blood pounding in my ears. I crawled out of bed and walked into the hallway. Instead of going to my mom's room like most kids probably would, I opened the door to Sam's room. He was sound asleep in his bed. I silently closed the door behind me.

I crawled into bed beside him, his slow breathing giving me slight comfort. The next thing I knew, I was waking alone in his bed the next morning. When I saw him later, I had to explain why he'd found me in his bed when he'd woken up. My face grew hot as I explained that I'd had another nightmare and needed to be close to someone I knew well.

"You can always tell me if something's bothering you," he said. "Remember, I promised that I'd endure everything with you, and I intend to keep that promise."

"Thank you," I replied, my face growing warmer. "I will remember that." I paused and then finally told him about the feelings of doom I'd been having.

"I've had similar feelings," he said, "but don't worry. Whatever it is, we'll get through it together."

For some reason, I didn't find any comfort in his words.

———————◆◆———————

That night I lay in bed awake again, staring up at the stars that covered my ceiling. *Another sleepless night,* I thought, sighing. *I wonder if I should wake Katie up. Maybe she'll help me with her sleep spell song.*

I sat up when I heard movement outside the house. When I heard nothing more I lay back down, thinking that my anxiousness was getting to me.

Should I die again? No, they'll just send me back right away like last time. I won't practice my hidden power again and risk another fire.

So I just lay there and listened to the silence. But there was a problem. It was too quiet. No wind rustled the bare tree branches, no small sound of an animal disturbing the fallen snow and leaves. Something wasn't right.

I heard a faint tapping at my window. When I turned, two small red lights glared at me through the glass.

My adrenaline pumping, I leaped from the bed just as the glass shattered. In a split second, three RUCAs surrounded me. For the longest moment, none of us moved.

The door suddenly swung open and Sam and my mom stood in the doorway, May and Katie right behind them. When I turned toward them, a RUCA grabbed me from behind and held my hands behind my back.

Mom ran toward us, screaming, "I'm not going to lose you for a second time!"

A RUCA blocked her and knocked her back with one arm, slamming her into the far wall. I tried to yell for her, but the RUCA pressed its paw over my mouth.

Katie quickly morphed into her wolf form and she and Sam attacked, trying to get to me, but the RUCAs were faster.

One socked Katie in the side, leaving her panting on the ground, and the other held Sam by the throat, suspended from the ground. The RUCA that held me shoved a thick bag over my head and then bound my hands together, despite my best efforts to fight him. Just like the first time.

I grew dizzy as I breathed heavily. That was about the time when things went black....

CHAPTER 58

Sam's point of view

Sam lay dazed on the floor among the shards of glass from the broken window. The RUCA had thrown him against a wall, and he'd watched helplessly as the sack was placed over Jay's head and her body went limp. The three RUCAs left through the window, taking Jay with them and leaving the rest of them behind.

Sam struggled to his feet and tried to follow them out the window. Someone tackled him from behind and held him to the floor.

"No!" he yelled. "We have to go after them! They'll kill her if we don't go now. Or worse, they'll take her back to the DAEL."

"We can't," Katie argued as he struggled. "That would be suicide."

"Do you think I care?" Sam continued to struggle against Katie's weight. When he couldn't budge her, he flicked his hands on. She instantly got off.

He stood again but Katie blocked his path, her lips pulled back in a snarl. A threatening growl vibrated deep in her throat. The lights around his hands went out.

He couldn't get past her to follow Jay and her captors. Instead, he walked over to the wall and slammed his head against it. *Crack!* And again. *Crack.* And again. *Crack.*

Blood began to splatter the wall and run down his face. *Why?* he thought. *Why did they take her? Why not one of us? Why not me?*

May pulled at his nightshirt. "Sam, stop it! You're going to hurt yourself. You're bleeding."

"I don't care!" he yelled, glaring at her. Hot tears blurred his vision. "They took Jay and I couldn't stop them." He felt a tug on the back on his pants.

Wolf Katie stared up at him. She glanced at May and raised her head. May whispered for Michelle to cover her ears. She and May held their hands over their ears and a low howl split the air. Sam had heard this sound before. His eyes grew heavy and his thoughts and movements became slow.

He crumbled and fell to the floor, asleep.

CHAPTER 59

My vision was blurred. I blinked to try to focus and instantly regretted that. I squeezed my eyes shut again.

No, not here. This can't be real. This can't be happening.

I sneaked another glance. Metal bars, a metal floor and ceiling. A cage. The surroundings, the smells, were far too familiar. I knew where I was. I was back where I started, the DAEL.

I stared through the metal bars. Dozens of hybrids and experiments surrounded me in cages of their own. Expressions of hopelessness were written across their faces.

As if on a cue, a scientist in the familiar white lab coat walked in. Someone was with him, but in the dim light I couldn't see the other person clearly. They walked down the aisle and stopped in front of me. They whispered to each other and then the scientist walked out of the room. The other person stepped closer so that I could see him better.

I sat up and pressed myself against the back of the small cage. Those familiar deceiving eyes stared at me through the bars, examining me.

"Hello, Jay," he said in a kind voice. "It's been a while since we've seen each other last."

I glared at him with both fear and anger. "Lewis," I hissed.

"Aren't you happy to be back home?" he said sarcastically. "You know, I've never seen so much hatred in your eyes before. It's beautiful." I said nothing, so he continued, "I will give you an explanation, knowing that fifteen hours from now, you won't be here."

I gasped and he smiled at my reaction. "All experiments are being recalled. The American public is coming too close to finding us out. Right now most people believe this place is a laboratory that studies the reasons for deformities in animals." He laughed. "They're not completely lying."

He continued seriously, "Every experiment is to be destroyed as soon as possible. Your friends who were hiding in the Cliffside, you remember them, have already been taken care of. Not one was found alive. And all were accounted for.

"Many others have also been eliminated. Like most of Katie's friends, for example, and Abbie, and that cat freak you called Sara.

"When I came back, I was punished for my failure to kill you and was interrogated on the best way to hunt you and your friends down. I told them that if they took you first, the others would fall apart and would become helpless and erratic. Then they can take the rest of you."

He paused before asking, "Have you ever wondered why you have those blind occurrences?" I remained quiet. "Have you also wondered how they kept finding you?" I again said nothing.

"Well, it's because of those blind moments. They implanted something surgically in your eyes the last time you were here. It allows the people here to see through your eyes, literally. The only problem for you is that it then disallows you to see."

The scientist stepped back in, telling Lewis that his time was up. Lewis started to leave and then turned back. "I've enjoyed this. I hope you now have a little to think about before you execution."

Fifteen hours! I thought. *I have less than a day to live?*

"Make that *less* than fifteen hours," someone said.

I whipped my head around to see who had spoken, but no one seemed to be paying any attention to me and Lewis was no longer in the room. And I knew it wasn't the voice in my head.

I reached my hand through the bars and groped for the lock. Maybe if I felt the shape of the lock and if I tried hard enough, I could make a key and get out. I found the lock but I couldn't find a keyhole.

"It's no use," the same voice said.

I pinpointed the voice this time and turned to the cage on my right. An emaciated boy with dark hair and eyes stared through the bars at me.

"It's a combination keypad lock," he said, exhaustion underlying his voice. "There's no way to unlock it without the right combination."

How did he know I was trying to escape again?

"I'm telepathic," he said. "Not to mention that every one of us has tried to get out. You're telepathic too, aren't you?"

I nodded. *I'm Jay. Now who are you and what right do you have to invade my thoughts?*

My name is Blue. And my right is that it's your fault for letting your thoughts wander out to be heard.

When he thought his name, I realized he matched the description Katie had given of her lover.

You know Katie? he asked.

Um, yes.

Blue eyes, brown hair, turns into a big wolf?

Yeah, that's her.

Oh, my God. How is she? Where is she? Is she okay?

Yes, she's fine. She's in hiding with friends of mine. Do you know that she thinks you are dead?

He lowered his shocked gaze. *I didn't know that. But it'll be true soon enough. I'll be gone any moment now.*

There were words of hope and wisdom that I wanted to give him, but I couldn't even convince myself that they were true.

About three hours passed. Two hours earlier the scientists had tried to feed us poisoned food. How dumb did they think we were? I didn't eat it.

Then another came in with a tray that held dozens of hypodermic needles. Reading the scientist's thoughts, I knew the needles were filled with lethal drugs, three times more than was needed to kill someone. One was for me and the other for Blue.

He grabbed my arm and plunged the needle in without the slightest remorse as to how much pain it caused me. The injection burned in my veins as the drugs raced through my body to my heart. He injected Blue next, and I watched as he gradually died before my eyes. His last thoughts were, *Jay, I know you hear me. If you see Katie again, could you tell her that I was alive and thinking of her till my last moments? Tell her that I love her and always will, even after death.*

Then he just lay there, his eyes half open and his body completely still. And I was still alive. How would I explain that to Katie if I ever saw her again?

More than an hour passed and I was still alive. Some lab technicians had already taken Blue's body, and I was deep in thought the way you can be only when you are on death row.

I looked up as a RUCA stepped into the room, accompanied by Lewis. They stopped in front of me.

I was taken aback when the RUCA spoke. "You are to destroy this one," he said to Lewis. "Do it any way you like, just get it done." It sounded like a recorded message on a failing answering machine.

"Yes, Alpha," Lewis replied, nodding slightly.

"I mean it. If you thought your punishment for your last failure was severe ..." It paused. "You already know the punishment for your second failure."

Lewis laid a hand over his chest. "I understand, Alpha."

"Good, don't disappoint me. You have one hour. Omega 3 will supervise and assist you." Alpha stormed from the room.

Lewis punched in a code on the keypad to my cage. He opened the door for me. "Come on, Jay. Your time has come."

I swallowed and stepped out of the cage. He twisted my arms behind my back, making me cry out, and led me out of the room. Another RUCA stood at attention just outside the door.

"Omega 3," Lewis commanded, "find some rope and lead me to B316."

Omega 3 bowed and walked off. Lewis pushed me to follow. We walked down a multitude of long corridors, stopping once at a room for the RUCA to get some rope. I feared what it would be used for.

When we stopped at another door, the RUCA unlocked it and we stepped inside. To my surprise, the room was empty except for a stool and no bigger than my bedroom. The walls were plain white and the floor was tiled in gray. Metal beams stretched across the ceiling.

"Omega 3, tie that rope into a noose," Lewis ordered as he let me go and closed the door. "Any final wishes or requests?" he asked me. "Questions maybe?"

"Why are you doing this?" I asked, my voice echoing off the walls.

"I was built to do this. I have no choice but to obey their commands," he answered. "If we don't follow orders, we will be either punished severely or destroyed. It's as simple as that."

"What do you mean by punishment?" I asked, watching as Omega 3 finished tying the noose and tossed the rope over an exposed beam.

Lewis turned and removed his jacket. He lifted the back of his shirt for me to see several wounds between his wings just beginning to scab over. The small feathers nearest his shoulder blades were clotted with dried blood. *His blood.*

"This was my punishment for not killing you and Sam the first time. Fifty lashes from an electrified cable whip. It slows even my fast healing abilities." He turned to face me and lifted the front of his shirt so I could see his chest. A metal device was in his chest, over his heart.

"My punishment, if I fail this assignment, is deactivation. This devise controls my heart and keeps me alive. They implanted it to keep me alive and they can turn it off to kill me." He lowered his shirt and replaced his denim jacket. "Now you see why I have to do this."

"Did you know when you tried to kill us that you missed me?" I asked, distracted by the RUCA. It had grabbed the stool and set it beneath the dangling rope.

"No, Jay, you're wrong," Lewis said, shaking his head. "At first I didn't know that Sam had survived. But one thing is for sure. I *never* miss. Not even by an inch have I ever missed."

He picked me up and set me on the stool, standing. He forced the noose around my neck, making sure the knot was in the right position so that I would suffocate rather than die from a snapped neck. I could tell he wanted me to suffer, so that he could watch the light drain from my eyes.

The rough rope cut into my skin as Omega 3 pulled it taut. Lewis stepped forward and looked straight at me with his evil, deceiving eyes. "Enjoy your real death, Jay, because this one is eternal."

Before I could react, he kicked the stool out from beneath my feet.

The rope instantly closed around my throat as gravity pulled me down. No air could get in, no air could get out. It wouldn't be long until I was strangled to death. I kicked instinctively as I grabbed at the rope. I flapped my wings to see if I could loosen the rope even the slightest bit for a gulp of precious air.

Over my strangled gasps I heard Lewis say, "I don't know how you survived that lethal injection, but this will definitely kill you. There's no coming back this time."

I seemed to hang there for hours, waiting to die, but it could have been only minutes. Lewis, however, got impatient.

With an aggravated sigh, he pulled his gun from its holster and cocked it. Raising it, he held it to my forehead. The cold metal stung my skin. He closed one eye, leaving his blue one open as if he needed to get it just right. Smiling, he pulled the trigger, releasing two bullets with two earsplitting bangs.

CHAPTER 60

When the second shot rang out, I was no longer in my body, but was watching from a distance.

I watched as my body went limp. I stopped kicking and flapping and my arms hung motionless at my sides. Blood dripped down my face. I looked like I was crying tears of blood.

The RUCA released the rope and my body hit the ground with a sickening thud. Everything sounded muffled, as if the room were enveloped in cotton.

Only then did I realize it was the exact image I'd seen in my vision.

My dream had actually been a premonition. When I was running through the maze with the warhound chasing me and no way out, it meant that my death was inevitable. No matter what I did, I couldn't avoid it.

I turned at the sounds of footsteps. Sara and Abbie stood behind me. I knew what they would say before they even spoke. I knew what was going on, and they knew I knew.

Sara stepped forward. "It's time to go, Jay. The others are waiting for us."

They each took one of my hands, and the room faded to the black plain I'd visited so many times before. I didn't feel cold this time, though. I felt warm.

I looked down. My clothes had changed to a long white dress. Three chains bound themselves to my ankles and legs, each pulling in different directions.

"What is this?" I asked. "What's with the chains?"

Sara started to walk away.

"Wait, Sara, where are you going?" Abbie called.

"I have some business to take care of," she replied. "I'll be back soon. I'll catch up later."

Abbie turned to me. "The chains are your decisions. Not all spirits get them. One links you to the earth and your body, and after a certain amount of time that will disappear, leaving you with only two choices. I have to show you the other two choices before the first chain is gone."

She took my hand and pulled me in one direction. The chains rattled and trailed behind me. They were heavy and made it hard to walk with them bound to my ankles.

Up ahead, a faint light shone. As we drew closer, I saw it was a tear in the blackness, like a slash in a piece of fabric. Abbie pulled the tear open wider to reveal a big white door. Upon closer inspection, I could see the door wasn't just white but was made from human skulls. The skeletons stared at me through dark eye sockets that bore through my heart. Their jaws hung open as they called out to the ones they'd left behind in the world of the living. Abbie hesitantly pulled the door open. Beyond it was a dark stone tunnel with a staircase that led downward. Fiery torches lined the walls, but they created little light.

I looked at her, silently pleading with her not to make me go down there.

"We must continue," she said, but she sounded wary.

She took the lead down the stone steps and I hesitantly followed. When we reached the end of the stairs, we stepped into a barren plain. The earth beneath my feet was dry and rocky. Scraggly grasses poked up through the cracks in the parched earth. The whole area was shrouded in a thick fog. Everything was bathed in a sickly shade of gray.

I shuddered as an ominous feeling of being watched reached me. I felt small and helpless. Goosebumps crawled over my arms and a shiver ran down my spine.

I whispered to Abbie, "Take me out of here. I don't like it here. I'm scared."

She nodded and together we hurried up the stairs as fast as we could manage. At the top we stepped back through the door and Abbie pushed it closed.

"What was that?" I asked.

"It's a place of many names, but I believe the most appropriate name right now would be the Underworld."

She led me across the black plain in the opposite direction. We finally came to another tear in the darkness. Behind this one was a marble door so heavy, it took the both of us to open it. More stairs lay beyond it, but these led upward and were well lit.

We practically ran up the stairs after Abbie exclaimed that I was running out of time. We reached the top and were greeted by grassy fields, trees, and a clear blue sky. The air was warm like springtime. Everything shone with a vibrancy of color.

"Normally," Abbie said, "more would be here, but we don't allow the spirits of others to affect your decision."

If you were smart, you would probably pick door number two, right? Well, I actually thought about it. I looked down at my chains. I still had all three, but I knew I had to hurry.

We returned to where we had started, and Melody, Jake, and Sara met us there.

"Have you made up your mind, Jay?" Jake asked.

"Yes, have you?" Melody asked with pleading eyes.

"I still have three choices, right?" I asked, not meeting their gazes. "I can still go back?"

"Yes, but you would have to hurry," Sara answered.

I thought quickly and said, "I'd like to go to heaven—"

"Yay! She's coming with us!" Jake jumped with joy.

"I'm not finished," I said. "I'd like to go to heaven with you, but I can't just leave my other friends and family behind, not without at least saying good-bye. They need me and I need them."

At first they looked disappointed but soon they accepted my decision.

"If that's the case," Melody said, "you'll need a lot of energy to get back. Jay, kneel down."

I did as instructed and everyone laid their hands on my shoulders. I felt new sets of hands touch my shoulders as well. Looking up, I saw Blue and two other people I didn't recognize. One was a petite girl with dusty brown hair and large brown eyes that were so dark, they looked almost black. The other was a tall, thin boy with pale green eyes and hair as white as snow.

Blue smiled. "These are Fawn and Zero." Fawn said hello while Zero just nodded. "When you see Katie," Blue went on, "tell her that we said hi and that we'll be watching out for her."

I nodded. My sister brought my attention back to her.

"Three days from now, more RUCAs will go to our mother's house to fetch the others. Your body will have to heal itself before you completely return and we don't know how long that process will take. If you have enough energy in your physical body when you wake, your body may reveal its true power. The spiritual enlightenment may unlock your full potential."

She nodded to me, and I closed my eyes as I took in all of the energy at once. The feeling inside went instantly from warm to burning.

I felt as though I was being pushed down through the thick blackness. I strained to go that way, but only after what felt like hours did I break through. I felt the usual sense of falling fast and hitting the earth hard.

CHAPTER 61

I gasped in a breath of air and nearly choked on the smells, the stenches of death, decay, and gasoline. My eyes opened and I was face to face with a rotting corpse. I tried my best not to scream. That image still clearly fills my mind as I write this.

The corpse's eyes were gone, leaving dark sockets wide open in an eternal expression of pain and suffering. The mouth was agape in a silent scream of agony. When I glanced around, I realized I was lying on top of a pile of corpses, my body twisted into an unnatural position.

I was in a metal room. Ash and soot covered the floor in heaps and piles.

Two days, Melody's voice sounded in my mind. *It's been two days. The RUCAs will be deployed to the cabin in two hours. You must stop them before then.*

I understand, but where am I?

The incinerator. They plan to destroy the bodies by burning them.

Why not before now?

Technical difficulties, she said.

I rolled my eyes.

A horrible hiss split the air. I pushed the corpse off me and stood, realizing that no one was watching. I had to get out.

I heard a click and then flames swirled around me like a whirlpool. The fire reached up to engulf me, but I felt no pain. I drew in a breath, and a new kind of energy filled me and warmed me to the core. I snapped open my wings. The fire licked at my feathers, turning them an ashen black. The flames touched the tips of my hair, blackening the tips. The flames never touched my skin, coming close but then flickering out.

The energy filled my body and threatened to take over. I tried to fight it, needing to regain control.

No! This time I heard Blue's voice. *Give into it. Let it take over. I've seen this before in my friend Zero. Let it have control, just let go.*

I did as he said, losing all control of my body as I stumbled to the metal door. I lifted my arm and threw it forward as Sam did to release his light. The flames followed my fingertips and ripped through the door as if it were paper. Was this my true power? Had the experience of seeing heaven and hell really done this to me?

Scientists stood stunned on the other side. I glared at them mercilessly. To them, I probably looked like the angel of death. They knew what they'd done. They knew the pain and torture they'd caused. And they felt no remorse for it. They tortured and killed innocent children and they felt nothing.

Rage boiled inside me. They could not be purged of their sins so easily.

I saw the fear in their eyes. They knew what was coming. Their fear urged me to go on. They deserved the worst of punishments.

I swung my arm again, and the fire followed my fingertips. The flames sliced through them like a burning blade, sending their blood splattering over me, themselves, and the walls and floors. Four were dead, an unknown amount left.

My body ran down the hallway. The fire followed me in a grand fiery halo, still flickering just inches from my bare skin and clothes. It consumed the walls and the scientists as they ran and I pursued.

Think "fast and deadly," Blue said.

What?

Just do it.

I focused as my body continued to run at high speed. A strange feeling filled and twisted in my stomach. My clothes shrank into my skin like Katie's did when she morphed into a wolf, and a coarse fur the color of ash replaced them. My wings shrank into my back and my hands and feet took the form of paws. I felt my body shifting till I was running on all fours. My muscles stretched beneath my dark fur. My teeth sharpened under my lips and my jaw elongated.

I poured on the speed, my claws clicking on the tile. Smoke, sparks, and flames streamed from my fur. I was a proud wolf and I was going to finish what should have been done a long time ago.

I turned another corner in the hall and skidded to a halt. My path was blocked by armed scientists in their white lab coats, rifles and shotguns raised to greet me. My flames went out as I stopped. I tried to turn around, but the scientists had fanned out onto all sides. I eyed them carefully. I could smell their fear. It was twelve guys, twelve guns, and only one me. That just wasn't fair.

One man cocked his weapon and I snapped into a blind fury. Bloodlust reddened my vision as I leaped at the nearest one, latching my powerful jaws around his throat. Blood gushed up around my lips and muzzle as he fell dead beneath me.

Another tried shooting me but ended up taking out two or three of his comrades.

I went from one to the other, killing each in turn. I never knew I was capable of such violence and destruction. And I never knew I could have such intent to kill. I never knew I was able to kill anyone, let alone a dozen people.

Paw prints of blood followed me as I ran on. An alarm had gone off and the high-pitched keening sounds of the RUCAs became stronger. I morphed back to my human form and, with my hands, created the flames that spread around me again. At least fifty RUCAs flooded the hall as I raced around the next bend.

I unconsciously let out a horrifying, rage-filled cry. The flames flashed and swirled and danced around me, growing bigger and bigger until they spread throughout the hallway. The fire engulfed them all, their false fur igniting on contact, leaving them as burning balls of fire. But the fires soon went out after their false fur had burned away, revealing the metal and wires underneath.

Now what? They can't be burned.

My body had other plans, however. Somehow I knew a large pipe that ran along the ceiling carried water. I stopped and raised my arms, and the ominous sound of creaking metal gave my enemies pause. When nothing more happened, they continued advancing on me.

The pipe strained under my power. When they were nearly upon me, the pipe broke loose. Water drenched me—extinguishing my flame—and the RUCAs, while also putting out most of the flames in the hallway.

Sparks and bolts of electricity jumped and danced across the water and crackled in the air. The electricity made my hair stand on end. All the RUCAs froze in place and fell dead in the streaming water. More RUCAs ran around the corner, first confronting what fire remained and then the spraying water. The same result: their fur was burned away and they died in the water.

Water? Water is their weakness? How pathetic.

Not exactly, Blue said. *They wear the fake fur to protect the wires and electrical cables from moisture, but the fur is highly flammable.*

Oh, I see now. At about that time I realized I mostly had control of my body back.

Don't get used to it, Blue said. *The energy's only building back up again.*

I heard splashes behind me in the ankle-high water. A single shot from a gun rang in my ears, and my right arm burned where a bullet grazed me. A trickle of blood seeped from the wound.

I turned, gripping my arm. Lewis stood ten feet away, his gun raised, the barrel faintly smoking from the blast. Even though he looked calm, I felt his shock.

How is it possible? he thought. *She was suffocated, she was shot twice in the head, and yet she survived? She was declared dead two days ago. How is she still alive? How did she kill all those scientist and RUCAs? It's completely impossible.*

I glared at him. "I'm going to kill you, Lewis, and you can't stop me."

He threw his head back and laughed.

Deadly, fast, kill, I thought. *Deadly, fast, kill.*

"What are you mumbling about in that demented head of yours?" he asked.

I said out loud, "Deadly, fast, kill. Deadly, fast, kill. Deadly, fast, kill!" My body began to shift again.

Sleek black fur replaced my clothing. A thin black tail extended behind me as my hands and feet morphed to black paws. My teeth pointed behind my lips, which I pulled back in a vicious snarl. A black panther, perfect.

I flexed my claws beneath the water as Lewis said, "That's new. An improvement if you ask me. So is this your true power?"

I tensed. I was losing control again. My tail lashed uncontrollably from side to side. The water sloshed about my paws and soaked my belly fur as it swirled around me in a whirlpool. My uncontrolled body let out a bloodcurdling yowl, and the water forced itself forward in a wave that crashed into Lewis, knocking the gun from his hand. I sprang forward while he scrambled to find his footing.

My paws pounded as I ran swiftly through the water, my claws scraping against the tile. I leaped off the ground and bowled into Lewis, knocking him to the ground.

My claws gouged his shoulders as I sank my teeth deep into his throat. I lashed out with my hind claws, slashing through his shirt, chest, and stomach. Blood drained into the water, turning it red.

I leaped off him and glared at him, daring him to stand. That attack would have killed a normal human, but he wasn't exactly normal or human.

He pushed himself to his hands and knees. A sputtering coughing fit wracked his whole body. Blood dripped from his mouth. He trembled as he gasped for air. Struggling to his feet, he pushed his soaked, untied hair from his eyes. A malevolent smile crept across his face as his wounds sealed before my eyes.

Damn, why didn't I remember that? I thought.

You couldn't control your actions anyway, Blue said.

Shut up!

Before I even saw it, Lewis ran at me, grabbed me by the throat, and slammed me into the wall. I lashed out with my claws but I couldn't reach far enough to inflict any damage.

Blood still dripped from the corner of his mouth, and the scent of blood was fresh on his breath. "Do you remember when we stayed in that one city? Where we met Katie? Do you remember the pile of corpses we found in the alleyway before the police found us?" He leaned closer. "I know who killed them."

He paused dramatically. "It was me. I killed them. I drained them of all their energy until they died, almost what I did to you at one point. And now I'm going to kill you the same way I killed them. This time, I'll be sure that you die and stay dead."

CHAPTER 62

His grip tightened on my neck, and I felt him stripping my energy away. As I lost my energy, I shifted back to my usual form.

I clasped my hands around his wrist. I could hardly breathe, could barely move. From the corner of my eye, I noticed that he stood with one leg forward and one leg back, and most of his weight was on the forward leg. That was my chance.

With as much strength as I had left, I kicked his front foot sideways, throwing him off balance. He released his grip, and I dropped to my knees. I whipped my head around, looking for something to use as a weapon.

Turning back toward Lewis, the only this I saw was his boot as he kicked me in the head. The force of the blow sent me flying through the water and into the piles of dead RUCAs.

At the rate this was going, I would *really* be dead before long. I couldn't lose, not if I wanted to see my mother and friends again. I turned to the RUCA scrap heap as Lewis slogged through the now knee-high water toward me.

I pulled at loose pieces of metal, the edges slicing my hands. I finally pried away a long jagged piece. I held it like a knife in my left hand as I stood to face him.

He had stopped, waiting for me to make the next move as if it were all just a game to him.

With my free hand, I made a flickering fire the same way I'd tried to make everything else. I swung my arm the way Sam did, sending blades of fire at him. As each one hit its mark, he staggered back a few steps.

I whipped my arm around, focusing on the water at my feet. I churned it into waves and whirlpools, sending each one at him until a particularly large wave bowled him over. I ran at him as fast as I could. Before he could push himself up, I pinned him so that he couldn't move his arms or legs. His face was almost completely under the water.

I pushed down so hard on his arms, I heard two loud cracks as I snapped his wrists. He cried out and took in water, spitting it back out.

I took the piece of metal in my right hand and raised it above my head, ready to bring it down for the killing blow. Then I looked into his eyes.

The red and blue eyes I'd known for so long were, for the first time, filled with fear, *real* fear. He feared for his life.

I remembered that I was still in control of my body, and I paused.

What am I doing? I thought. *I'm about to kill this boy who I loved and who tried to kill me on* their *orders. But why do I want to kill him? Because he hurt me, and, worst of all, he hurt my family. Do I want to kill him? No, I* have *to kill him, so he can't hurt us or anyone else ever again.*

I closed my eyes and brought the blade down on his heart, on the devise that kept him alive. He cried out in agony as sparks ran up the metal and my arm and through the water. My heart raced from the intense shock.

Lewis stopped struggling and went limp beneath me. Bubbles rose from his mouth as he fell back into the water and released his last breath.

I jumped up and backed away. I was trembling. I'd actually killed him. I took in every horrifying detail: his glazing eyes, his stillness beneath the water, and the blood, so much blood, some of my own mixed with his.

I had killed others, but that hadn't really been me. I looked down at my hands. Blood. A bloody shard of metal. I threw the weapon away, watching it splash and sink into the rippling water.

I tensed as the energy took over for the last time. Without a thought, my arms turned to wings and my skin to feathers. My whole body shrank as my face changed, and the end result was a hawk who, with a flap of my wings, took off over the water and down the hallway.

I turned sharply and flew down a set of stairs. A growl of engines came from up ahead. I cried and my flame ignited again, lighting my path. I burst from the tunnel of the staircase and into a cavernous room full of machines and generators and boilers. I guessed this was where the DAEL got its power because, remember, it's in the middle of nowhere.

A stack of wooden planks stood along one wall along with several cans of fuel.

I morphed back to myself and knocked over the gas cans. I even picked one up and drenched some nearby machinery with its contents. The fire began almost immediately because of the flames that still surrounded me.

I bolted up the steps, leaving a few fiery footprints behind.

I heard Abbie's voice this time. *Get out. The place will explode in, I'd say, about thirty seconds.*

I fell forward as I reached the top of the stairs. My fire licked at the wall behind me. Finally back in control again, I leaped to my feet and ran from room to room, looking for one with a window. Not much time was left.

When I found one, I ran right into it, shattering the glass on impact. The shards cut my skin but I paid no attention. I had to get away fast.

I unfurled my wings as I felt the freezing air on my soaked skin. I beat my now ashen-colored wings heavily, trying to get as far from the impending explosion as I possibly could. After two strokes, a fiery roar erupted behind me. An enormous boom nearly shattered my eardrums.

A wave of heat pushed me away, and I glanced back.

Half of the building was completely destroyed, and the other half was in flames, black plumes of smoke rising steadily to the dark sky. Nothing would be able to survive that blaze.

I turned back around and focused. I could sense which direction I needed to go in order to get home. That was another great thing about being part bird—an internal compass.

Clouds lay thickly over the night sky, not even a breeze stirring the icy air.

Go swiftly, Jay, or another familiar life may be lost, Melody warned.

My eyes widened, and my first thought was, *Sam!* I knew I felt something toward him. What was it? What made my heart skip a beat at the thought of him being in danger? Why did I feel this way?

Swing your arm in front of you in a big circle, Jake instructed, *It will get you there much faster.*

I swung my arm around in front of me, probably looking completely ridiculous. Out of nowhere, a big gust of wind pushed me forward, chilling me to the bone. I kept swinging my arm around, realizing it made me slightly warmer and that I was creating the wind.

Are these all of my true powers? I asked. *To transform and to control water, fire, and the wind?*

Yes, Jay, they all said in unison. *That's what we've been showing you.*

Awesome.

I flew on. I needed to get home. I had to save my friends and family from whatever danger was stalking them.

CHAPTER 63

Sam's point of view

The snow had turned to rain a few minutes earlier. Sam walked alone through the dark streets, the occasional lamppost lighting his lonely path. It had been nearly three days since Jay had been taken. The others had kept him locked in his room, afraid he would try to go after her. But after the first full night without Jay, he stopped trying to get out. He just gave up all hope.

He'd had a dream that first night without her. He was in the mysterious black plain that she had once described to him. Sara, of all people, came to him, the girl he'd killed to protect Jay. She looked happy and healthy, but a somber look lurked in her bright green eyes.

"Sam," she said, "I forgive you for that long ago incident, but I come now bearing sad news. Jay has died. She is no longer among the living. The death was real and nearly painless. I'm sorry to be the one to tell you, but it seems it would be best that you be told first. You may share the news with the others or keep it to yourself, whichever you choose."

She had faded into the blackness, and he had woken in tears. He'd never gotten the chance to tell Jay how he felt about her.

As he walked alone through the rain, he thought, *I don't even remember why I'm doing this, but I feel that I need to. But why? To relieve my anger? To try to forget? Or is it suicide?*

Almost a week earlier, before Jay had been taken, he'd gotten into a fight with a man in this same area when he'd been out and alone. Only when the police intervened did the fight stop.

"I'm going to get you, punk. You just wait," the man had yelled as officers pulled Sam off him. Both of them had been taken home in separate police cars.

Sam wanted that fight *now*. And he knew how to find it.

He turned down another street, ducking into a dark alleyway as a car rolled down the wet street. He made sure his black hood was still up and continued walking. He turned down another alleyway that was draped in blackness between four-story buildings.

A scruffy man sat on top of a metal trash can, a cigarette in his mouth and a beer can in his hand. Crushed cans lay scattered on the ground around him. The man wore torn jeans, an old, stained T-shirt, and a worn denim jacket.

He looked up at Sam and threw his cigarette to the ground. "What'd you want, kid? You need help?"

Sam walked closer. "No," he said.

"You lost or something?" the man asked.

"No."

The man got off the trash can. "What's your problem, kid? You *looking* for a fight?"

Sam smiled wickedly, stopping an arm's length away. "Actually, yes." He threw a punch, hitting the man square in the nose and sending him flying into the wall behind him.

Blood gushed from the man's nose. *No powers,* Sam thought. *Just an old-fashioned fistfight.*

"Dammit, kid, I'm going to kill you for that!" the drunken man yelled. He ran at Sam, arm cocked back and ready to throw a punch.

Moving like a shadow, Sam easily dodged the blow. It wouldn't have hurt him even if it had hit him. He swiftly evaded each attack and got in a few hits of his own, but the man's adrenaline was kicking in, and he was gaining speed.

Sam dodged a punch to the left but miscalculated the one to the right. The blow hit him square in the jaw and knocked him back a few paces. As he straightened again, he narrowly avoided another blow. Another soon followed, and while Sam ran from it, he stumbled on a beer can.

He rolled to brace the impact of the ground, instantly swiveled, and was back on his feet. He turned and found himself staring down the barrel of a gun. Seeing it so suddenly, made him think back on the note he'd left on his bed for the others to find:

> To Michelle, Katie, and May,
>
> Guess who forgot to guard the window? Anyway, two days ago, I learned that Jay has died or has been killed. I know this is sudden, but I'm struggling with this fact too.
>
> I left to clear my head. I have some minor business to take care of.
>
> From,
> Sam
>
> P.S. I'll be back soon … maybe.

As he stared from the man's gun to his scarred and bruised face, he found that he'd lost this battle. This had been suicide all along, and he wouldn't even get to say good-bye to his new family.

Tears welled in his eyes as he fell to his knees before the man.

"Go on," Sam said, his voice shaking, when the man didn't move. "What're you waiting for? Do it, I lost."

Still the man did not move.

"Please," Sam cried. "You'd actually be doing me a favor!"

He reached up and took hold of the gun's barrel. He pulled it closer and pressed it to his forehead, tears streaming from his eyes.

"Please, do it. The one I love is gone. She was taken from me. They took her, and they killed her. I have no reason left to live. I never even got to tell her how much I love her. If you do it, I'll be with her again." He paused. "So do it already. What're you waiting for? Pull the damn trigger!"

CHAPTER 64

I ran into a strange rainstorm only a few minutes from home. The rain slowed me down as I flew as fast as I could over the small town nearest our house. My mind went blank for a moment when I thought I heard Sam's voice from below. I paused, hovering in midair.

I heard a commotion going on below me. I followed the sounds and landed on top of a building near the noise. I looked down over the edge of the roof.

I saw Sam. He was on his knees but he had his back to me so I couldn't see his face. A scrappy-looking man loomed over him, a gun in his hand. Sam held the barrel of the gun to his head.

Sam was crying. I couldn't hear what he was saying at first, then his voice got louder.

"She was taken from me. They took her, and they killed her. I have no reason left to live. I never even got to tell her how much I love her."

That word. It made it all click into place. That was why he'd been so kind to me, why he'd kissed me. That was what I felt toward him, love. I loved him, and he loved me!

I snapped back to what was happening as Sam yelled, "Pull the damn trigger!"

"No, Sam!" I shouted. "Don't do it!"

He turned and looked up at me. "Jay?" he said, both disbelief and happiness in his eyes.

The man pulled the gun from Sam's grip. He swiftly backed away from Sam and aimed at his original target. He pulled the trigger three times. *Bang, bang, bang!*

Sam's gaze went blank, and he seemed to fall onto the wet pavement in slow motion. I called to him, but he didn't move. Leaping from the rooftop, I used my wings to slow my decent. I landed beside him and laid a hand on his back.

His breathing was slowing already. I could see only one eye. It had no expression and was beginning to fade. With care, I rolled him onto his back.

There were three bullet holes and blood, a whole lot of it, all in his chest, near his heart.

His gaze slowly focused on me. "Jay, is that you? I thought you were dead. Are you here to take me to heaven?"

I couldn't respond, couldn't speak. Sadness and rage whirled within me, a turmoil churning and twisting in my stomach. I turned my head to glare at the man.

He'd backed up to the opposite wall and was trembling, the gun still raised and pointed at me. To him, I probably looked like death itself, bent over the body of a dying boy.

The water that lay in puddles at his feet crawled up his legs at my silent command. When it reached his hands and face, it froze on his bare skin. He couldn't move. I'd frozen him in place.

I stood and got face to face with him. "I ought to kill you right here and now. I won't because you've severely hurt my friend and if I don't help him now, he'll die in a matter of minutes."

I walked back over to Sam. He was unconscious now and if I didn't hurry, he'd die right there in my arms.

I turned back to the frozen man. "Don't think I won't come back, because I just might."

Fast, strong, I thought. *Very fast and very strong.* My body shifted again, my hands turning to big paws and my skin covered in a thin layer of yellowish fur. The frozen man looked like he was going to faint—or maybe wet himself—when he witnessed my transformation into a lioness.

I picked Sam up by the shirt and lifted him gently onto my shoulders. I willed him to stay on as I took off running, out of the alleyway and down the road.

Not much time was left, but my adrenaline poured into my speed.

Once we made it past all of the buildings, there was nothing but trees on the path ahead. Low branches and twigs scratched at my face and hidden rocks tore at my paws. The rain stung my eyes, but I pushed on.

My claws dug through the frozen soil as I ran. I didn't care about the burning in my lungs or the roar of blood in my ears. Then I caught a scent of it on the wind: home, my friends, my mom, even Nicky. I raced into a clearing and skidded to a halt on the dirt driveway.

Letting Sam slide off my back, I sniffed him all over. The smell of death was creeping over him, and his breathing was labored and shallow.

I could hear barking inside. I roared loudly, calling for Katie or Nicky or anyone who could understand me. Almost all of the lights flicked on at once in the house. A few seconds later, the front door flew open.

My vision was growing blurry and doubling. I lost all feeling in my legs and collapsed next to Sam. The last things I saw were our friends rushing to the rescue and Sam's chest no longer moving before the whole world faded to black.

CHAPTER 65

I bolted upright, instantly awake, and then cringed at the soreness in my arms, legs, and back. Even my wings were sore.

I whipped my head around and took in my surroundings. I was in my bed, my bedroom, my home. What had happened?

Late afternoon light filtered in through the new window. My wounds had been bandaged, even my torn-up hands, and I was dressed in new clothes.

I was still wondering about the dent in my wall and the faint red splotch when I forced myself out of bed. I leaned against the wall for support as I inched my way to the door. I opened the door and walked out into the hallway. May walked out of Sam's room at the same time. She stared at me in surprise.

"Jay, you shouldn't be up and out of bed yet." She took my arm, trying to turn me back into my room. "Go back to bed."

"I have to see Sam." I tried to walk to his door, but my legs wobbled and I fell to my knees.

She helped me stand up, but I pulled away and limped down the hall. She pulled at my arm. "Sam's fine. He's still asleep like you should be. Now go back to bed."

"It's okay, May." Sam's voice came from the other side of the closed door. "Let her in. I want to see her."

I accidentally overheard her thoughts. *He's awake? Already? But I just left him and he was completely asleep.*

I pulled away from her and opened the door, walking into the dimly lit room. Sam lay in bed, his blankets pulled up to his chest and his arms lying at his sides. An IV was connected to his right hand and he looked sickly pale and exhausted.

"So it's true," he said, his voice almost a whisper. "You *are* alive. It wasn't only a dream." As I walked slowly to his bedside, he asked, "Are you doing okay?" A weak smile crossed his face.

I smiled back. "Don't worry about me. I'm fine. I'm just so happy you're still alive. I thought … I thought you had died. Right there … in front of me."

He reached up and touched my face. "No, I'm still here. Jay, I survived because I'd found my reason to live again. I knew you were alive and that you'd be waiting for me when I came back."

Tears pricked my eyes at his gentle words. He paused and seemed to look past me for a moment. He moved his hand from my cheek to my hand, resting on the blanket.

"When that man was about to shoot me, I realized I'd never told you how I feel." He paused and laughed a little. "You never were one to take a hint. I didn't know how many times I would have to show you for you to get it. I guess … What I'm trying to say is—is that … I love you."

I leaned forward and pressed my lips to his before he could say anything more that would make me cry. Too late. Tears streamed down my bandaged face. He tensed but then quickly relaxed.

I pulled back. "I love you too, Sam! I know that now. I've felt something for so long, but I only now know what it is. And—"

He pulled me back for another kiss, making me forget what I had meant to say. When he released me he said, "You talk too much. The power of love is much greater than that of death. I know that better than anyone because you've brought me back from death not once but twice.

"You know," he continued, "I liked you even before we met. I would look at you through the bars of our cages and at night, I'd go to sleep thinking that as long as I saw you wake up the next day, I'd be fine."

He stopped and looked me over carefully, and then he touched my feathers. "What happened to your beautiful wings? They're gray now. They look like they're made from ash."

"It's a really long story," I replied, lying next to him, careful not to bump into him.

"I think we have time." He smiled. "We're finally free, aren't we?"

"Yes, I think we are."

Epilogue

I set the laptop computer on the bed, powered it up, and opened a blank document.

Mom had loaned the computer to me. After all this time, she'd finally asked what had happened to us before she met us in Chicago. My response: "It's a longer story than you know." She got her laptop, showed me the basics about using it, how to type on it, and told me to use it to write out the story for her.

Just before that conversation, she'd found my birth certificate. After I did the math, I found that I was really fourteen, no longer thirteen. Just thought you might find that interesting.

Sam had healed from his injuries, mostly. I'd even found him asleep in my room one morning. His head and arms had rested on the foot of my bed, the rest of him on the floor. We've been talking about ourselves and our feelings, and things are going steadily.

Katie was devastated when I told her about seeing Blue alive and then his death. She stayed in her room for the whole day, not even coming down for a meal.

So I sat on my bed with the laptop in front of me, staring at the little blinking line. There was so much to write, so much to remember, so much to get down.

How to begin a story such as mine?

I laid my fingers on the keyboard and began to type, one key at a time.

It was a dark beginning. We were stuck in a dimly lit room, each of us locked in our individual cages.

CPSIA information can be obtained at www.ICGtesting.com
Printed in the USA
LVOW06s1219120913

352015LV00003B/4/P